Special thanks

E, you were a wonderful help, thanks for the insights and drive.

Red, you are my muse, always striving to make you proud.

Baby, you are my inspiration, my life, my passion.

D1607689

EARTH 2.0
Part 1: The Arrival

By S. Ganley

Scott Ganley
© 2021, S.Ganley
sganley@yahoo.com
Earth 2.0 Series

CHAPTER 1

Finn's head felt cloudy and his limbs weak as he shook off the effects of long-term hibernation. His eyes blinked open slowly and his vision took several moments to focus on his surroundings.

He was lying flat on a bed, a wool blanket pulled up to his chest and surrounded by an array of machines all blinking, beeping and whirling with mechanical noises. A tube running from under the blanket connected to an IV port in his wrist, the cool fluids steadily entering his body causing an uncomfortable chill.

"Well, there he is." A warm feminine voice cooed from somewhere beyond the edge of his vision.

He felt a hand pressing gently on his shoulder as Dr. Lauren Epperson came into view, her mouth turned up in a welcoming smile as she gazed down on him.

"Wh…where?" Finn stammered, his parched throat crying out for relief.

"Easy there." Lauren said as she slightly increased the pressure on his shoulder, "You're in the med bay on the cryo deck. You're still recovering from the effects of hibernation. Your head probably hurts and your throat is raw, both are common at this stage. You've got an IV drip with a hydrating compound that will start making you feel better very soon. Just lay still and try to relax for now."

Tilting his head slightly to the side he was able to see a row of matching beds lining both sides of the large, open bay. Every bed was currently occupied as a dozen nurses and medical technicians rushed from one bed to the next, checking the equipment readings and tending to the patients. It seemed chaotic but in reality, was a carefully choreographed and well-practiced scenario.

"Your people." Lauren said before he could ask the question. "Everyone's coming along

3

fine, well within parameters. You're with the first batch we're bringing out of hibernation, it will take another two days before the entire security element is up and around."

The hydrating effect of the IV was doing its job and Finn felt his head clearing and the dry, strangling sensation in his throat was rapidly receding. Slowly and deliberately he tried speaking again, "where are we?"

Sliding a wheeled metal chair next to his bed, Lauren took a seat alongside him, "We'll we made it. We're in orbit around our new home if you can believe it."

As Finn's head continued to clear he took note that as the chief medical officer she was giving him a level of personalized attention that no other patient seemed to be receiving from any other medical staff. He felt a warm sensation spreading within that helped temper the frigid IV fluids coursing through his veins.

The news that they had completed their long journey added to the warmth while also filling him with anticipation and elation.

"How long has it been?" He asked, his voice now steadier and gaining strength.

"Fifteen years, three months and change." Lauren replied.

"Unbelievable." Finn mused.

"Yeah, it's pretty incredible. I'm both terrified and electrified with excitement all at the same time." Lauren confided.

"But…" Finn started, clearly searching for words as he looked at Lauren, "you haven't aged a day. You look exactly the same as you did when we launched."

Lauren's cheeks blushed pink for a moment as she smiled broadly in response,
"Well thank you my dear sir." With a wave of her hand across the side of her face she continued "better than Botox wouldn't you say?"

4

His hand brushed the side of his own face where he noted a small growth of stubble but otherwise nothing that would indicate a sudden fifteen-year jump in age.

Lauren produced a small mirror from a nearby drawer and held up for him.

Finn was thirty-four years old on the day the Resolute launched, his reflection was exactly the same as he remembered, no added wrinkles, no graying to his closely cropped brown hair. It was as if the entire journey had never taken place and he was simply waking from a long afternoon nap.

"How do you like that?" Lauren said, "just as ruggedly handsome as the first day we met."

Finn started to pull himself up into a sitting position but Lauren held him steadily in place.

"Take it easy. Your muscles are weak and it will take a little while before you can move about freely."

Easing back against the pillows he sighed in agreement.

"I've got to make my rounds. You relax for about another hour, let the IV finish and I promise you'll start regaining your strength." Gesturing towards a pile of clothing and equipment neatly arranged on a shelf next to his bed she added, "Its 1100 local right now. Commander Tilley has called for a briefing in the op center conference room at 1800. In the meantime, try to take it slow. Once the charge nurse releases you, get something to eat and make sure you stay hydrated."

~~~~

CHAPTER 2

June, 2026

8 months before launch
Kennedy Space Center, Merritt Island Florida

Finn took a long pull from the camelback hydration pack. The water was warm, bordering on hot but even still the moisture soothed his dry throat and helped keep dehydration at bay. It was only 0900 and the outside temperatures were already closing in on 100 degrees with forecasts calling for highs closer to 120 near midday. It was early June in Florida and things were only going to get worse with each passing day.

He thought back to his early childhood. He must have been six or seven and his parents had rented a beach house not far from Miami. It was summertime but he could never recall if it was early or late in the season. The weather had been nice back then, hot but not oppressively. They had spent long days on the beach, swimming, collecting shells and building sand castles. It was the last family vacation he remembered before his father left on deployment and never returned. That was back before global warming tipped the scales against them. The beaches were all closed now, the blistering sand so hot that the soles of shoes would actually melt. Sea life routinely washed ashore, some of it dangerous and still alive for periods of time. The world had changed so much since his youth, it had become a strange and unforgiving place over the years.

"Gonna be another hot one." 1SG Tayte Sheppard exclaimed as he strolled up alongside.

"You have one hell of a grasp of the obvious." Finn shot back as he wiped a sleeve across his brow.

All around them members of the 194th Military Police (MP) company manned checkpoints and roadblocks across the Merritt Island Causeway. Awnings had been pulled into place to provide much needed shade but otherwise there was little that could be done to protect the soldiers from the intense heat.

They were standing on the grassy shoulder off the Causeway, the looming gantries of the Kennedy Space Center serving as a captivating backdrop. Hundreds of workers pressed on night and day putting the final touches on one the most ambitious space programs mankind had ever embarked upon.

Based out of Fort Campbell, KY, Finn's company had been tasked for a six-month rotation to provide armed security around the Space Center. With access to food and clean water becoming a daily struggle all across the planet, the massive stocks of supplies earmarked for the upcoming launch had drawn thousands of desperate people in search of a handout. There was a growing level of hostility with those who considered the program a blatant waste of valuable resources that could be put to better use here and now. Blasting them deep into space on what many considered a suicidal fool's errand was simply a waste.

"Eight days and a wake up." Tayte mused as his eyes darted back and forth observing soldiers at the nearby checkpoint. He was a notorious watchdog constantly on the lookout for slackers especially while on duty and in the public eye.

While Finn knew the man cared deeply for the troops under his charge, the snarled look he always carried across his deeply scared face, booming voice and perpetual thousand-yard stare struck fear into the hearts of even the most battle-hardened troops under his command.

The scars Tayte carried across his face stretched down over his chest and his abdomen. The wounds from a roadside bombing in Afghanistan that nearly took his life were forever carried as a badge of honor for the service he had dedicated his life to.

"Oh hell yes." Finn replied quietly not wanting any nearby troopers overhearing such a casual conversation between the company commander and senior NCO. "It will be nice to stand down for a period and pass this mess off to someone else."

"Your change of command is set for next month." Tayte said, "any word from DA on your next assignment?"

"No, nothing. It's unusual, I should have heard something long before now. How about you? Your set to PCS not long after me, you looking forward to duty in Korea again?" Finn replied.

"You know me. I'm happy wherever the army sends me."

Finn didn't want to admit that he would miss his old friend dearly. They had grown up together, joined the army together and served in several units together including combat tours in the middle east. It was only when Finn put in his packet for Officer Candidate School (OCS) that their lives and careers began to drastically diverge. The 194th was their first opportunity to serve together in nearly eight years, Finn as a Captain and company commander and Tayte as the unit's 1st Sergeant. They made a great team and it would be hard to find someone to fill Tayte's shoes wherever the Army decided to send him next.

"Tell you what. I'm going to take a break for an hour or so." Finn said. With his days starting long before sun up and his nights running well past midnight, he was feeling himself starting to drag. The nearby visitors center had been converted into a community facility for the islands guard force. With air conditioning, snacks, comfortable seating and several televisions, it was a popular place to kick back and relax for a short time when the opportunity presented itself.

"You do what you need boss. I've got it covered." Tayte replied his eyes growing wide as he locked his gaze onto a particular soldier who thought he was being sneaky.

"Anderson!! Special Anderson!!" Tayte thundered as he stormed off towards the checkpoint. "Why in the name of god am I seeing your bald head out there on guard duty? Who told you it was ok to remove that damn helmet!?"

Finn grinned as he walked off towards the community center, it was always a pleasure to see a master at work.

The blast of cool air as he stepping inside brought instant relief and also a small measure of guilt. Deep down it bothered him when he found such a guilty pleasure while soldiers under his command stood a vigilant watch under the relentless heat.

Helping himself to a cup of fruit juice, Finn found an empty seat on a small couch off to the side of the room and plopped down to take a load off for a few minutes.

On a wide screen wall mounted television a cable news network was starting a special report. Recognizing the backdrop as the nearby space center he grabbed a remote from a side table and turned up the volume.

The reporter and his guest sat in a pair of high back chairs in an open field under the shade of a canvas awning. Industrial sized fans off to either side helped circulate the stagnant air but the growing sweat stains on both their shirts demonstrated it was a losing battle.

Over their shoulders and centered in the frame of the camera, the towering central core of the spaceship Resolute dominated the backdrop as workers clambered up and down the gantries surrounding the ship like an army of worker ants.

The show's host, the widely popular and well-spoken investigative journalist, Grant Lovelace, was interviewing a short, slender, serious looking man who appeared visibly uncomfortable in the sweltering heat. Finn thought to himself that when he'd agreed to the interview, the guest most likely thought he'd be sitting inside a comfortable air-conditioned studio somewhere. It was part of Grant's MO in many of his segments to put his guest in an uncomfortable position where their guard was lowered and he could capitalize on that distraction by swooping in with the toughest of questions.

"Greetings from the Kennedy Space Center here in Merritt Island Florida. On today's segment we will be speaking with the head of the US Scientific Advisory Board, Dr. David Parra."

Extending his hand to his guest, Grant and Dr. Parra heartily shook hands while offering a broad if not disingenuous smile for the camera's benefit.

"Thanks for having me today, my wife and I are big fans of the show, and please, call me David."

"Well, David, its wonderful you could join us here today. We're here to talk a little not only about the upcoming launch of the Resolute, the incredible work of space engineering that it is, but also about the circumstances facing our planet that has brought us to this particular point in time."

Rifling quickly through a folder on his lap, Grant referred to the top page of a neat stack of papers as he opened the interview.

"As we all know, the world has now not only reached but surpassed the tipping point in terms of a climate crisis. The effects of global warming are now seen in every corner of our planet. Extreme heat waves and drought or intense periods of heavy rain have drastically impacted all levels of agriculture leading to food shortages and rationing on every continent. Predictive models have shown that within another two to three generations, this planet will no longer be able to support life as we know it."

It was a well-established and widely accepted premise that man had ignored the damage caused to our climate through the use of fossil fuels, chemical and industrial contaminates for too long and the impact was now irreversible.

"Twenty-five years ago, a twinkling star in a distant galaxy was discovered by a NASA deep space probe. From that point we learned that another habitable exists within the limits of our technology to actually reach it. Earth 2.0 as it has come to be known, was found to have not only a favorable atmosphere but the presence of carbon dioxide further suggests the existence of life in some form. At a minimum the planet is known to have a significant amount of plant life and many in the scientific community believe that animal life may also already exist there.

Seven years later the first manned colonization effort to this new world was launched. Five hundred daring souls were launched into space with the goal of laying the groundwork for the first human colony on another planet. That ship, the Discovery, demonstrated the most advanced technical achievements of the day. Fifteen years later the world rejoiced in celebration when it was announced that a signal was received from those colonists and that they had successful reached their new home.

Now, we stand on the precipices of the next mission into space. One where 2500 colonists will take to the heavens and set down roots on a new home in that distant galaxy.

What can you tell us about the technology involved that allows us to travel between worlds like this?"

Dr. Parra took a long sip from a bottle of water as he composed his response.

"Several recent advances in different fields have led to this point. First and foremost, in the area of propulsion, the use of fusion generators allows us to propel large vessels across incredible distances without a need to pack along large quantities of less stable materials such as nuclear cores.

Secondly, we look to the journey itself. Fifteen years in space is a long time, a crew of any size would require massive stores of food and supplies. With the introduction of cryogenics however, we can send large numbers of people on that same journey where they are sustained by supplemental means that require very little space. In addition, those in a suspended state are not impacted by the passage of time. For them, they go to sleep here at home, wake up fifteen years later on a new planet and awake as though they only took a long nap."

Through a window facing the front parking area, Finn spied a Humvee pull up to the front of the building and a uniformed Air Force officer stepped out. After stopping a few soldiers in the parking lot and asking questions the officer was directed to the community building.

Finn picked up the remote and muted the TV as he watched the officer enter the building and glance around until he noticed him and immediately started towards him.

The officer, a Major, bore the insignia of the Unified Space Command (USC) on the sleeve of his pressed and perfectly appointed uniform. The USC was a newly appointed arm of the Air Force, taking the place of the failed Space Force venture. A joint effort with European, Asian and NATO allies across the globe, the USC was spearheading the missions to send humans to colonize Earth 2.0.

"Captain Finnegan?" The Major stated as he approached.

Finn rose respectfully and offered, "Yes sir."

"Captain, your presence has been requested in the Operations Center."

~~~~

Finn sat nervously across the desk from the Air Force three star General. It wasn't every day he found himself ordered to gather his personnel records and report to such a high-ranking flag officer and his mind was whirling with questions. The name tag on the General's utility uniform said Blackwood, but Finn was unable to place him in the chain of command and had never heard the name mentioned before.

"Captain Brian Finnegan." General Blackwood began after spending several minutes paging quietly through Finn's records before setting them off to one side, "do you know who I am?"

"Sorry sir, I'm afraid I don't." Finn replied unflinchingly.

General Blackwood offered a sly grin as he continued, "Didn't think you would. I head up the USC North American mission out of Peterson Air Force Base in Colorado. I've been serving as the principle liaison between the Pentagon and NASA for the Earth 2.0 mission. We prefer to work behind the scenes, so to be perfectly honest I would have been surprised had you said I was familiar to you."

"Can I speak freely sir?" Finn asked politely.

Settling back in his chair, General Blackwood waved offhandedly and replied, "of course, please do. Feel free to speak your mind Captain."

"As an Army officer, I fall under the command of the Department of the Army, not the Air Force or the USC. Why exactly am I here?" Finn asked pointedly.

Offering a broad smile, General Blackwood replied, "you certainly are direct. I like that in an officer. Let me begin by reviewing a few basics."

The General made a point of leaning forward in his chair and locking eyes with Finn as he spoke from memory.

"You are thirty-four years old, you've been in the service for fourteen years six of those an enlisted man where you reached the rank of Staff Sergeant. After enrolling in and completing the officer's basic course, you received your commission and quickly moved up the ranks to your current position as a Captain and Company Commander. You have three combat tours during which you received two purple hearts, two bronze stars with valor designations and numerous commendations. You are single with no close family, parents deceased, no siblings or other direct ties, you are in excellent physical condition and possess what most would consider above average intelligence."

Finn could feel his face beginning to flush. The two minutes of record review he'd witnessed was clearly nothing more than theater, the General knew much more about him than was contained in the personnel folder Finn had provided, the entire scene suddenly felt like an elaborate set up.

"No disrespect intended General. However, what exactly is your point here?"

"My point Captain, is that I am charged with vetting personnel to join the Earth 2.0 mission. We are on a tight schedule with a launch window looming in the next few months. As you are aware, the Discovery mission was designed to lay the foundation for a colony on this new planet. That mission has been publicly lauded as an unprecedented success."

Finn nodded his agreement but remained silent.

"What you and the rest of the world don't know however." General Blackwood continued, "is that contact with the Discovery has been lost."

He knew his face registered a brief moment of surprise at hearing that news. For two years the public had been hearing nothing but positive reports on the successful mission along with a growing hope that no matter what, humanity had at least some kind of future on another world.

"Communications over such a large distance is tenuous at best, but with the use of digital data packets, it was possible to establish limited contact although with a delay of up to twenty days. We know the mission succeeded in reaching the planet and to the best of our knowledge they were able to land on the surface and begin laying the groundwork for a settlement. Several months ago, however, the Discovery suddenly ceased sending updates and has since failed to reply to multiple queries. The only remaining contact is from their automated locater beacon, a device intended to serve as a road map for follow up missions."

"Clearly this information has been kept from the public at large." Finn mused.

"Exactly." General Blackwood replied, "there could a hundred reasons for the loss of communication, anything from atmospheric issues to equipment failure on their end. We simply don't have enough information and felt it best to not erode what little public hope in this endeavor still exists."

"That's all well and good sir and trust me when I say I understand classified information and know how to keep my mouth shut. But it does beg the question, what exactly does any of this have to do with me?"

"I'll cut to the chase Captain. We don't know what happened to Discovery but the importance of the Resolute and subsequent missions can't be understated, the future of our species depends on it. Therefore, it has been decided to include a 200-man security element to help cover all bases. I want you to lead that element."

A period of uncomfortable silence enveloped the room as Finn tried to process the information. In his wildest fantasies he'd never considered the opportunity to join the Resolute mission. It was a lot to take in and as he churned it over in his head, the General sat back in his seat and quietly allowed him those moments of consideration.

"Sir, I don't know exactly what to say. I have responsibilities here, an active command."

Nodding to a nearby folder General Blackwood said, "the paperwork for an immediate transfer of responsibility has already been drafted. The Pentagon has approved a capable replacement to take immediate control of your unit here. As an officer with line experience myself, I completely understand and appreciate your hesitancy based on a sense of loyalty and duty. I give you my word however, that if you accept this offer, your men will be well taken care of and your units mission will continue without interruption."

"If I were to accept, how soon would I be expected to receive orders and report?" Finn asked.

Tapping the folder once again General Blackwood replied, "the orders have already been drafted. If you accept right here and now, your transfer will be effective after close of business today and you would be required to report to in-processing and medical screen within 48 hours."

Finn visibly flinched at the response, for a branch of the government, especially in dealing with military personnel, to move so quickly was simply unheard of. Noting the response, the General offered, "you must understand, this mission is a top priority, nothing else takes precedence over this. Yes, I understand the transfer is short notice, but the clock is ticking and to get personnel trained and ready for launch we need to start yesterday."

"Sir, I know I am not in any position to ask for special consideration here, however, if I were to accept this offer, I'd like to ask that my unit 1st Sergeant be transferred along with me."

General Blackwood smiled and opened another folder that had been sitting off to one side.

"This blank general order only needs my signature and the names of any specific personnel you request. I can personally guarantee it will be fast tracked through channels and approved before you report for in-processing."

It was an opportunity he would never forgive himself for passing up. Finn knew what he had to do, "In that case sir, I accept."

48 hours later

Finn dropped his gear against a wall in the clinics waiting area and collapsed in a nearby seat. He was allowed two bags, one parachute cargo bag and a tactical assault pack. Inside he had the only worldly possessions he would be taking with him. There were a few changes of clothes, toiletry items, cold weather gear and some of his preferred tactical equipment. All in all, not even half the amount he would have brought on a standard deployment and now he found himself leaving for good. Space aboard the Resolute was limited and personnel had to keep their luggage to a minimum.

All the issued gear had been provided brand new, at no cost, a luxury he was unaccustomed to but was grateful for since there wouldn't exactly be a chance to run out shopping or place online orders once they reached their destination.

It had been a nonstop whirlwind of activity since accepting the transfer to join the Earth 2.0 mission. Hours of grueling paperwork updating his will and assigning dispositions of his personal property. He didn't have much but he provided for liquidation of all his assets with the balance divided equally between the families of seven soldiers who had fought and died under his command.

"Mr. Finnegan? Mr. Brian Finnegan?" A female voice beckoned from an open doorway behind him.

Finn turned and caught himself as he was about to snap back the correction of Captain for his proper title but the words caught in his throat as his eyes fell on the woman.

She was unremarkable in every way possible, average height, maybe a few extra pounds but nothing excessive, dirty blonde hair pulled back into a scruffy ponytail, black rimmed glasses framing a set of brown eyes with a complexion that offered the slightest hint of a sun tan. Her brow was scrunched in thought as she studied the chart in her hand waiting for a reply. Something about her momentarily struck him mute for the first time in his life.

Catching his eye, Finn was the only one in the waiting room, she offered a friendly smile and asked, "you must be Mr. Finnegan then?"

"Yes ma'am." Finn awkwardly stammered back.

"I see that you are a member of the security detachment." She added, Finn simply nodded back in agreement. "I'm Doctor Lauren Epperson. I'll be part of the medical team joining the mission. It's nice to meet you Mr. Finnegan."

The tenor of her voice had changed in the last few seconds, where it had started with the detached decorum characteristic of a medical professional, it suddenly took on a much more personal and friendly tone.

"Finn. Please, just call me Finn." He said as he collected his gear and started towards the door.

"You can leave your gear here, Finn." She replied, "as soon as you are medically cleared, you know, no tropical diseases or contagious bugs, you will be assigned a room for the duration of orientation and training."

Dropping his gear once again Finn replied, "thank you, Doctor."

"Call me Lauren. We're going to be spending a lot of time together in the future, I think we can safely dispense with all the formal nonsense, don't you?" She replied, her cheeks reddened slightly with the tiniest hint of a blush and her eyes brightened with a noticeable glimmer.

Holding the door open, she gestured towards another door a little further down the empty corridor.

The exam started off as routine as any other he'd experienced, blood pressure, temperature, check the ears, reflexes and a review of his medical history. During that review Lauren took things a little off script as she said, "I see you underwent surgery about five years ago in Germany. Several pieces of shrapnel were removed from your lower back. I assume that was a war injury of some kind?"

Finn rarely discussed the incident, it was a trauma in his life that he would have just as soon forgotten but he found himself drawn to this woman and eager to open up more so than ever before.

"I was in Afghanistan; our compound was hit by mortars. I was wearing a vest but some shrapnel found one of the few weak spots and tore into my back. I was lucky though, doctors told me that another quarter inch to the right and it would have severed my spine."

"Can I, um…." Lauren began, her voice suddenly turning sheepish as she indicated for Finn to pull up his shirt allowing her to inspect the wound.

Pulling his shirt over his head, Finn turned his back to her and allowed her to examine the scars and surgical marks that marred his lower back.

"Good stitching work, looks like they kept the incision minimal. They were right though, the entry wounds are very close to your spine, you could have been killed or crippled for life." She tried showing nothing more than a detached medical interest as though it was nothing more than a routine part of the exam. As her fingertip gently traced the outline of the scars and then ran its way across the four entry wounds, Finn noted a tenderness in her touch that he sensed involved something more than simple professional curiosity.

Noting the tattoo on his shoulder of a pair of crossed flintlock pistols with a cluster of dog tags hanging from the barrels she asked, "is there a special meaning here?"

Pulling his shirt back on he explained, "the cross pistols are the insignia of the Military Police. The dog tags, each one represents a soldier who lost their life in combat while under my command. There are seven in total, seven names I will always carry with me."

It was a somber moment adding a sudden discomfort to the chemistry they had both felt up to that point. Lauren was quick to recognize the change in temperature and passed Finn a metal tray with empty sample jars and paperwork. "If you would please take these to the restroom at the end of the hall and follow the instructions to fill each, there is a drop off window in the restroom where you can deposit them. If you'll let the nurse at the reception desk know when you're done, she'll take you into another exam room to draw some blood."

Finn studied the three containers and asked, "ok wonderful, so urine, feces and then what's the third one for?"

Struggling to suppress a grin, Lauren replied, "Semen. Basically, if it comes out of you, we need to take a look at it."

~~~~

CHAPTER 3

"Well, that certainly wasn't steak and potatoes, but after fifteen years in cold storage I could eat shoe leather without complaining." Tayte exclaimed as he pushed his plate aside and concentrated on a cup of coffee.

"We've certainly had worse over the years. Remember the soup in that Afghan village that turned out to be rat meat?" Finn replied as he munched down the last of the ham slice.

"You know, after two weeks of eating dirt and shit rations, that slop wasn't actually that bad. As long as you didn't think about what was in it." Tayte fired back with a toothy grin.

They were in the level seven chow hall, a sprawling room with row after row of bench seating and Formica tables that also served as a meeting and common area. A buffet style serving line provided a choice of MRE ham slice, spaghetti or tuna sandwich along with garden fresh salad options from the ships hydroponics bay.

Several dozen people milled about enjoying a meal, chatting in small groups or off in their own thoughts. Most were members of the security force and they offered both Finn and Tayte respectful nods or salutes as they passed.

So far only security and a small contingent of mission critical personnel had been awoken for the initial stages of their mission.

Finn was feeling much better now that he'd had a chance to shower and shave. When he had finally pulled on his military fatigues in place of the flimsy gown they'd all worn during hibernation he started to feel like his old self and was eager to begin the next phase of their long journey.

Attached to his right wrist, he wore the standard issue Personal Data Assistant (PDA). The microcomputer with touch screen, included a next generation virtual reality program packed with a wealth of knowledge rivaling the Internet back home. The system also provided them with traceable locators and long-range communications. Of all their equipment, the PDA's were their most important instrument the moment they stepped foot on an alien planet.

They followed a winding corridor surrounded on all sides by various cryo chambers or storage lockers until they reached the nearest lift and selected the control center from the list of destination options.

A minute later the doors slid open with a hiss and they found themselves on a platform overlooking the ships bridge. Crew members manning work stations below went about their duties without looking up or paying them any attention. Finn led the way along the platform until they reached a door labeled, *Conference 1*.

A large oval table surrounded on all sides by chairs took up most of the large conference area. Three of the surrounding walls were occupied by large screen monitors while sealed view port covered the entirety of the forward most wall. To the left of the door a table had been arranged with coffee, water and an assortment of small snacks. Several people milled about filling cups and making small talk turned to look as Finn and Tayte entered.

Finn counted seven people in the room, a few he vaguely recognized, others he did not. Most surprising of all was seeing Lauren already seated at the table nursing a cup of coffee and offering him a sly smile and a curt wave.

After a few moments a door on the far side of the room slid open and Commander Brian Tilley, along with two uniformed crew members strolled in and took their places at the head of the table.

Finn was immediately taken aback with Commander Tilley. He'd had the opportunity to meet the commanding officer of the Resolute on a handful of occasions during training prior to launch. With the international nature of the mission many of the crew and colonists came from any number of member nations, Commander Tilley hailed from the British naval ranks. He recalled the man as a strong and highly capable officer in his early to mid-forties. The man he saw now was much older and nearly frail in stature. His thick head of black hair had been replaced with a balding mop of closely trimmed gray stubble. Deep wrinkles marred his cheeks and surrounded his mouth and eyes along with deep, dark circles that spoke of many, many long sleepless nights.

While Finn and the other colonists had peacefully slept the years away during their journey, Commander Tilley and a crew of thirty remained awake piloting the ship and servicing the equipment designed to keep the rest of them alive. It was a necessary trade off that a handful must suffer the ravages of time for many others to have the chance of a new life.

For Commander Tilley and his crew, their role in the mission was nearing its end. Once the offloading of personnel and equipment was complete, the Resolute would be abandoned in space and the crew would settle into a restful retirement where they would enjoy their golden years on a brand-new world.

Gesturing for everyone to take their seats, Commander Tilley began, "Ladies and gentleman. First off, I trust everyone is well on the way to recovering from your long nap."

There was a slight chuckle around the room but otherwise the atmosphere maintained a professional air.

"There's a great deal to cover and I'm afraid time is not our friend."

Tapping a command into a tablet computer, the monitor to his right sprang to life with a graphic rendering of the Resolute in orbit around Earth 2.0.

"I will start off with the news of the day. As everyone is aware at this point, we have successfully arrived at our destination and are now in orbit above Earth 2.0."

There was a collective round of cheers and applause around the room. Finn and Tayte however shared a sideways glance, both sensing that the other shoe was about to drop based on the sour looks from the ship's officers.

For their part, Commander Tilley and his people sat quietly and allowed the brief moment of celebration to sweep the room before continuing.

"Unfortunately. That is the extent of the good news." Commander Tilley said.

"Here it comes." Tayte whispered.

"First we need to discuss damage the Resolute has suffered during the voyage. Approximately two years ago, we passed into an uncharted ion storm. That storm subjected the ship to stresses beyond its design limits, resulting in structural damage in many areas that we have, for the most, been able to compensate for. The worst damage however was to our Fusion reactor. Without getting into the specifics of the engine design, the reactor relies on twelve independent fusion cells to maintain and distribute electrical power to all systems. Eight of those cells were damaged beyond repair."

The wind was suddenly knocked out of the celebratory sails around the room as each face registered the worst was yet to come.

"Our mission protocols call for a period of up to twenty-four months in orbit. A length of time that was supposed to allow us to assess the situation on the surface and if necessary survey planetary conditions for alternate landing sites. That's no longer an option. Running on only four cells we have calculated no more than six months of electrical power if we immediately scale down to minimal functions across the board. After that the ship is dead in space without the capability of supporting life."

"Ok, then why not simply accelerate the offloading procedures. Surely six months is more than enough time to complete waking the rest of the colonists and getting them and our equipment to the surface?" A man seated on the far end of the table chimed in.

Finn vaguely recognized the paunchy, bespectacled man. He was a bit older, maybe in his early fifties and presented himself as an academic.

Noting the empty looks around the table, Commander Tilley offered in way on introduction, "for those who may not be aware, Dr. Hughes here is heading up the scientific aspects of our mission. Anyways, while I would tend to agree with you in principle Doctor, this brings me to the next portion of the briefing. As you are all aware, contact with the Discovery was lost some time prior to our launch. While we are continuing to register their locater beacon on the planet's surface, we have had no direct contact with the crew in over sixteen years now."

There were nods of agreement around the table, the loss of contact had been the primary reason for including a security element to the Resolute compliment.

Commander Tilley continued, "Five years into our trip, we received an update from back home that they had finally received a digital voice message from the Discovery. The message was brief, consisting of only two somewhat garbled words…*stay away*."

That news visibly shook everyone in the room, but what Commander Tilley followed up with slammed into everyone like a brick.

"Shortly after we received that update, we learned that conditions back home were rapidly deteriorating. Russian and Chinese military forces were standing to and diplomatic efforts to prevent a wide scale invasion of Europe were breaking down. We lost all communication with Earth shortly thereafter and have heard nothing since."

There were audible gasps around the room as it sank it that the Commander was saying they had now gone ten years without any word from home. The implications were obvious but the question was inevitable, Lauren was the one who broke the silence to ask it.
"What does that mean?"

Commander Tilley sighed deeply, his shoulders sagged and the wrinkles on his face seemed to grow deeper as he replied, "the consensus with my senior officers is that with resources growing scarce and climate conditions only worsening, a large-scale war between world powers broke out. While we have nothing to substantiate it, it is our belief based on the evidence at hand that a nuclear exchange may have taken place. For all intents and purposes, life as we knew it back home has ceased to exist."

The room fell silent as everyone took in the shocking news in their own way. More than a few teared up and others excused themselves to the restrooms or to refill their drinks. For the next half hour, they took a break while everyone collected their thoughts and pulled themselves together.

For Finn, the news hit hard. While he had no immediate family remaining back home, there were many good people he had served with in the military who would have been on the front line of any major conflict. He suddenly found himself with mixed feelings about running away across the galaxy in relative safety while others put their lives on the line. Deep down he knew that the worst part of all of it was that they may never know for sure what actually happened back home, but it was within their nature to assume the worst.

Sipping absently from a cup of water, Lauren stood alone in a far corner of the room staring blankly at a plastic plant in a small decorative vase.

Finn eased up quietly beside her, "You ok?"

Sniffling and fighting hard to keep her tears at bay and failing, Lauren replied, "My parents lived near Washington, DC. They are both in their mid-70's and things had been tough for them; the rationing had really taken its toll you know?"

Finn remained quiet only nodding his head in understanding as he recognized her need to unload what she was feeling.

"When I was first approached to join the mission, I was actually going to turn it down. I felt my place was near them but they convinced me otherwise. My mom told me how much they wanted a better life for me and my dad expressed how proud they were of my accomplishments. They wanted me to leave with the Resolute and find a life on another world."

Finn could see the pain and anguish behind her swollen eyes, it was his first glimpse of a tender and more personal side to her.

"I mean I knew once I left on this mission, I'd never see them again. I knew their time was short. Part of what held me together about them is that I would never really know and always remember them as they were the last time I saw them. Now I find it nearly impossible not to think of them dying horribly in a nuclear explosion."

Reaching out and taking her hand, Finn offered, "None of us know for sure what happened. Right now, your mind is absorbing speculation from others who are simply grasping at straws when there is no further information available. No matter what, your parents were together and proud of you. Try to remember them the way you last saw them."

He barely believed what he was saying himself but knew he had to offer something in the way of reassurance. It would take some time but eventually she and the others with family back home would learn to bury the dead and move on. Right now, it was critical to get their heads back in the game and concentrate on the things they could do something about.

Finn was grateful when Commander Tilley finally cleared his throat and called the meeting back to order.

"As much as I would like to allow everyone some time to adsorb that distressing bit of news, I'm afraid time is not a luxury we have in abundance." Commander Tilley announced as he motioned for everyone to resume them seats for the briefing to continue, "unfortunately the rest of the information I have is not much better, so it's probably best to simply lay it all on the table up front."

Referring to the monitor showing a rendering of the Resolute in orbit around the plant, he used a laser pointer to highlight a specific region of the planet's surface. "Based on the beacon from the Discovery, we have narrowed the most probable location of where they landed to this region."

"Makes sense." Dr. Hughes interjected, "climate models show that area to be temperate, with easy access to multiple sources of water along with a high likelihood of arable land. It's along the rim of a major rain forest where timber and other natural resources should be found in abundance. I am somewhat confused though Commander, I was under the impression that the Resolute was equipped with external sensors that should provide a better look at the surface. Have you not attempted scanning this area for signs of life?"

"You're correct Doctor, the Resolute is well equipped with an array of sensors that should give us a wealth of information along with close-in imagery of the planet's surface. Unfortunately, all of our scans are being reflected back, even orbital imagery is scrambled and useless. We are essentially blind."

"Reflected back?" the question came from a stout young woman who up to that point had sat quietly by herself at the opposite end of the table. Finn had noted her inclusion in the meeting as somewhat odd, she didn't appear to fit in with any part of the crew, medical or scientific teams. He guessed she was somewhere in her early to mid-twenties, she appeared fit if not even somewhat muscular in a form fitted t-shirt and well-worn cargo pants. At first glance she was easily mistaken for a man with her closely cropped hair and rugged facial features.

"What do you mean by reflected back Commander?"

"Exactly what it sounds like. Every form of electronic, digital or micro burst transmission is reflected back to the source. It's like the entire planet is shielded in some way from every known form of scanning technology." Commander Tilley explained.

"Any idea who she is?" Finn leaned in close and whispered to Tayte.

"Oh yeah, that's Dutch. I remember her from training. A sure-fire example of looks being deceiving, she's a grade A engineer, a regular genius in the field. We're lucky to have her."

Finn was caught off guard by Tayte's evaluation of the young engineer. In all the years he'd known the man, he could count on one hand how many times he'd shown a level of respect and admiration for someone else's abilities. Finn found himself intrigued with the woman.

"Not only does this interfere with our on-board sensor arrays, it is also preventing us from launching orbital satellites." Commander Tilley continued. "Without direct control of those satellites during their initial insertion, we won't be able to place them correctly and risk losing them."

This was a setback that Finn hadn't anticipated. The satellites carried by the Resolute were designed to provide them with a wealth of data including GPS guidance, communications, weather and terrain modeling not to mention critical monitoring capabilities for dangerous wildlife or atmospheric situations. Those satellites could pretty much track an individual fish in the open ocean and from a security standpoint were a pivotal resource he had been counting on having at his disposal.

"Do you suspect some kind of atmospheric interference? Possibly magnetic or solar?" Dutch continued.

One of the officers alongside Commander Tilley shook his head and replied, "I'm Lieutenant Commander Bob Patterson, formerly with Air Force intelligence. I have a background in Electronic Warfare and what we are seeing in terms of how our scans are being reflected back is indicative of intentional jamming."

"I don't understand." Dutch fired back, "how is that even possible? I mean our people on the surface wouldn't have any reason for jamming us."

"Not only would they have no reason but they would also lack the equipment or specialty within their ranks to do so. No, we believe the jamming has nothing to do with our people."

This hung in the air for several moments as everyone considered the implications. Dr. Hughes was the one to finally break the silence, "You believe an intelligent alien species could be involved? Why has atmospheric interference been discounted so easily?"

"We are leaving all options open at the moment Doctor." Lt. Commander Patterson replied. "What we do know is this. Our scanning equipment modulates to different frequencies on a wide spectrum in order to overcome interference. What we are now referring to as jamming comes into play several moments after a frequency skip. We're talking fractions of seconds but still measurable. Naturally occurring interference, be it electromagnetic or atmospheric would flood the spectrum with continuous noise. In this case those small fractions of a second breaks show that some form of technology is locking onto and blocking the returns."

Both Dr. Hughes and Dutch were about to jump out their seat with an animated reply when Commander Tilley raised his hands and took the floor.

"We can speculate until hell freezes over and ultimately get nowhere. The fact remains, we have no means of scanning the surface and before we offload our passengers and equipment we need boots on the ground to determine what we could be walking into down there."

Directing his gaze towards Finn he continued, "Captain Finnegan, this is where you and your people come into play. We will need you to organize a landing party to survey the projected colony location. Your goal should be to ascertain the status of the crew and passengers from the Discovery and determine any potential dangers on the surface. We can't go home and with our ship running out of power we can't search for another planet. Whatever we find on the surface, good or bad, we are going to have to figure out how to deal with it."

"You can count on us Commander." Finn replied stoically.

"Now, I know that how you conduct this mission is at your discretion as the ranking security officer. However, there are some caveats from our end that you need to take into consideration." Commander Tilley added.

"Shit." Tayte muttered, "always a catch."

Finn shot a sideways glance at the senior NCO but remained silent as he waited for more information.

Commander Tilley continued, "Your goal will be to secure a landing site on the planet's surface. Once that is accomplished, we will begin ferrying a work force along with supplies to construct any necessary shelters and facilities needed to sustain us long term. We know the Discovery crew landed on the surface and at a minimum laid the groundwork for a settlement. While we don't know what happened to them, securing that settlement is our best option for the immediate future."

It was far from an ideal arrangement, but under the circumstances they were simply too short on time to scour the surface for another location.

"With that being said, we don't know much about conditions on the surface so it would be prudent to include Dr. Epperson, Dr. Hughes and Ms. Dani Kirkman to provide an engineering perspective on available resources."
 With a wave of introduction along with a curt smile the young engineer said "I prefer Dutch if it's all the same to everyone."

While he didn't like the idea of being micromanaged in such a way, Finn understood what the Commander was trying to accomplish. The personnel he mentioned could very well prove useful for their initial mission to the surface. He offered no objections and gently waved Tayte to do the same as he sensed the NCO preparing to fire off a rebuke.

"Excellent." Commander Tilley went on, "we all seem to be on the same sheet of music. Launch prep is already underway, Captain Finnegan if you will assemble the rest of your team and gear you can meet the flight crew in the forward launch compartment tomorrow morning at 0800."

Standing and moving to the fall wall containing the sealed view screen, Commander Tilley said, "now that all those cards are on the table and seeing that there are no immediate questions. Ladies and gentlemen, it's time for you to have your first look at our new home."

With a press of a button, a section of wall began sliding down into a compartment in the floor and a collective gasp filled the room as Earth 2.0 came into view.

The planet filled the screen and necks bobbed up and down as everyone struggled to find one particular area to focus on. Unlike their home where blue seemed to be the predominate color when viewed from space, this planet was bathed in a brilliant explosion of greens. The heavily forested surface areas stretched from one horizon to the next. While wide swaths of open oceans divided a handful of continents, it was the surface areas of those land masses that simply stole the show.

"Oh my god." Lauren exclaimed, "I've never seen anything so beautiful in my life. It's like the most brilliant green emerald."

Finn found himself lost for words as he took in the dazzling scene. The planet was at least three times the size of their own but contained many similar features that were easily identified even from orbit.

Sprawling white capped mountain ranges stretched for hundreds of miles in dizzying patterns in places dipping down until they joined with wide-ranging swaths of what he was sure were deserts. Gentle rolling plains brimming with picturesque valleys and broken in places by long and meandering rivers glowed with so much brilliant colors that he could almost picture flowering plants, flowing seas of grass and towering fields of wheat. Incredible ocean vistas separated nearly a dozen vast continents. Across the entire planet however it was the bright green forestry of lush rainforest's, dense jungles and fertile woodlands that gave the planet its predominant colorization.

For several long moments the crushing news from back home and failing shipboard power systems were simply pushed aside as everyone found themselves lost in the beauty and majesty of their new home.

It was at that moment that Finn understood that no matter what challenges they may face on the planet, they would be overcome and this was where the human race would begin anew.

~~~~

CHAPTER 4

The shuttle was roomy and actually fairly comfortable with heavily padded seating, backrests and wide shoulder restraints. Compared to the modes of transportation Finn had experienced throughout his military career he was pleasantly surprised to see tax dollars going to such a creature comfort.

Both shuttles carried aboard the Resolute could carry up to a hundred and fifty passengers and several tons of cargo. For their initial expedition Finn had elected to bring only a fifty-man security team with the rest standing by in reserve in the event they ran into trouble.

To his right, Tayte sat slumped in his seat, the ability to simply close his eyes and drop off for a quick snooze was a habit ingrained in many career soldiers. To his left, Lauren busied herself reviewing everything they had on record concerning the atmosphere of the planet. As the chief medical officer, she was making it her business to be ready to confront any potential medical situation they could encounter.

"The atmospheric readings are actually better than we could have hoped for." Lauren mused aloud.

"How so?" Finn asked curiously.

"Oxygen levels are at 32%, that's a big jump from less than 20% back home. At those levels, the human body should, theoretically at least, recover from injuries much faster and display a higher level of endurance. I wouldn't be surprised if the increased oxygen also results in denser muscle mass after a short period on the surface." Lauren explained. "The thirty-four-hour day cycle will also be interesting."

"Yeah, I was wondering how that worked. If I understand correctly, the breakdown of night and day differs across the planet based on where you are."

"Exactly." Lauren replied, "Where we are heading that should be a 20 to 14-hour cycle, with daylight lasting longer than night."

Sitting on the opposite side of Lauren, Dr. Hughes was listening intently and jumped in to the conversation at that point, "the long-term impact of that cycle will be very interesting. I suspect in terms of agriculture we will see impressive yields well beyond anything back home. In fact, I wouldn't be surprised if harvest cycles double or even triple in frequency."

The shuttle bucked and jumped as it entered an area of turbulence in the lower atmosphere, the pilots quickly compensated and the flight smoothed into a steady ride. Finn found himself surprised that the descent through the atmosphere hadn't been more jarring. The pressurized shuttle had eased through the border of space with little more than a minor jolt.
They were dropping through a layer of clouds and the planet's surface was becoming more detailed as it rushed up to greet them. Conversation inside the shuttle suddenly ceased as all eyes turned to the view ports and studied their new home.

"It's too overcast to see very far." Dr. Hughes bellowed dejectedly. "I can make out some mountain formations to the East and what could be a very large lake to the South."

They were over a heavily forested region, the thick tropical canopy towering more than 300 feet above the forest floor blocked their view of any specific details below.

"It's all so familiar." Dutch mused dreamily as they dropped below 1,000 feet and onto a course following the Discovery's homing beacon. "The trees are just like back home. I can see furs, pines, cedars and maybe even rubber trees down there."

"It's incredible." Lauren replied. "But these trees are so much larger. It looks like you could build an entire neighborhood of homes from just a single one."

"Two-minute warning." The pilot announced over the cabin intercom.

Finn noted with satisfaction that each member of the security detail took that information and immediately began checking their gear, making weapons ready and silently forming into a pair of lines at the shuttle's rear cargo ramp.

"Ok, Lauren, Dr. Hughes and Dutch, stay inside the shuttle with the flight crew until I signal that we have an effective security ring around the landing zone." To his team he added, "heads on a swivel out there. We don't know what we are walking into but there could be friendlies in the area. Remember your rules of engagement and only fire if you witness a hostile action."

Glancing down at his own weapon, Finn marveled at the futuristic pulse rifle. Similar in appearance to the M4 rifles he was accustomed to, the pulse rifle used electrical energy to generate and fire a charged particle. A dial on the side of the weapon allowed the user to increase or decrease the amount of charge for each shot, giving them a range of options from a small caliber impact to a heavier hitting round like a .50 caliber. The higher the setting, the faster the weapon was drained of energy. Standard issue was six capacitors per soldier for an average load of fifty shots per capacitor at a mid-range setting.

"How you feeling boss?" Tayte asked as he tested the weight of his own rifle and made one final adjustment to his equipment harness.

"Ready to do this thing." Finn replied.

Forward movement stopped as the shuttle came into a hover and slowly descended into the center of a wide clearing. They could feel the struts deploy and lock into place moments before there a gentle bump as they touched down.

The crew chief positioned himself near the controls for the cargo ramp and listened intently in his head set as the pilot informed him they were safely on the ground and conducting engine shut down procedures. With a press of a button there was a loud hiss of escaping air and the door split upwards and downwards like the jaws of a living beast. The lower half of the door formed a nonskid ramp onto the ground and before it even finished its descent the first of the troops were rushing out, weapons held at the ready, eyes scanning their assigned sectors.

It was a textbook deployment, in less than thirty seconds the security team had formed a protective perimeter out to a hundred meters all around the shuttle. With no immediate threats in sight, the men all took a knee and began keeping watch.

Finn stepped off the shuttle's ramp and into the grassy meadow. His first thoughts were amazement at how earth like their surroundings were. They were in a large field surrounded on all sides by dense forest. The grass at his feet rose to knee height and was exactly the same as that in any similar setting back home.

Taking a deep, exaggerated breath he felt his lungs filling with a flood of cool and refreshing air. The feeling was exhilarating and impossible to describe. His entire life back on earth he had grown accustomed to the acrid aftertaste of various pollutants in the air he breathed every day. While the recycled oxygen aboard the Resolute, while breathable and somewhat refreshing compared to the polluted mess back home, contained a noticeable metallic bitterness to it.

This was a sensation unlike any he had experienced. The absolute pure, cleansing feeling from a lung full of fresh and unfiltered air was astounding. The sun felt warm on his skin and there was a soft breeze blowing gently across the meadow. The air carried a slight bit of humidity with temperatures leaning towards the warmer side. It was just a beautiful, mild spring day, on an alien planet. Finn could close his eyes and almost imagine he was back on earth, many years past, on a hike in the woods far from civilization where the air was clean, clear and as yet unspoiled by man.

Following behind him, Lauren, Dr. Hughes and Dutch clambered down the ramp and began looking around in amazement.

"Incredible." Dr. Hughes exclaimed as he crushed a handful of seed clusters from a patch of grass, rolled it between his fingers and studied the remains. "This is hairgrass. Even without a microscopic analysis I can tell you without any doubt this is the same as average meadow grass back home."

Gesturing towards the edge of the nearby forest he added, "even from this distance I can already identify oak, pine, maple and beech trees in the woods. While they are much larger than we would find back home, the bark, leaf structure and flowers appear identical."

"Listen." Dutch said, "do you hear that?"

"What is it?" Finn asked suddenly alert, "I don't hear anything."

"Just close your eyes and really listen." Dutch offered as she squeezed her eyes shut and craned her neck to one side, "Crickets, frogs, birds chirping and even some kind of insect, maybe cicadas? It reminds me of a camping trip my dad took us on when we were kids, the sounds of the forest are the same."

The rest of them joined her in closing their eyes and soaking in the sounds in the background of the scenery they had all simply taken for granted up to that point.

"She's right, my god." Lauren mused, "This planet is alive in every way imaginable."

Dialing his wrist mounted PDA into a map put together aboard the Resolute from high orbit topographical photos Finn marked a point representing the spot they had landed. "According to our readings the beacon originated in this sector. The problem is with interference from the surface we can't narrow it down more than a twenty square mile radius."

Studying the map, he tapped his finger on a point six mile to the north west.

"This should be a good spot to start looking. There's a river passing through here and some flat open ground that would be perfect for cultivation. If I were to pick a settlement location around here this would be the most likely spot."

Dutch disappeared for a few moments along the side of the shuttle where she dug through a storage compartment and pulled out a suitcase sized metal case.

Opening the case, she quickly assembled a small rotary drone and ran through a series of tests.

"Ready to take a peek?" she asked eagerly.

"Alright Dutch. I know you've been chomping at the bit to play with your toys. Let's see what's out there." Finn said.

With a handheld control panel, Dutch launched the drone and directed it to treetop level following a steady path to the north west. "Ok, the feed should now be available on everyone's PDA. The more eyes the better."

"What's the range on the drone?" Finn asked.

"It's modeled after a military drone and rated to 25 miles, however with the jamming on the planet's surface, its capabilities are limited. I should be able to push it out to eight miles on local control. None of the onboard sensors will work however, all we're going to get is a live video feed, so we can only see below the forest canopy when there are gaps in the leaves."

"I'll take whatever help we can get." Finn replied, "let's get the show on the road."

All eyes were glued to their wrist displays as the drone made its way across the tree top canopy.

"Amazing." Dr. Hughes mused as he studied his viewscreen. "Those oaks are nearly 300 feet tall, that's almost double the size back home."

"Wow!" Cried Dutch, "Did you see that?"

Adjusting the controls Dutch reversed course on the drone and dropped it into a gap between trees until it was hovering almost a hundred feet over a winding stream. Continuing slowly upstream she guided the drone until a half dozen four legged creatures came into view.

The animals were huge, the largest nearly the size of a city bus. They were low profile squat creatures their heads and torsos covered in thick armored plating with long lizard like tails extending behind. The ends of each tail topped with a thick flat plate ringed on all sides with menacing looking spikes. Four of the group were casually lapping away at the flowing stream while the other two grazed mouthfuls of leaves from the surrounding foliage.

"Ankylosaurs! Right off the pages of an encyclopedia." Dr. Hughes exclaimed, "absolutely amazing."

"A dinosaur?" Lauren mused, "that's an actual earth dinosaur from millions of years ago. But how?"

"I can't say for sure, but based on what I have seen thus far, I am starting to form a working theory. I need to see more before I'm comfortable presenting it however." Dr. Hughes offered.

"Are they dangerous?" Dutch asked as she marveled at the creatures on the screen in front of her.

"They're primarily herbivores, plant eaters, but each weighs several tons and they can swing those tails with deadly precision. It would be advised to stay out of their way. If we leave them be they shouldn't be any bother."

"I thought you were a botanist?" Finn asked.

"I am, but paleontology has always been a passion of mine." Dr. Hughes replied indignantly.

Finn recognized a smugness in his voice that he had an immediate distaste for. For the moment he pushed those feelings aside as he concentrated on the mission but he made a mental note that Dr. Hughes was someone he needed to keep a better eye on.

They watched the armored dinosaurs continue to drink and graze for several more minutes before Finn directed Dutch to move the drone back on course.

Thirty minutes later the drone approached a large clearing split on one side by a wide, gently flowing river.

"This looks like the spot." Finn said. "Bring it down below the canopy and start panning around, let's see what we will see."

"Look, there." Tayte exclaimed tapping excitedly on his PDA's screen. "There's a walled complex."

At the drone dropped lower into the clearing they started to make out the details of a sprawling village surrounded on all sides by a towering wall of thick tree trunks with sharpened tops. Metal and wood sided buildings of all sizes and shapes were arranged in a pinwheel fashion on either side of the river with a number of small bridges connecting each side.

Dutch deftly maneuvered the drone over and around each building as everyone kept their eyes glued to their screens.

"Incredible amount of work." Finn mused. "Those metal sided buildings must be the prefab deals from the remains of their ship. The rest look hand made."

Finn had spent long hours studying the planned designs of the community they expected to build on their new home. He identified bunk houses, storage facilities, agricultural buildings, community and common areas along with blacksmith works and a host of support areas. The framework for many follow up structures had been laid out and were in various stages of construction. It was clear that that the Discovery team had put in a great deal of effort to make this place livable.

The drone had reached the edge of the village where they could now see large swaths of weed choked land that had once been cultivated for farming. Animal pens, feed storage areas, barns and even a number of windmills were all easily identified and in the process of being reclaimed by the landscape.

"Yeah, but it looks like it was abandoned a long time ago. Everything is overgrown and there are no signs of life." Lauren added.

"Either way, it's a starting point. We're going to check it out." Finn replied.

After assigning a small detachment of security officers to remain with the shuttle, Finn organized them into a column with the bulk of their security people staggered to the left and right giving them all around coverage. Picking their way cautiously into the tree line, they moved out and began the trek towards the settlement.

~~~~~

CHAPTER 5

Finn called a halt some hundred yards short of the compound. They were at the edge of a plowed but overgrown field that still bore the remnant of corn stalks from the last harvest. The security force immediately spread out and took up defensive positions in a full 360-degree perimeter.

The terrain had been tough and unyielding forcing them to follow a zig zag course around insurmountable obstacles that had added time and distance to the trek.

With a fully laden MOLLE kit consisting of a three-day assault pack, hydration carrier and equipment vest all riding over a built-in layer of dense ballistic fiber, the humidity inside the rain forest was amplified several times over. Despite the discomfort of the heat and dripping sweat,

Finn did find that his muscles were handling the extended hike much better than he would have anticipated. Whether it was a direct benefit of the oxygen rich atmosphere or the excitement and anticipation of where they were and what they were doing it was impossible to know for sure but he felt good.

A slap of skin on skin followed by a muffled exclamation caught his attention.

"Mosquitoes?" Tayte said as he held up the palm of his hand displaying the bloodied remnants of a small insect. "Did we really travel to the other side of the damn galaxy only to find alien mosquitoes??"

Finn was about to reply when a slight breeze carried through the air and he caught a faint but familiar scent. He immediately felt his senses go on high alert as his hands gripped tight to his rifle and he raised it to a low ready position.

"You smell that?" Finn asked, his eyes scanning side to side through the brush off to his right.

"Oh yeah. Camp fire, charred meat, certainly not what I would have expected here." Tayte replied his own rifle now up and ready, his eyes focused and alert.

Using hand and arm signals only, Finn directed six men to follow along with Tayte and himself as they cautiously stepped into the dense foliage towards the source of the smell. Twenty or so feet into the brush and the smell grew even stronger. Finn held his right hand over his head and opened his fingers indicating for the small squad to spread out alongside him.

Keeping his body low to the ground and moving with slow, deliberate steps, he crept forward until he was behind the low hanging branches of a thick oak. Several feet in front of him the woods opened up slightly into a small clearing, the smell of smoke was even stronger now, they were right on top of the source.

Raising their rifles to the ready position Finn and Tayte exchanged nods and quickly stepped out into the clearing sweeping their weapons around from side to side in a well-rehearsed pattern.

They found themselves facing a roughed-out camp site. Several lean-to's put together with long branches and logs were held in place with vines and roots. Inside each of the primitive shelters they noted bedding cobbled together with dried leaves and large palm fronds. In the center of the camp site a smoldering fire pit was overflowing with ashes and burnt logs. Suspended between a pair of trees directly over the pit was a drying rack for meats and animals hides, several pieces of both remained in place over the center of the pit.

"Still warm." Tayte exclaimed as he bent down and examined the fire. A smattering of loose dirt along with a puddle of water along one border of the fire pit indicated someone had made a hasty attempt at extinguishing the flames. Picking up a stick he poked it into the charred remains of logs noting glowing embers underneath.

"I'd say we missed whoever was here by no more than 10 or 15 minutes."

Finn studied each lean-to taking a count of the makeshift bedding, "looks like there were at least eight people camping here for quite some time."

"They were having one hell of a barbecue." Tayte mused as he poked a rack of animal ribs resting on a wooden spit over the fire, "doesn't make any sense though. Why would someone be camping out so close to the settlement?"

"That's a damn good question." Finn mused. "Let's make a search of the settlement, maybe we'll get lucky and find someone who can answer it."

Seeing the log wall surrounding the colony on their small PDA viewscreens was one thing, to be standing at the base of the structure was something else entirely. The work, craftsmanship and effort that had gone into the construction was hard to imagine. Rising 30 feet tall, the top of each log carefully carved into a menacing spike and the base driven several feet into the ground, it was clear the first group of settlers had realized their new world held dangers no one had anticipated.

The images the drone had provided had failed to properly capture some of the more striking details of the condition of the settlement. As they approached the main gate along a well-traveled and packed dirt trail, it was clear that in addition to the ravages of time and overgrowth of the surrounding rainforest, the settlement had suffered more ominous sources of damage. Large sections of the wall were missing, the scorched remains on the surrounding portions hinted at fire damage.

As they entered the compound, Finn directed his team to spread out and conduct a search of every building. It quickly became evident that the colony had been abandoned but not necessarily by choice. Many structures had additional signs of fire damage, some burned completely to the ground while others were missing a wall here or a doorway there. While the indications of fire damage raised alarms, it was the pock marks across the doorway of one particular building that caught Finn's attention even more.

"What do you think?" Tayte asked as the two men studied the holes burrowed into the wood.

"What I think is simply impossible." Finn replied as he drew a long Kbar knife from his utility belt and approached the front of the building. Probing with the tip of the knife into a pock mark, he dug into the wood and pried loose a small metal object. Examining the object in the palm of his hand he felt the color drain from his face as he continued, "it's a bullet fragment, no question about it. Steel jacketed, high caliber, probably a rifle or automatic weapon of some kind. Someone shot this place all to hell."

"That doesn't make sense." Tayte replied, "other than a handful of pulse rifles, the Discovery wasn't carrying any firearms and certainly nothing that fired a steel projectile, rounds like that were rare as hell back home."

"Exactly." Finn countered, "but here we are and someone sure as shit fired this place up with some old-fashioned firepower."

Throughout the complex they discovered a number of buildings that bore the same markings both inside and out that indicated a large amount of gun fire had taken place.

"Captain. We've got a body out here sir." Finn's PDA sang with the incoming report from one the security personnel.

The body was resting half in and half out of a crawlspace under one of the largest of the buildings. It was adult, but other than that it was hard to tell much more as there was nothing more than a few skeletal remains left, the skull, ribcage and one arm, the remaining pieces were nowhere to be found.

"I found the medical center, it's still in pretty good shape all things considered." Lauren reported as she joined the small group of them all standing around and viewing the weathered bones, "I'll get a body bag and we can move the remains there, maybe I can determine a cause of death or at least a time line."

Several hours later and the sun was starting to set in the distant skyline. The entire settlement had been searched from top to bottom confirming that it had been deserted for some time. The remains of nine additional bodies has been discovered in various buildings. Those remains had all been carefully transported to the medical center where Lauren was taking charge of the examinations.

With guard rotations established, Finn called for a meeting inside one particular building they had identified as a command center. Computer equipment, maps, communications gear, and other essential items made it clear that the facility had once served as the operational nerve center for the Discovery mission. While some of the equipment had been damaged or even destroyed, the center was in surprisingly good shape and the building remained structurally sound.

"What's the word Dutch? Any luck with the power?" Finn asked as Dutch strolled into the command center.

With a sly grin on her face she marched across the room and flipped a switch turning on the overhead lights.

"You doubted me?" Dutch replied sarcastically.

"Not in the least." Finn said.

"It's going to take some time to get the rest of the colony powered back up." Dutch explained. "Lot of cut wire, damaged or missing solar panels and only a handful of converters still operational. I'm going to need supplies from the Resolute to finish repairs and a few extra sets of hands would be helpful."

"Well done." Finn exclaimed. "Even a little power will make life easier. We'll make sure everything you need is included on the first load of equipment to the surface."

Everyone called to attend the meeting was now filing in and Finn motioned for them to take a seat around the conference table.

"Lauren, why don't you start us off, what have you learned from your examination of the remains?"

"Quite a bit actually. While I've only had time to conduct exams on four sets, DNA analysis has concluded that they are from the Discovery mission, as we expected. The records of every person from our crew and the Discovery are maintained in our database." Lauren explained as she opened a tablet computer and reviewed the rest of her notes, "they've been dead quite a while, between 17 and 18 years."

"That goes right along with the time line of when contact with the colony was lost." Tayte interjected.

"Exactly." Lauren continued, "and from the looks of things, these people each met a violent end. Two of them died from blunt force trauma to the head and upper torso, one from sharp force trauma and the forth took three bullets to the chest."

While it fit with what they had discovered so far, it did little to help solve the mystery of why and by who these settlers had been killed. What was made clear was that at some point there was a hard-fought battle within the walls of the settlement. Until those questions were answered Finn had to assume that dangers continued lurking around every corner on the planet's surface.

"Now, the remains also showed a significant level of animal activity. With the passage of so many years, I can only assume that the handful of bodies we've recovered are only small part of a much larger story here."

"It certainly opens the door to a lot of questions, but at the same time it tells us that security needs to be maintained at all times. There are threats on this planet that we have yet to identify." Finn said as he nodded towards Tayte to pick up the briefing with his own findings.

"I've had squads out conducting patrol patterns all around the compound. We discovered another camp site to the north very similar to the one we found earlier. Tracks throughout the area seem to indicate that someone has been keeping a close eye on things here." Tayte said. "All signs inside the compound itself seem to indicate a sudden and violent event several years back. From Lauren's briefing we know that several villagers were killed during that incident. We've searched every single building on the grounds and found clothing, supplies, tools and equipment for the most part left completely undisturbed. What that tells me is that no one from the Discovery crew returned here after that incident."

"You're saying that all 500 people from that mission are likely dead?" Dr. Hughes interjected his voice shaking with unease.

"I'm saying their unaccounted for." Tayte corrected, "we've recovered and identified only a handful of remains. As to the rest of that mission, we don't have enough information to base any solid conclusions at this time."

"Alright then, security will continue to be our number one priority." Finn said. "Tayte, let's get word to the shuttle crew and have them return to the Resolute. I want the rest of our people on the ground as soon as possible. We also need work crews to start repairs throughout the colony. Get with Dutch and Lauren after this briefing, find out what supplies and equipment they need and ensure everything is included on the next shuttle."

Turning back to Dr. Hughes, Finn continued. "You've conducted preliminary testing on atmospheric conditions, is there anything hazardous that we should be aware of?"

"Quite the opposite in fact." Dr. Hughes replied, "the air is clean and fresh, water safe to drink, even background radiation levels are several times lower than what we saw back home. Everything about this planet is as close to perfect as one could hope."

"Well that's certainly a welcome piece of positive news." Finn interjected.

"What about the dinosaurs?" Dutch asked, "Don't they pose a significant threat making our situation a little less than perfect?"

"Potentially, yes." Dr. Hughes continued. "So far, we've identified a handful of species, all fairly innocuous for the most part other than their size. It does stand to reason that along with those species this planet is also home to more dangerous, carnivorous animals that would be a much greater threat to all of us."

"It's something to keep in mind." Finn said, "the most important thing right now is that we keep our guard up at all times. The power situation on the Resolute being what it is, we don't have the luxury of scouring the planet for a more hospitable home. For now, this colony has shelter, cleared lands for planting, easy access to a clean water supply and with a little work a secure defensive wall that will help provide at least some protection from threats."

"Sure as hell didn't help the last guy." Tayte blurted.

Finn shot him a disapproving look. He had long ago grown accustomed to Tayte's willingness to openly speak his mind on any topic and in any setting. While his comments were often ill-timed and even borderline inappropriate, on reflection Finn realized they bore a measure of truth that it was important all of them take to heart.

"He's right." Finn said bluntly, "while we still don't know what dangers we face here, we have the benefit of hindsight in realizing they exist. Now, with that being said, it's getting late. Everyone get some rest; the real work is about to start."

~~~~

CHAPTER 6

Finn awoke shortly before dawn, his internal clock seemed to sense the impending sunrise and pulled him from a deep and restful slumber. His cot was arranged in a private office inside a large bunk house with row after row of roughed in frames for beds stretching along both sides of a long and wide common area. Only a handful of beds has been completed, but it was clear this building had originally been designated as one of several that would serve as temporary housing for new colonists until permanent structures were constructed.

Pulling on his boots, he was about to step into a communal washroom when his PDA crackled to life with the excited voice of one his security people.

"We've got movement in the tree line at one o'clock from the north entrance."

Grabbing his MOLLE vest and rifle, Finn sprinted for the exit. He vaulted down the steps and had just hit the ground when the distinct pop of gunfire ripped across the peaceful morning air. The sounds of electrically charged bursts from pulse rifles were joined by the eerily familial crackle of semi-automatic and automatic small arms weapons.

"What's going on?" Lauren shouted as she stepped out from the door of a nearby bunk house. Finn watched with horror as a chunk of wood exploded off the side of the building only inches from her head.

"Get back inside!" He shouted as he darted past her waving frantically, "we're under attack. Get inside and stay down."

Sliding to a stop at the corner of the exterior wall, Finn joined four other security officers as they raked the sights of their rifles back and forth across the landscape searching the rapidly waning gloom for targets.

Across the field and from the trees beyond came the steady rattle of gunfire, several single shots and then a short, sustained burst from an automatic weapon. Dirt at their feet kicked up in small fountains as a spray of bullets passed close by.

"What they hell happened?" Finn exclaimed as he pressed his rifle into the stock of his shoulder and squeezed off a handful of return shots at the distant muzzle flashes.

"Not sure sir." The senior officer replied. Finn recognized the man, one of their section leaders, a former SWAT officer from Chicago. "We were just returning from a walking patrol around the exterior perimeter. Almost reached the main gate and then all hell broke loose behind us. Started taking fire from several positions in the woods out there."

"Injuries?" Finn asked.

"Two walking wounded, I sent them towards the medical building."

"Alright, good job." Finn replied and then taped the comm link on his PDA, "Tayte, you in position yet?"

The reply came in the form of two squawks of breaking squelch letting Finn know that the Quick Response Force (QRF) was in position and ready to bring the fight to the enemy, whoever that enemy may be.

"Ok." Finn said addressing the small group of security officers, "on my lead, we are going to draw fire and give the QRF some cover. Everybody ready?"

With a quick check of their weapons, all four signaled they were ready. Finn drew in a deep breath, brought his rifle to bear and then stepped from cover and began sending a stream of pulse beams into the tree line. The response was an immediate and heavy volume of return fire. Finn and his small force held their ground and kept up the pressure as they tracked muzzle flashes as a point of reference.

"Ugh!" An officer stammered as he staggered back and crumpled to the ground in a heap. Finn took a step towards the wounded man when he felt something slam into the center of his chest with the force of a sledgehammer. He stumbled and dropped to his knees where he quickly assessed himself for injuries. A single round had struck the armor mesh over his breastbone but failed to penetrate. The kinetic force of the impact left him short of breath and wondering if any of his ribs had been broken.

The tempo of outgoing fire intensified as more defenders along the perimeter took up the call and poured a stream of deadly charged beams into the trees and brush.

Rising to his feet on wobbly legs, Finn spotted a pair of figures moving from behind a tree into the open in a rush towards the gate. They held familiar looking rifles in their hands and were firing blindly from the hip as they charged.

"Targets!" Finn yelled as he looked down his telescopic sight and tracked the approaching figures.

Finn and two additional officers fired almost simultaneously. Pulses of energy stabbed out across the open ground slamming into the torsos of both targets. Their bodies stumbled and wavered but still they came.

"What the hell?" Finn mused aloud. The hits from the pulse rifles should have been more than enough to drop anyone in their tracks.

With his eyes continuing to track the targets, he let loose a carefully aimed three round burst into the chest of the closer of the two. This time the body pinwheeled sideways, dropped into the knee-high grass and lay still. The two security officers finished off the other target with a succession of bursts

From inside the line of trees Finn noted bursts from pulse rifles cutting through the brush from the east and knew that Tayte and his QRF force were hitting the enemy on the sides and flank.

"Shift fire, shift fire!" Finn called out as he adjusted aim further to the west along the avenue the enemy would need to use to escape the sudden ambush.

Moments later the wood line exploded with brilliant bursts of weapons fire. Dancing strobes of energy charged particles were answered by a steadily dwindling return of muzzle flashes from the as yet unidentified enemy force.

Finn and his small contingent of security personnel continued adding their own wall of fire to the carnage sending steady streams of pulse blasts across the enemies' line of retreat.

The firing slowly withered down to a few scattered shots here and there and Tayte's voice crackled through the airwaves. "Hold fire, all units hold fire."

This was followed seconds later with calls for medics.

"Lauren. We've got wounded coming in, need you at the medical center right away." Finn called into his PDA.

"Already there, get the injured here as soon as possible. Seconds count." Lauren replied.

Finn wasn't surprised, deep down he knew that despite his warning for her to remain inside the bunk house she'd completely ignored him and made her way across the compound to be ready for this exact scenario.

~~~~

By all accounts the fighting had last no longer than ten minutes, but they had taken a toll in terms of casualties even in that short of time. Finn stood over a row of six body bags arranged in a line in the corridor outside the medical center.

The shadows on the wall were starting to grow longer as day slipped way into evening. Finn was having a hard time accounting for all the hours throughout the day. Following the firefight, there had been a rush to get the wounded to the medical center. Along with Lauren, five medic trained security officers had worked tirelessly throughout the day fighting to save lives.

When all was said and done the casualty count came to six dead and eight wounded, two of those critical cases with severed limbs.

"Ok, strip off that shirt." Lauren exclaimed as she stepped into the hallway snapping on a fresh pair of gloves. Her surgical gown remained splattered with blood and gore from the latest surgery. She looked on the verge of exhaustion and as Finn studied her eyes he could see that she was also fighting back a flood of emotions as she took each life loss as a personal affront.

"I know you were hit and I want to check your injuries."

He knew better than to argue the point. He was learning that she was as determined as she was stubborn.

Unhooking his vest resulted in a wave of pain that nearly knocked him off his feet. With considerable effort he unbuttoned his uniform top and slipped his t-shirt over his head.

"Left quite a mark." Lauren mused as he studied the dark purple fist sized mark on the right side of his chest. With tender hands she probed along the edges of the bruise. Even though he struggled to avoid flinching it was clear the examination was causing him pain.

"You're lucky." Lauren eventually proclaimed. "Doesn't look like you have any broken ribs. They may be bruised and tender, but nothing life threatening."

"Yeah, hurts like shit, but I'm pretty sure it was just a ricochet. We found out that whatever ordinance they were sending our way punched right through our armor like a hot knife through butter."

"That explains the number of casualties. Most of the fatal wounds were through the torso where body armor should have helped." Lauren replied. "Have we learned anything about who attacked us?"

"About to find out." Finn replied as he keyed the radio on his PDA. "Tayte, what's your status?"

"Approaching rally point bravo. We lost the trail about three miles out, they just up and vanished into the woods like ghosts."

Noting Lauren's questioning look he explained, "There were a few survivors who fled into the woods. Tayte took two squads to try and follow and see where they went."

"Roger. Stand by, I'm enroute to you now." Finn said into his PDA.

Ten minutes later Finn and Tayte stood across from each other looking down at a line of bodies that had been collected and dragged out into the edge of the clearing.

"What the hell am I looking at here?" Tayte asked.

There were sixteen bodies in total, eleven male and five female. Four others were known to have escaped into the woods. The bodies were all dressed in a motley collection of tattered rags and animal hides. They were gaunt, pale and appeared malnourished but that was far from the most remarkable feature.

Each of the dead were fitted with electronic implements covering their left eyes and attached to different locations on their body.

"Cyborgs." Tayte mused aloud, "honest to god Cyborgs."

"I'm not exactly sure what they are." Finn replied as he dipped down to one knee and carefully studied the remains of a middle-aged man.

"The way this is sunk into his head, it's not just covering the eye. I bet its serving as a replacement."

Upon closer examination he could see that a dark orb fitted perfectly into the eye socket. The central piece, where the eyeball should be, appeared flat and dark but also had a near transparent appearance. "It actually reminds me a little of a camera lens."

Gesturing towards a fitted piece of metal and wiring protruding from the exposed chest he continued, "this is directly over the heart. I wouldn't be surprised if most of the major organs are being artificially controlled or manipulated in some way."

"Might explain why these bastards were so hard to take down." Said Tayte as he pointed out the multitude of injuries on each body. "Most of them took anywhere from five to ten shots center mass before they finally dropped. I've never seen anything like it, a single blast from a pulse rifle anywhere to the torso is more than enough to drop most men, even with body armor."

"Yeah, I saw some of that myself. Two of them broke cover and it took several of us to finally bring them down." Finn replied.

"The cyborg aspect aside, their weapons are another puzzling issue." Tayte continued.
Along with the bodies, a crew of security personnel had scoured the woods and surrounding fields recovering weapons and equipment. Everything was now stacked in neat rows next to the bodies. Knives kitted out in leather scabbards had long, curved handles that appeared to be carved from animal bones and connected to thick and razor sharp ten-inch blades made of a dense metal that they couldn't readily identify. The fire arms included infantry rifles and belt fed machine guns, the structure of each stood out as very familiar to both men.

"These are old school World War II era British weapons." Finn mused.

"My thoughts exactly." Tayte replied as he hefted a machine gun, opening and closing the bolt release, "Bren light machine guns and Enfield rifles. Both firing a .303 round. Shit load of stopping power right there."

Finn hefted one of the rifles and studied it closely. The wood grain stock and metal finish appeared nearly brand new and well maintained. A five round cartridge seated in the magazine well still held two rounds. Finn popped one of the rounds from the magazine and examined it.
"These are machined cartridges. Right off an assembly line somewhere."
Stacks of additional magazines and belts of ammo for the machine guns lay next to the weapons.

"They were certainly loaded for bear." Tayte added. "Other than a small quantity of food rations and knives, they were only carrying weapons and a large loadout of ammo each."

"Alright, let's get all this policed up and secured. Get a detail out here with stretchers and get these bodies to the med center. I'm going to see if I can get Lauren to perform autopsies, maybe she can learn something more about these people." As an afterthought he added, "let's get a few of these weapons over the Dutch in the machine shop, maybe she can tell us a bit about where and how they were manufactured."

~~~~

"Well cyborgs may not be the most clinical term I've ever entered into a report, but it's the closest definition I can find at the moment." Lauren offered as she dropped into a chair in the command center conference room.

Finn knew she was running on fumes at this point. After a long day struggling with the wounded, Lauren had spent the better part of the night conducting autopsies. Finn pulled up a seat next to her while Tayte helped himself to a cup of coffee from a pot brewing on a nearby table. They were soon joined by Dutch and Dr. Hughes both of whom appeared equally haggard and worn down from a long and sleepless night.

"Let's hear it." Finn opened with a gesture towards Lauren.

"Ok, I've only completed eight autopsies so far. Normally I would have had them all done by now, but what I've found is just so far out in left field that I'm struggling to fully understand it." Lauren said.

"They're aliens aren't they?" Dutch asked excitedly, "actual aliens right out of a sci-fi movie."

"Well, no, not exactly." Lauren continued, "while I haven't completed all the autopsies, I did run genetic tests on them and have identified several as members of the Discovery mission." She tapped away at a tablet and connected remotely to one of the wall mounted screens that were powered and still working. The biographies, backgrounds and official photo of nine individuals were displayed for all to view.

"They sure look a hell of a lot different now." Tayte whistled, "but I don't get it. I mean how did they get like this and what about the others? Who are they??"

"I'm afraid my examination and report are only going to raise more questions then they will answer, but I'll lay out my findings all the same." Lauren said. "In each autopsy I found duplicate cybernetic enhancements to the left eye, heart and lungs as well as the brain stem and spinal column. The purpose of that equipment is well beyond my specialty, but I can say that whatever it was for, it allowed these individual to function at a level well beyond typical human endurance."

"Does that explain how we shot them multiple times and they still kept coming?" Tayte asked.

"Exactly." Lauren replied, "no matter how you go about it, there are basically two definitions of death in humans. Interruption of circulatory and respiratory functions as related to the heart and brain death following cessation of all brain functions. These enhancements appear take over once those organic functions cease following any catastrophic injury, it allowed them to push well beyond a normal person. In addition to that, I suspect they would also possess superior strength, endurance and agility all without experiencing pain or fatigue."

"So, were dealing with some kind of super soldiers here?" Finn asked.

"I don't know about that." Lauren replied as she gestured towards the biographies still displayed on the screen, "farmers, construction workers, metallurgist, even a nurse. None of these individuals have any background suggesting a familiarity with military or police activities. No, I think it's more a conditional situation. The cybernetics are merely a conduit, the programming behind it is what is driving these people to do what they do. It's likely they have no idea what's happening to them or the ability to stop it. Of course, this is just a theory at this point, as I've already stated, the equipment is well beyond my field of expertise."

"Dutch, after this meeting why don't you take a look at that equipment and see what you can learn." Finn said with a nod to the young engineer, "Lauren, what can you tell us about those that weren't part of the Discovery, any clue who they are or where they came from?"

"No, nothing at all. I mean, they're genetic profile is not on file in any database I have access to." Lauren explained, "and believe me, I have a comprehensive record set for everyone on the crew of both Discovery and The Resolute, these people were not part of either crew."

"Ok, another mystery to add to the growing list, but they are human, correct?"

"Oh yes, in every sense of the word. There was one additional factor that all of them share that needs to be addressed." Lauren continued, "their DNA has been corrupted. By this, I mean, I believe they have been the subject of some kind of medical experiment involving the extraction of genetic material that was 'altered' in some fashion and then reintroduced to their bodies." There were audible gasps around the room as everyone took in the disconcerting news. Lauren paused for a moment to glance down at her notes, her eyes moist and her lips trembled slightly as she recounted the rest of her findings.

"This accounts for their gaunt and pale appearance, its actually not far removed from the type of damage we would find in someone suffering from radiation sickness, although there were no traces of radiation or toxins in their systems."

"Medical experiments?" Finn asked, shock mixed with rage in his voice as he struggled to keep his emotions in check, "for what possible purpose and performed by who?"

"No idea on either account." Lauren sighed, "I can only report my findings, the who, why, how, what and where are questions I simply don't have enough data to even attempt answering yet."

"There's one last thing you should know." She sucked in a deep lung full of air and steadied herself before delivering what she considered the most uncomfortable piece of news.

"As you know, there were several women included with the attackers."

That single sentence sent shivers up Finn's spine. While he wasn't exactly sure where this was heading but he knew they were about to hear a distressing piece of news.

"There are indications that each of these women have undergone further experimentation in terms of their reproductive systems. There are indications of a number of miscarriages and even abortions." Lauren's voice wavered as she spoke, but she was able to gather her wits and push ahead to lay it all out of them. "They have all suffered various forms of uterine damage to the point that they would have never carried a child to term. In my opinion, these women were subject to rapes as well as forced pregnancies, to the point of infertility."

Slumping backwards in his chair Dr. Hughes exclaimed, "My god."

"Exactly." Lauren countered, "while we don't know what we're dealing with here. It should be clear that the stakes are much higher than simple survival of our species."

An uneasy silence descended on the room as everyone absorbed this latest turn of events.

"Alright, that's a lot of heavy information. It's clear we are dealing with something we don't fully understand. I know it's hard to hear these kinds of things, but believe me, it's important to help us learn how to deal with and overcome the dangers we are going to face on this world." Finn said.
"Dutch, how are things going with establishing comms with the Resolute?"

"Unfortunately, I'm still unable to get past the jamming. While local, short range communication with hand held units and our PDA's seem unaffected, we still can't get a signal off planet." Dutch explained.

"That's an issue." Finn replied. "What are you going to need to help get around it?"

"Honestly, we need to locate the jamming source and shut it down. Beyond that, we're dead in the water as far as comms and orbital surface scans, both of which would be very helpful."

"Understood, that's on our list of priorities." Finn noted with a grimace. That list was steadily growing larger and faster than their available resources, he would need to get a handle on that sooner rather than later.

"Tayte, how's our security situation looking?"

"Thin I'm afraid. I've got every able-bodied individual standing to and pulling round the clock guard shifts. We're running two, eight-man patrols at random intervals out to the four-mile marker. I'll feel a lot better when we get some more boots on the ground and engineering work on the perimeter, lot of holes in that wall that need patching."

Finn nodded his understanding, "If everything goes according to plan. The next two shuttles should arrive day after tomorrow. That will bring us the rest of our security force as well as the initial contingent of workers and supplies. From there it shouldn't take long to extend the perimeter, close those gaps and add some additional elements to help with security."

~~~~~

CHAPTER 7

Lauren followed a worn dirt trail through a thin screen of trees along the banks of the stream. Even after years of growth and lack of care it was evident that this expanse of land had offered the colonist a place of peaceful refuge within the walls of their new home.

The trail took her to a small open pasture on a slight rise several feet over the stream. Large sections of tree trunks had been beautifully constructed into makeshift benches randomly scattered about where they could take advantage of shade from overhanging branches. It was a beautiful little oasis that she had discovered the day before when she went looking for a quiet place of reflection.

As she rounded the bend and was about to step out into the open she stopped short as she realized she wasn't alone.

His back was too her as he rested in one of the delicately carved benches. His concentration was split back and forth between typing into a computer tablet and moments of pause where he looked up and stared out over the tranquil view across the stream. His rifle was leaning within easy reach against his knee, a reminder that even in such a peaceful setting there were dangers all around them.

Her intent wasn't to be sneaky and she knew it wasn't wise to surprise him from behind, but for a just a moment she remained frozen in place as she watched him from a distance.

From the first moment they met she had recognized an attraction between the two of them. It was actually somewhat puzzling to her, he was far from the type of man she usually went for. Her dating history was punctuated with a handful of broken relationships with academics, medical professionals and even a six-month stint with an ambulance chasing lawyer. She never exactly fit into the dating world and long ago had resigned herself to growing old all alone.

Something in her changed when she met Finn for that first time though. He was rugged and certainly rough around the edges with a military bearing that she never thought she'd find attractive. But in the depths of his eyes she saw something that drew her in with the comforting cloak of a warm blanket. As she got to know him during their training before launch and certainly during the short time on the surface of their new home, she found herself drawn to him in a way that was both exhilarating and eerily scary at the same time.

"You know, you're not the secret ninja you think you are." Finn called out over his shoulder.

Lauren felt her cheeks grow flush as she stepped into the meadow and approached him, "Sorry, I wasn't intending to spy or intrude. It didn't look like you wanted company, I was trying to make up my mind whether to leave or stay."

"Please, stay. I would actually enjoy the company." Finn replied.

As she neared she caught a glimpse of what appeared to be a letter he was typing into the tablet.

"A journal?" She asked, her curiosity getting the better of her.

"No, letters actually. Six men died on my watch. I'm writing to their families."

Her face betrayed her puzzlement at that.

"Of course, I know I can never deliver them. I guess it's more for me than anything else." He explained.

"I think I understand." Lauren replied as she eased herself down onto the bench alongside him. "Everyone deals with loss in their own way."

"Actually, I think this is different." Finn countered, "I once told you about my tattoo and how it memorializes soldiers I lost in combat back home."

Lauren offered a nod but also chided herself at the selfish thoughts that filled her head as she recalled the toned canvas carrying that particular piece of ink.

"I think deep down those losses hit me harder only because they were really unnecessary."

"Unnecessary?" Lauren asked, surprise evident in her voice.

"Those wars, Afghanistan and Iraq. When we first sent troops into those countries it was in response to a direct action against our country, the 9-11 attacks. I guess you could say they were retribution." Finn's eyes drifted away from her as he searched for the right words. "After a time, it seemed those wars lost their focus and we shifted from payback to nation building. Myself and other officers started to feel that the lives of soldiers lost in that effort were simply wasted in some futile political bullshit. That's why those losses hit me so hard, I suppose I saw them used like pawns in a game we were never expected to win."

"I never really thought about it." Lauren replied, "the wars always seemed too far away and I hate to admit it, but after a time they kind of got lost in the shuffle of climate change and other worldly events."

"Don't beat yourself up about it, that was actually pretty common. After the first year or so, those wars became old news, well, except for those of us eating sand and dodging IED's on a daily basis. I'll always remember being home between deployments one time. There was a headline article about some actor breaking up with his girlfriend for one reason or another. All the major news services were carrying it. That same day five soldiers died in action during a twelve-hour firefight in Afghanistan. That article was half a paragraph long and carried on page two of those same papers."

Finn's eyes fell on her and in them she recognized a spark of emotion, an ember of passion that filled her with an unfamiliar warmth as he continued.

"I suppose my point is, the deaths of those soldiers as well as the men under my command were pointless in the larger scheme of things. It's different now. The men I lost the other day died defending our home. Those deaths had meaning. While we may not yet fully understand why it had to happen, I know deep in my gut that it served a greater purpose. There was true honor in their sacrifice."

"And the letters help?" Lauren asked.

"I think so. It's my way of ensuring that their sacrifice is never forgotten. We are just starting here and there will be many more trials and tribulations to come. I don't want them to simply end up on page two one day down the road."

Finn reached out his hand and grasped Lauren's. There was a chemistry between them, something building towards a crescendo that he felt powerless to deny. He shifted towards her and bent his neck slightly as he leaned in for a kiss.

A rustling in the bushes across the stream along with the unfamiliar growl of an animal thwarted their moment.

Releasing her hand, he snatched his pulse rifle and bolted to his feet. His eyes tracked the sound through the brush until locking in on a swaying branch some fifty feet away. Bringing the rifle to bear, he spied something large moving slowly and methodically through the scrub. Between breaks in the undergrowth he could make out a squat round hump lumbering along almost lazily through the thin screen of woods. As they watched in amazement, the figure passed through an opening in the trees and the hump materialized into the armored shell of a large four-legged creature.

"Oh my god, it's a giant turtle!" Lauren exclaimed as she barely contained a burst of uncontrolled laughter at the unexpected interloper.

It was roughly the size of a small car with the crown of the shell rising to shoulder height of a full-grown man. Finn estimated that it must top the scales at close to a ton. As it moved across the opening between trees he took note of the thick, matted fur covering its reptilian legs and neck along with a pair of rodent like ears that twitched back and forth like a nervous mouse.

"Actually" Finn offered, "It might be more closely related to an armadillo. An extremely large armadillo."

Moments later the creature lumbered past and deeper into the brush where it disappeared from view.

"It's a truly amazing place." Lauren mused as she stared into the woods after the departing creature.

"Amazing, but dangerous in so many ways we simply weren't ready for." Finn replied, "we have a lot of work ahead of us. We really can't afford to have minivan sized animals like that simply wandering around inside the walls with us."

Lauren's PDA crackled with an incoming message from the medical center. Her presence was requested as soon as possible.

She stood and turned to look at him. "This was nice, let's do this again sometime."

With a beaming smile she hustled off back down the path and out of sight.

Finn walked the long and circuitous route along the inner perimeter. Stopping at each checkpoint he checked in with the guards, making sure they were alert and focused on their assigned sectors.

As he made his way through the middle of the compound towards the command center he was passing by one of the bunk houses when he heard a clanking sound followed by a raised voice and a string of muffled curses.

"Damn piece of worthless shit." A husky female voice exclaimed from the communal shower area.

Finn pushed open the door to find Dutch straddling the top of a ladder, half in and half out of the ceiling as she strained against the handle of a large wrench and a length of pipe.

"Dutch? What's going on?"

Continuing her struggle, she groaned back, "damn bolts stuck, rusted shut."

Pushing her full body weight into it and nearly falling off the top of the ladder in the process, the wrench began moving ever so slightly and Finn heard the unmistakable sound of water begin flowing overhead.

"Wait a minute, you actually got running water to the sinks and showers in here?" He asked excitedly.

Giving the bolt one last turn, Dutch looked down at him and smiled, "not just running, why don't you turn on one of the faucets."

Finn walked across the tiled floor and tried a faucet at one of the sinks. After a few seconds spitting misty air, a steady stream of water flowed into the bowl. Moments later he couldn't believe his eyes when he noted a mild bit of steam beginning to rise from the stream.

"Shit Dutch! Hot water? How did you pull this off?" Finn exclaimed.

"Well, I really can't take all the credit." Dutch replied as she climbed down from the ladder and began putting her tools back in their box, "the Discovery crew really set things up nice around here. They put in an underground feeder system tapped directly into the stream. I traced the lines and found that they have it set to run into a series of 50-gallon wooden barrels set out alongside each bunkhouse. The barrels are all lined with solar sheeting to heat the water."

"Unbelievable." Finn replied, "I didn't really expect we'd see running water, let alone, heated water for a long time to come, if ever."

"They were pretty brilliant in the design, I would never have thought of a gravity fed system like that. They re-purposed metal and PVC piping from their ship and even took advantage of local bamboo for some of the longer runs. It's simple, yet extremely effective. It's been sitting idle for so long, it just needed a few tweaks and there you have it." Dutch replied with a wave of her hand towards the steady stream still flowing from the sink, "all the comforts of home."

Finn rinsed his hands under the steaming stream and marveled as the grit and grime quickly melted away to reveal his callous and chapped hands. "Every little bit helps."

"It's a start anyway." Dutch continued, "still a shit ton of work that we need to do. Power being the number one priority. I could only salvage a handful of solar panels and a single wind turbine. Its barely enough to keep our equipment charged and a few lights on."

They were interrupted by a thunderous clap high overhead, followed seconds later by a second identical clap. With a broad smile Finn replied, "Fear not, help is on the way. That should be our shuttles with personnel and equipment."

Stepping outside they scanned the sky overhead until they spotted the approaching shuttles. Finn considered them ungainly looking craft, bulky and utilitarian lacking any of the sleekness or artful designs he'd always pictured space ships would one day possess. The main body was built like an oversized double decker bus sitting atop a pair of extra wide cargo containers. With four engine couplings, two per side and extended several feet away from the main body, the boxy craft would never win any beauty awards. But he had to admit, what they lacked in aesthetics they made up for in cargo capacity and durability.

As they drew closer the engine cowling's rotated to face downwards as the pilots began to slow their descent. They were targeting the fields on the outskirts of the colony, with one ship heading north and the other towards the south. The ships went into a hover at a hundred feet above the surface as the pilots made final adjustments and lowered the landing struts. A minute later the first of the craft touched gently down, kicking up a billowing cloud of dust that filled the sky and billowed high above the trees. Finn shuddered at the thought that along with the sonic booms, this was a beacon visible for miles all around, but one that couldn't be helped. Moments later the second shuttle settled onto the ground in a similar cloud of dust and debris.

Tayte joined Finn at the edge of the compound and they watched as the cargo ramps at both the front and back of the northern most shuttle dropped slowly to the ground. First down the ramp was a massive looking individual, standing a good six foot six and topping the scales at nearly 300 pounds, the ramp under his feet appeared to nearly buckle with each footstep. Solidly built with muscles developed from years of construction and heavy equipment operations. One of only a handful of German's to join them, Phoenix Zimmermann was an easy-going colossus, quick with a smile and someone who took great pride his work. They'd met several times during pre-launch training and both Finn and Tayte had come to like and admire the gentle giant.

"Well, I hear you boys needed a hand around here!" Phoenix bellowed as he approached and took first Finn and then Tayte's hand in his own massive paw offering each a hearty shake. Finn had to suppress his laughter at the Texas accented English. His mother was German and his father American, during his early childhood, Phoenix had spent some time in Texas where he learned English along with the accompanying drawl.

"You're a welcome site." Finn replied, "Got a list of chores that need your special attention."

Workers and security members were now streaming off the shuttle in orderly lines. Tayte excused himself while he went to meet the rest of their security force and get them organized with housing and onto the guard rotation.

Finn guided Phoenix a short distance away from the growing commotion as work crews began organizing to start unloading cargo. Reaching into a back pack, Phoenix pulled out a tablet computer, "Commander Tilley wanted me to give you these updates first thing." Firing up the computer he opened an image file of the planet taken from orbit. The picture included an overlay depicting the location of the settlement. Finn's eyes were instantly drawn to a swarming mass of dense clouds some distance to the east of their location.

"That looks pretty rough." Finn said.

"Yeah, they've been watching this thing form over the last few days. These pictures are only a couple hours old. Shipboard sensors are still coming up blank with surface readings but visual tracking puts the colony right in the bullseye for this storm."

Casting a glance towards the eastern sky Finn took note of the first wisp of darkening clouds far off on the distant horizon. A gentle breeze through the trees was pushing leaves towards them, a clear indication that the storm front was steadily making its way in their direction.

"Wonderful. Was there any good news to pass along?"

"Not much I'm afraid." Phoenix continued, "they've tried everything possible to get around the jamming with no luck. The Commander believes it's going to take someone on the ground to actually locate and shut down the source before they can complete a full planetary survey."

Typing commands into the tablet, Phoenix brought up a document outlining a schedule of future landings. "They're still looking at a six-month window for orbital operations until the Resolute is completely drained of power. With the supplies and equipment we need to offload, that equals a shuttle mission every two to three weeks just to bring down materials. It will take another month of steady operations to get all the colonists and crew to the surface."

"We'll be cutting it close." Finn mused.

"Yeah, but it's doable. Since you've had a chance to review conditions down here. You let me know the priorities you want us to concentrate on. I've got five complete work crews. With a rotating schedule we can keep three full crews running around the clock."

"Excellent, that's going to be a big help. Why don't you get everyone offloaded and checked into quarters." Finn said as he gestured towards a bunkhouse where a squad of security officers were standing by ready to pass out housing assignments and provide directions to the newcomers.

Over Phoenix's shoulder Finn spotted Tayte jogging in their direction, by the strained look on his face he could see that something was up.

"Go ahead and get yourself situated Phoenix, I've got some things to tend to. We'll meet back up a little later and discuss priorities."

"Trouble." Tayte exclaimed as he drew within ear shot, "a patrol ran into a pack of wild animals, a flock of large birds and their nesting area."

"Shit, casualties?" Finn asked.

"Not too bad, a few cuts and bruises. But that's not the worst part." Tayte explained, "During the scuffle, the patrol got divided in two. All but three returned to the rally point. They waited a couple hours but when the others didn't return or respond to calls on the radio, the rest of the patrol beelined it back to report in."

Finn could tell that there was more to come, "what else?"

"Alright look, Dr. Hughes has been on my case to let him off the leash and join a patrol to check out the wildlife. He's one of those missing."

"Great!" Finn exclaimed, he was angry but at the same time he understood. The good doctor was a persistent pain in the ass and had he been in Tayte's shoes its likely he would have given in as well. "Ok, what's done is done. I need you to stay put and get things organized here. You know the security situation and Dutch is up to speed on the construction needs. Once Phoenix and his people get situated, I want you and Dutch to sit down with him and get him up to date on things. I'll lead a team to backtrack the patrol route and see if we can find our stragglers."

~~~~~

CHAPTER 8

Finn cinched the draw string on his day pack tight and hefted the bag over his shoulders. Filled with extra rations, ammo and a change of clothes, it would hold him over in case the patrol ran overnight.

He was joined at the south gate by a ten-man security element, including two from the wayward patrol.

As he organized his personal gear, the senior patrol member, former Marine sergeant Jenna Conway performed a quick inspection of the rest of the patrol. Finn was glad she would be joining the operation, she had a stellar military record and her performance during training and since arriving on the planet's surface had been commendable.

"Ready when you are Captain." Jenna announced as she hefted her pulse rifle with a practiced ease.

"You weren't planning on leaving without me, were you?" A voice called from behind him.

With a pack strapped to her back and outfitted in fatigues and a pair of jungle boots, Lauren locked eyes with him and held her gaze as she readied herself for an argument. A holstered pistol at her side along with spare charge packs, a Kbar knife and a utility pouch all attached to a set of standard issue web gear, told him that Tayte was more than likely responsible for her outfitting.

While he was able to think of a thousand reasons why it would be a bad idea for another untrained civilian to leave the compound, he knew the argument would be futile and serve no purpose other than wasting more time.

"Alright Jenna, lead on." Finn said.

Nearly three hours later they were almost five miles out when the first claps of thunder were followed by a steadily increasing blanket of rain. Finn knew the storm had been approaching but the thick canopy of trees overhead had prevented them from tracking its progress until it was right on top of them.

"Close it up." Jenna ordered, "intervals of no more than twenty feet apart, make sure you have eyes on the man to your front and rear at all times."

They were pushing their way through thick brush, the rain continuing at a steady pace and Finn could feel a rapid drop in the barometric pressure, a sure sign that the worst of the storm was still to come.

From the front of the column Finn spotted the lead man raise a balled fist over his head, the hand signal for everyone to halt. Jenna broke ranks and jogged forward to see what was up.

"Sir, we've got a body up here." Jenna's whispered voice crackled over his comms, interference from the storm now starting to impact even short-range transmissions.

With Lauren following close behind, Finn pushed his way through the brush and joined Jenna at the head of the column where they found her kneeling down and picking through the shredded and bloodied remains at her feet. It was a grisly sight, pieces of tattered uniform and equipment intermixed with chunks of flesh, gristle and exposed bones. A pulse rifle lay nearby, a severed hand still clutching the trigger guard.

"It's Taylor." Jenna announced to no one in particular as she held a pair of bent ID tags into the air.

Lauren crouched down next to the remains and made a cursory exam. "There's not much left, intestines, part of one arm and about half the ribcage. He was attacked by an animal judging by the teeth marks in the soft tissue and bone. A pretty large and very strong animal to do this kind of damage in such a short period of time."

"That's where we ran into the animals." The lead security officer exclaimed gesturing into the driving rain towards a massive tree trunk with a huge split running nearly twenty feet up its base. "I recognize that split tree trunk."

"What the hell were you even doing out this far?" Finn asked as he experienced a frustrated sense of anger at yet another senseless loss of life under his command. "This is well beyond the established patrol range."

"Sorry sir, I tried to explain that to him, but he insisted on exploring this particular region, he thought it held promise for some interesting wildlife."

With an exaggerated roll of his eyes Finn said, "Dr. Hughes brought you out here, didn't he?"

"Yes sir. He was very insistent on extending the patrol, I was only trying to keep him happy." The officer explained as he squared his shoulders and said, "I take full responsibility, this was my patrol, I should have turned back at the four-mile marker as instructed."

"Nobody's casting blame here." Finn replied, "Dr. Hughes can be a pain in the ass. But for now, him and at least one more of our people are missing somewhere out here. Let's find them and bring them home."

"Finn." Lauren said, her voice a harsh whisper as she struggled to be heard over the increasing tempo of the storm while also trying to keep her voice measured and low. "There's something in the brush over there."

With a nod of her head, she directed Finn towards a clump of brush several feet closer to the split tree trunk. Lauren's eyes were open wide, her brow creased and her hand moved steadily towards the butt of the pulse pistol holstered at her side. Finn could feel the tiny hairs on the back of his neck rising up as his senses responded to imminent danger.

He slowly raised the barrel of his rifle and pressed it into the stock of his shoulder as he tilted his head and sighted through the optics. Scanning from side to side he concentrated on the clump of brush, there was something there but it was difficult to make out in the gloom. A brilliant flash of lightning flashed in the distance and his eyes locked onto a pair of glowing orbs staring directly back at him. The creature was perfectly camouflaged, its large, flowing feathers spread gently to each side where they blended seamlessly with the branches and leaves.

It stood nearly eight feet tall, bipedal with a pair of long spindly arms ending in three stubby appendages topped with curved and topped with menacing claws. His immediate impression was that of an extremely large bird, its long, blunt beak jutting several feet from its domed head. In the few seconds of illumination provided by the lighting Finn discerned a reptilian tongue snaking in and out between rows of razor-sharp teeth.

He had no idea what he was looking at but instantly recognized it as a dangerous predator. As his finger began wrapping around the trigger a blood curdling scream sounded from behind him startling him and throwing off his aim. His initial shot went low, blasting a rut in the mud at the creature's feet.

In a blur the beast shot from its hiding spot and careened across the short distance separating them like a linebacker in a desperate sprint for the opposing quarterback. Another scream from behind him was followed by blasts from multiple pulse rifles, out of the corner of his eye he spotted flickers of movement as a pair of identical creatures sprung from the woods and into their ranks.

His brain processed the ambush in a split second, the remains of the fallen officer had been left on display to draw them in and they had walked directly into the trap. As these thoughts fired across the synapsis in his mind, his body reacted on autopilot to the approaching threat. Adjusting his aim, he centered on the largest portion of the target, flicked the selector on his rifle to burst and squeezed the trigger.

A trio of pulse beams shot forward hitting the creature square in its chest. The force of the blasts caused it to stagger slightly but failed to penetrate the thick muscle and scaly armor hidden under the dense outer covering of fur and feathers. As it closed to lunging distance, Finn let loose another three-round burst at point blank range into its neck and the underside of its snarling beak and then flung himself towards the ground.

He hit the mud and began to slide, his momentum carrying him under and beyond the creature as it launched itself ahead where Finn had been standing an instant earlier. This time the pulse bursts found purchase in the softer tissue under its beak, punching through its leathery hide and drawing a shower of blood. The creature bellowed a tortured roar as the sudden shock of pain threw it off balance and it stumbled drunkenly between Finn and Lauren before slamming headfirst into a thick tree trunk.

The beast was quick to recover and turned to find Finn slipping and sliding in the mud trying to stand back up. Finn saw it coming and knew in that instant that it was over for him, his rifle was tangled up under his own body weight and there was nowhere to jump clear of the snarling teeth and claws.

He felt a soft whisper of disturbed air as something shot past only inches from the side of his head. As the beast reached out a clawed hand ready to slash at him, the shaft of a long, finely crafted arrow suddenly embedded itself deep in the recesses of its right eye. The creature's head turned skyward as it let loose one final, strangled roar that quickly dissipated into a high-pitched screech and it toppled over onto its side where its chest rose and fell twice more before all movement finally ceased.

The fighting between the rest of the patrol and the other creatures ended abruptly when the remaining beasts recognized the dying scream of their companion and scampered away into the thickest of the brush out of sight.

Through the driving rain and murkiness, Finn's eyes fell on three unfamiliar figures, each holding long bows with arrows nocked and drawn. He reacted on pure instinct. Tucking and rolling off to the side, he untangled his rifle from his gear and came up onto one knee while swinging his weapon up and ready to fire.

Finn paused, his finger on the trigger and ready to fire. The three figures standing in the rain a hundred feet from him stared back at him their weapons raised by not directly threatening him or any of his people. The rain, wind and gloom made it difficult even at that distance to clearly make out details. What he could discern was more puzzling than any direct threat any of them posed at that moment. Two of the figures towered a good couple feet over the third, one male and one female judging by the outline of their bodies. They were broad shouldered, heavily muscular and sparsely dressed in hand crafted animal hides. The male was shirtless, his immense chest richly covered in thick, dark hair that appeared more like animal fur. While the male's face sported a flowing beard, the females was smooth and clean although the bone structure of both their heads and faces were similarly rugged and animal like.

A clap of lightning, much closer this time, lit things up, giving Finn a better look at the newcomers. His eyes caught the reflection of metal on the face of the smaller of the three.

"Contact rear!" Finn shouted as he recognized the cybernetic implant similar to those that had attacked without warning only days earlier.

A flurry of movement in the brush behind the tree was accompanied by excited shouts "don't shoot, don't shoot, don't shoot!!"

The voice was strained and out of breath but familiar enough that Finn relaxed his trigger finger as he called out, "hold your fire."

Dr. Hughes appeared behind the three figures, he was soaked to the skin, covered in mud, his clothes torn and filthy. He was out of breath, shaking and on the verge of collapse as he waved his arms wildly and continued yelling for them to hold their fire.

"What they hell is going on here Doctor?" Finn demanded.

As Dr. Hughes struggled to catch his breath but before he was able to answer, Jenna's strained voice cried out from a tangle of brush, "Medic! Medic! Man down over here."

Lauren was on her feet and moving in seconds. Following the calls for help, she pushed her way through the underbrush until she found Jenna along with two officers kneeling on either side of a prone and bloodied figure. The injured man was fading in and out of consciousness, his hands grasping desperately at bloody mess around his midsection. A substantial gash exposed portions of his intestines and left them hanging freely as he tried to tried to push them back into his body.

Pushing past the other guards, Lauren crouched beside the wounded man and began digging into her day pack pulling out equipment and supplies while shouting hurried commands at the onlookers.

"You! Hold that IV bag up at shoulder height."

Rolling up the injured man's sleeve she stabbed a needle directly into his arm and in seconds had the connection set for the lifesaving fluids.

After a quick check of his vital signs, she prepared a needle with a mild pain reliever and injected it directly into his hip.

"This should help with some of the pain. I wish I could give you more but your blood pressure is dropping and I can't risk it." She offered softly, her soothing voice doing more to help calm her patient than the medication she was administering.

Removing a sheet of plastic wrap and a roll of gauze, she carefully dressed the wound, giving special care to the exposed organs. Placing the man's hands over top of the dressing she said, "maintain pressure here, not too hard though, just enough to help slow the bleeding."

Looking up and locking eyes with Finn she pleaded, "I can't treat him out here. He'll die of infection just as sure as he will of blood loss. We need to get him somewhere dry and clean where I can work on him or we're going to lose him."

Gesturing to a pair of officers, Finn ordered, "get out your ponchos and prepare a stretcher with some tree limbs."

The wind was picking up to hurricane force bending the tops of the trees and adding fragments of branches and twigs to the stinging rain. "It will take a couple hours to get back in this weather, can you stabilize him that long?"

Still working on securing the dressing around the man's waist Lauren glanced back over her shoulder, the distressed look radiating from her eyes answered his question.

"There's another place much closer." Dr. Hughes called out over the roaring wind and rain. Finn had nearly forgotten the doctor and his new friends. As he glanced back he saw Dr.

Hughes standing a few feet behind him, having finally caught his breath he continued, "it's really not far, it's safe and dry."

Sensing Finn's hesitation as his eyes shot from him to where his companions remained several yards further back looking on quietly, Dr. Hughes added, "your other man is there, he's hurt as well and needs attention."

Gesturing towards the body of the slain creature he added, "those raptors are highly intelligent. That's their pack leader laying there, they'll be back any minute in greater numbers."

"Alright, we don't have a lot of options." Finn snorted.

~~~~

CHAPTER 9

Dr. Hughes had been true to his word, after a trek of less than thirty minutes, they emerged from the dense forest along the banks of a wide and rapidly flowing river. Following the bank upstream a short distance, they rounded a bend and were confronted with a marvelous sight. A waterfall rising hundreds of feet up a sheer wall of granite dumped majestically into a deep reservoir that fed the river beyond. Had it not been for the urgency of tending to their wounded and escaping gale forces storm winds, they may have taken a few moments to marvel at their surroundings.

"Almost there." Dr. Hughes assured him.

Their three companions had served as guides through the forest and so far, had remained silent, for his part Dr. Hughes had not offered anything in the way of introductions or explanations, the weather making normal conversation nearly impossible.

They continued following their guides to the base of the granite wall where they found a well-worn path hidden behind thick knots of ferns leaves and heavy branches. The path was narrow and steep forcing the stretcher barriers to strain under their burden while struggling to keep their footing as torrents of ankle-deep water flooded past.

They climbed steadily until eventually reaching a wide, rocky ledge and a cave entrance.

Behind them the waterfall flowed relentlessly with a deafening roar while providing an impenetrable camouflage screen from the valley beyond.

Flanking the cave entrance, one to either side, the two larger guides extended their hands and motioned for everyone to enter. Unsure of what they were walking into, Finn suggested that Jenna assign a few officers to remain at the entrance to keep watch. He locked eyes with the larger of the two strangers who merely nodded, shrugged and continued gesturing for the rest of them to continue inside.

The ground under their feet and walls were all smooth limestone adding a cooling effect the moment they ventured beyond the threshold. Their footfalls and hushed voices echoed back at them as Dr. Hughes and the cyborg led them deeper inside the mountain. A short distance later, the path began to widen and suddenly opened into a sprawling cavern stretching hundreds of yards into the distance. It was so large they were unable to even see the walls at the back of the cave. What they could see however stopped them dead in their tracks.

The cavern housed a sprawling village tucked away and safely hidden from the outside world. Individual caves climbed the walls four stories in height, dirt paths or wooden ladders providing easy access up and down. Wooden structures of different shapes and sizes had been constructed in a wagon wheel pattern all around the base of the open cavern. The inhabitants milled about mostly uninterested in their group. Finn noted that there was a mixture of the larger, hairier ape like people along with a smaller number of cyborg humanoids. It was like something pulled right from the script of a Planet of the Apes movie, but it was real and there they were standing right in the middle of it.

"This way to the aid center." Dr. Hughes directed as he took the lead and headed off towards a two-story building in the distance.

The air was thick with sounds and smells, the alien mixture assaulted and overloaded their senses. Finn could make out the unmistakable odor of cooked meats intermixed with what he thought might be tanning animal hides all mingling with the scent of unwashed bodies and animal waste. Conversations floated on top of one another, nearly impossible to follow as they skirted the side of the village approaching the aid center, Finn was able to pick out a few words and scattered phrases here and there. He found himself astonished to realize that everyone appeared to be speaking either in English or one of several recognizable Hispanic or European languages.

Inside the aid center they were confronted with even more surprises. The building was artfully constructed, a small anti room led directly into an open bay lined on one side with a dozen raised cots. IV stands, trays of medical supplies and even electronic medical components all stood by at the ready next to each cot, the blinking of power lights and displays showed that the building was fully powered.

Three cots were already occupied. Their missing security officer occupied one, his heavily bandaged arm and face visible from under a blanket, his eyes tightly closed as he slept, blissfully unaware of their presence. The other cots were filled with cyborg humanoids, one male and one female, also sleeping but with no outward sign of injury or impairment. A pair of females from the larger ape species moved between the patients checking the readouts on the equipment and administering medications. It was eerily reminiscent of any hospital wing he had every visited back on their own Earth, but it was an alien planet and the people were alien beings, it was a scenario he was having trouble wrapping his head around.

"Get him on the bed." Lauren directed, her entire focus on their wounded man and nearly oblivious to her alien surroundings.

Once he was in place Lauren set to work gently removing the field dressing as one of the ape women wheeled a cart loaded with medical supplies alongside her.

Lauren regarded her unexpected assistant for a brief moment before returning to doctor mode, "can you start a central line on him?"

"Of course." The ape woman replied in accented but understandable English. "Saline solution, correct?"

"Yes, perfect." Lauren replied as she continued stripping away the bandages and exposed the gaping wound. Her eyes quickly surveyed the array of supplies offered on the cart and she nodded with satisfaction as she realized that anything she needed was right at her fingertips.

In the clear light and out of the weather she noted with some relief that the injuries, weren't as bad as she had first thought. The creatures' claw had cut a near perfect incision across the man's abdomen completely through the stomach muscles and exposing the intestines, but had not ruptured any of the underlying organs.

"I need everyone to clear out." Lauren said as he continued working, "infection and distractions are our greatest enemy now."

~~~~~

Finn accepted the steaming cup of the dark brew and took a tentative sip. The coffee had an unfamiliar yet pleasant sweetness to it that he thought he could grow to like.

They had followed Dr. Hughes and his new friends halfway across the cave complex to a smaller building near the center of the village. Along the way they passed through throngs of locals, mostly of the ape like variety and from the polite nods, friendly waves and occasional welcome greetings, the sense was that they were amongst friends and were openly welcome within the colony.

Finn was joined by Jenna after the remaining guards were tasked with securing the outside of the aid station while their wounded comrades underwent treatment.

The inside of the building was sparsely appointed, groups of wooden chairs surrounding matching tables were scattered throughout. Soft iridescent light from recessed ceiling lighting filled the room with a comfortable and adequate glow. A long serving table built into one wall offering a selection of glass and wooden jugs filled with a variety of beverages as well as plates of fresh fruits, berries and nuts. Finn had the sense that this was something of a community building where people could come together and meet for official or social occasions.

Dr. Hughes took a seat at a table directly across from Finn while his new friends, eased into seats to either side of him.

"I suppose introductions are in order to start things off." Dr. Hughes began. Gesturing towards the large hairy male and female to his right he offered, "This is Linc and Rune, they're from a race of people who call themselves the Revati."

The pair nodded in turn as they were introduced. Despite their impressive stature, they had a gentle and kind look in their eyes, their facial expressions remaining neutral, non-threatening. Their ape like appearance looked less animal like in their current setting, the prominent forehead, wide and pronounced cheek bones along with copious amounts of thick body hair suddenly seemed like nothing more than genetic variations found in any other population of people. Their extraordinary height and larger frames were mitigated as they sat comfortably at the table with the rest of them. Finn inwardly chastised himself for his earlier conclusions that they were more closely related to animals.

Next, Dr. Hughes gestured to his left and said, "this is Marcela, she's a surviving member of the Discovery mission, part of their IT support crew."

Inside with better lighting, Finn now had a better look at the female cyborg. Unlike those they'd fought back at the colony site who appeared emaciated and sickly, other than the obvious tech implants, Marcela appeared much healthier, clean and in relatively good shape. She looked a little younger than him, somewhere in her early thirties, with dark black hair pulled into a tight ponytail and eyes to match.

"Thank you doctor." Marcela said as she turned her attention to Finn and Jenna, "Captain Finnegan. No doubt you have many questions. I will do my best to answer what I can."

"First and foremost." Finn replied, "what happened here? Where is the Discovery crew and colonists?"

Marcela's eyes misted over, it was evident that this was a story she did not relish revisiting, but it was also one that had to be told, "some are dead, a few are here in the colony. The rest are, well...."

She choked and the tears began to flow, "they are far worse than dead."

She relived the tail in graphic detail. The Discovery's successful arrival in orbit, the ship damaged beyond repair after passing through the same Ion storm that the Endeavor had encountered. Communications back home remained spotty at best but the crew offloaded and carried on with the mission. The settlement eventually grew to a thriving community.

"It was eight years after arriving that we realized we weren't alone here." Marcela explained. "The wildlife is one thing, I mean dinosaurs of all things, who would have guessed? But we built the walls and learned quickly how to hunt the smaller ones while keeping clear of the larger and more dangerous species. Have you run into a Rex yet?"

"A T-Rex?" Dr. Hughes asked excitedly edging forward in his seat in anticipation.

"Exactly." Marcela continued, "Huge, fast, deadly. Very territorial, so you usually only encounter them alone or in pairs during mating season. Anyway, between them, raptor packs, and several other nasty predators, it's safe to say this planet isn't exactly the Garden of Eden we had hoped for. Well, predatory animals aside, it was the other people we encountered that turned out to be the most dangerous of all."

Finn rubbed unconsciously at his throbbing ribs where he was still recovering from the earlier firefight, "yeah, I'm pretty sure we have already had the pleasure of meeting them."

"They just attacked, late one night, without warning, it was a small group at first but we didn't have a great deal of weapons. Thankfully the wall held and we were able to push them back, but not before we lost over thirty people."

Finn had questions but he held them for now sensing that it was important for Marcela to tell the story in her own way without interruption. She went on to explain how the attacks continued over time, with each incursion growing more intense, until finally the walls were breached and the colony overrun.

"I don't understand." Finn finally stopped her to ask, "it clearly wasn't the Revati who attacked you, so who then?"

Marcela rose and poured herself a cup of water before continuing, "others, like us. Just people who came looking for a new world. For centuries this planet has served as a beacon of hope for hundreds or even thousands of other civilizations. They came, they built, they settled here and in turn they were all eventually attacked. Many were killed but most were captured and subjugated into a life of unconscious slavery and servitude."

"Wait a minute." Jenna interjected, "what other civilizations? Are you talking about alien races?"

Dr. Hughes, unable to contain his eagerness replied, "no, not alien at all. Other Earths! Planets nearly identical to our own. All containing human life, exactly like us, all evolving in similar fashions. In fact, we got it all wrong. This is not Earth 2.0, this is the original Earth. Earth 1.0."

So incredible was his story, that Finn and Jenna hung on his every word as though listening to a master story teller spin an intricate tale. But this wasn't fiction or fairy tale, this was real and it was unbelievable to hear.

"This planet is where life began for us, millions, maybe even billions of years ago. This is where it all began, right here. However not only for us, but countless other planets all across the solar system, all originating from this particular planet."

"Ok, this is incredible and also way outside my wheel house." Finn replied directing his comments back towards Marcela, "but for the moment, let's set aside the talk of other Earths and other civilizations. Who attacked you? You said most of your crew was taken, where were they taken? What happened to them?"

"Others just like us, those that came from different worlds, the other earths. There are hundreds of thousands, maybe even millions of them all over this planet. All the survivors from Discovery, my closest friends, the only family I have left, all of them are being held. It's a massive slave army, they have no control, no individual thought, they're unable to speak or communicate in any meaningful way, their implants control over them completely. After a time they are lost forever, their humanity completely wiped away and all that remains is a mindless husk that lives only to serve its master."

"Ok, wow, that's pretty incredible" Finn exclaimed, "but slave to who? Who are the masters."

The reply came from an unlikely source, for the first time Linc opened his mouth and spoke two simple words in a deep, thickly accented English, "The Creators."

"Few have ever seen them." Marcela explained, "but the Revati call them the Creators. Their culture lacks any formal religion as we would recognize it, but they do view these beings as deities to some degree."

"So, you're saying god like beings are pulling the strings here?" Finn asked, a snippet of skepticism in his voice.

"No, not exactly. Personally, I think it's another race humanoid, something far advanced of our own. You have probably noted that the planet is shielded against electronic sensors and communications are severely limited. Well, we believe that this other species, the Creators for lack of a better name, are behind it. Did you track in a beacon, one that appeared to be from the Discovery?"

"Yes, we followed it right to the colony's doorstep." Finn replied.

"Well it wasn't ours." Marcela said, "our beacon was disabled in the Ion storm. It wasn't until several years after we were on the surface that we first registered it. But we could never track the source. Some thought it was an atmospheric phenomenon. I'm convinced the Creators are behind that beacon and used it to lure you here."

"Like a spiders web." Dr. Hughes added hearing this part of the story for the first time himself.

"Exactly, and it's a system they have repeated for generations. Drawing the inhabitants of countless other Earths into the same trap." Marcela said.

"You said you were captured and taken away, where did they take you?" Jenna asked, her voice trembling as though she had to know the answer but at the same time was terrified of what she would learn. "What happened to you?"

Running her fingers along the cybernetic implant over her eye Marcela shuddered visibly as she said, "we were force marched for days through the jungle. Eventually we reached the base of a mountain range. We were herded into underground labs and sedated. I'm pretty sure this is where the Creators stepped in and why we don't remember them, they kept us drugged and in and out of consciousness that whole time. I remember only small fragments, snapshots but it's too jumbled in my head to pull together or even try to explain."

She was trembling now and her voice began shaking. It was clear that reliving the experience was as traumatic as the events themselves. Both Jenna and Finn tried to interrupt and offer her a chance for a break to pull herself together, she waved them off and pressed ahead determined to get it all out.

"When we woke, days…weeks…months later, no one ever knew, our bodies had been violated in the vilest manner one could imagine. The implants were in place and we no longer had direct control over our conscious selves. Then came the experiments, blood and tissue extractions as well as insertion from foreign sources. We underwent medical experiments of all kinds. It was horrible, a living nightmare where you were awake the whole time but lacked any control over your own body."

"But you escaped?" asked Finn.

"No. No one escapes." Marcela corrected, "I woke up one afternoon in a muddy field near the base of the mountain where we were originally taken. Forty-three of us where there, all dazed, confused and sick. We wandered into the forest and eventually happened upon a Revati hunting party. They took us in and over time nursed us back to health. We've been with them ever since."

Gesturing towards Linc and Rune she continued, "As you have likely guessed, this planet bears a number of characteristics similar to our own ancient Earth. The Revati tribe are the native inhabitants of this world. In our own history, they would be considered the missing link in human evolution. What that means is that while we share a common ancestry of sorts, our DNA is not compatible with each other. They are for all intense and purposes, a chain of human evolution which evolved independently of our own direct and ancient descendants."

"Were you the one who sent us the warning Marcela?" Finn asked, "The one that told us not to come here?"

Marcela's face fell as though a painful memory had suddenly struck her, "No, it wasn't me. Terry was a crew member from the Discovery, he was sort of our leader for a time after the Revati took us in. We knew there would be follow up missions with more colonists, he was obsessed with finding some way to send a warning."

Her solitary eye teared up again as she spoke, Finn knew he was pushing her hard but at the same time it was important that they learn as much as possible about what they were dealing with.

"We knew there was some kind of underground relay device not far from where we were released. We suspected its part of a chain of devices they use for their electronic jamming. Terry and nine others broke in and sent that message, only one of them made it back out."

Marcela was clearly exhausted at that point, the emotional toll of reliving some of the most painful memories in her life had pushed her to her limits.

The deep bark of thunder reverberated through the rock walls of the cavern reminding them that a hurricane level storm was still bearing down all around them.

"The storm will likely last all night. Food and sleeping quarters will be arranged for you and your people." Marcela said as she stood and motioned towards their Revati hosts.

"In the meantime, Linc and Rune have offered to show you around the colony and answer any questions you may have."

Both Finn and Jenna found themselves mesmerized with the architecture, creativity and efficiency that had gone into designing the Revati's cave complex. Dr. Hughes was like a school kid on a field trip firing off questions so fast and furious that Finn eventually had to ask him to settle down and simply go with the flow and allow Linc and Rune a chance to speak.

They learned that the colony was home to nearly eight thousand Revati along with another five hundred rescued colonists from home worlds all across the galaxy. Salvage efforts to one of several abandoned homesteads had provided them with a wealth of equipment and supplies, including everything they needed to construct and maintain an intricate hydroelectric system built along the rim of the waterfall. The cave system itself was much more complex and far reaching then they had initially thought. With the central chamber as the main hub for the community, several side tunnels branched out for miles in different directions. Additional housing units, storage areas, and production facilities were located throughout those different branches. When they asked about agricultural efforts and food production, Linc lead them down one particular tunnel while he offered general information about their surroundings along the way.

It was a fascinating experience to see how the tribe lived, they passed building where masons, carpenters, pottery makers, glass blowers, bakers, tanners and other artisans worked and lived. Revati children reminded them of little ones back home, the way they ran in groups, playing and living their lives, stopping and staring in curiosity as the group of strangers passed them by.

Finn found Linc to be a surprisingly likable individual. While he was guarded with his words, he spoke with a deep yet insightful voice that was contrasted with his physical features and appearance. He was further astonished to learn that the Revati people were fluent in a number of familiar languages all stemming from a common root of Latin. While thickly accented they were easy enough to understand and presented themselves as an intelligent and well-educated people. He inwardly scolded himself for allowing the term 'ape like' to enter his mind, even unspoken he felt it was an unfair and incorrect comparison.

They learned that Linc and Rune were coupled, while the Revati had no actual concept of marriage, they did tend to pair off for a period of time. During such pairings, couples often worked together in a single primary field. For Linc and Rune they were part of the tribe's warrior and hunter faction. With lifespans extended on Earth 2.0 to two or three hundred years, these pairings only last several decades, long enough to produce and raise offspring before each moved onto new partners and different fields of work.

While Linc was their primary guide and current spokesperson for the tribe, Dr. Hughes interjected himself whenever an opportunity arose, desperate to impart some nugget of information into the conversation. As they walked a tunnel branch, he droned on about his theories of how the caverns were formed.

"These are likely natural caves formed in the base of an ancient volcano. The volcano itself has been dormant for hundreds of thousands of years, but the geology here shows us that at one time it was very active with multiple eruptions throughout its lifetime. The tunnel we are in now will lead us to the inactive caldera." Dr. Hughes offered before adding, "it's truly a sight to behold."

Directly ahead of them loomed the opening to the ancient caldera and as they crossed the boundary into the crater they stopped and stared in astonishment.

The crater was huge, stretching at least two miles long by nearly a mile wide. The collapsed dome of the original volcano had formed a depression half a mile down from the outer rim towering high above them. Over time, decayed plant and animal sediments formed a soil base on top of the rocky surface. This nutrient rich soil provided an ideal location for crops and animals. The Revati had taken full advantage of it and turned the entire caldera into a productive agricultural hub. Crops, including corn, beans and several others they weren't able to readily identify filled the majority of the open ground. Along the periphery, animal pens were filled with chickens, cows, pigs and even a few smaller dinosaurs, although Finn couldn't even imagine their purpose. Dozens of Revati along with a handful of human/cyborg survivors worked side by side tending to the operation.

"Many of the crops and animals here have come from the villages of your people." Rune offered. "I understand your ships carried frozen eggs from animals on your home world. An incredible scientific effort."

It was the first time she'd spoken other than the occasional grunt of agreement or disapproval during their earlier conversations. Just like with Linc the sound of her voice was far from what any of them expected judging solely by her outward appearance. She had a soft, feminine quality to her speech along with a soothing tone that if they were to close their eyes and listen, they would have never pegged her as a seven-foot-tall Neanderthal cave woman. Her English was better than Linc's, more refined and with less of an accent.

"These animals are easy to handle and provide an excellent food source. The crops are a wonderful delight and with preservation they keep us fed through the longer winter months."

"This is astonishing." Finn mused, "it looks like you have a really good set up here. But aren't you concerned about the Creators and their cyborg army?"

Linc regarded Finn as he considered the question, "we fight when we have to."

Rune explained that the Creators and their slave army did not actively seek out the Revati and their wayward conscripts. On occasions when encounters did occur the result was always the same, savage fighting with heavy losses on all sides. To Finn's way of thinking that meant they were allies in a common fight and his ultimate goal would be to form a solid alliance with their hosts.

They wrapped up the tour an hour later back in the main chamber where Linc led them to a path which climbed the back wall where several cave dwellings had been set aside for them. Food, drinks and clean bedding awaited them and after a hearty meal, some light-hearted conversations along with a few mugs of a sweet homegrown nectar with an abnormally high alcohol content, they found themselves dead on their feet and ready for a few hours of down time.

Outside, the storm raged on and the steady drumming of thunder carrying through the rock walls around them helped lull them all into a restful slumber.

~~~~~

CHAPTER 10

"He's not completely out of the woods, infection and shock are still serious concerns. I'm reasonably optimistic of his chances though." Lauren said as she shoveled a spoonful of eggs into her mouth and chased it immediately after with a swig from a citrus type drink that reminded her of orange juice but was brown and had most certainly not come from an orange tree.

The storm had passed early in the morning and they had enjoyed a comfortable night sleep. Awaking refreshed and ready to start a new day each of them had a more optimistic outlook on their new home now that they had laid the groundwork for a relationship with a potential ally.

"We should start back as soon as we can." Finn said as he enjoyed a plate of eggs, sausage and something close to hash-browns but flakier with an unusual texture. He had learned long ago not to ask the source of unfamiliar foods, best to try everything he could and let his taste buds and stomach decide what was palatable or not.

"He can't travel." Lauren replied, "at least not for a few days. I'd like to stay here for a while anyways. It's my understanding that these people have been without a doctor for a long time. As a gesture of good will, I'd like to lend my services in providing checkups and overseeing some training. The nurses who helped me last night are good, no doubt about it, but with a little help they can really take things to the next level."

"It's not a bad idea." Finn mused, "we have medics that can handle most issues that may come up. I would insist on leaving a few security guys here with you though."

In response to her raised eyebrows and before she could voice her protest he added, "consider them extra hands to help with whatever you might need. It would really set my mind at ease."

~~~~

The hike back to the settlement was much faster and easier going in the light of day without hurricane force winds and rain holding them back. Linc, Rune and Marcela had all agreed to return with Finn, Dr. Hughes, Jenna and two security officers while the rest of the team remained behind to provide security and help with anything Lauren may need.

It was closing on midday when they entered communications range shortly under four miles from the colony.

Instead of directing them to enter the colony, Tayte requested a meeting in an open meadow half a mile from the main gate.

When Finn entered the meadow to find Tayte waiting with a small patrol force he called out to instruct them to hold their fire as they were approaching with friendlies. The wide eyed and slacked jaw reception at seeing him in the company of not only their first Revati tribesman but also a cyborg hybrid was not unexpected.

"I see you found some new friends." Tayte offered as he met Finn half way across the meadow.

Introductions were made and Finn promised a more detailed briefing once they were all back behind the colony walls.

"So, what's up?" Finn asked.

"We resumed our regular patrol patterns early this morning after the storm blew through. One of them found something that I think you should see." Tayte replied.

Leading them nearly half a mile to the east, Tayte directed them to a spot alongside the stream that passed through the colony. In the soft mud where the swollen waters were starting to recede they found themselves staring at the footprints of an enormous creature. The three toed prints were clearly visible in the muck, sinking nearly a foot into the ground they were close to four feet in length and two and half feet across. A normal sized man could almost use any one of the prints as a shallow swimming pool.

"T-Rex" Marcela exclaimed as she clutched tightly to her bow and scanned the surrounding forest. "We should get out of the woods as soon as possible."

Linc bent down and studied the print, "buck, very large."

"That's bad." Marcela added, "the males are much more aggressive than females. They also claim a huge territory and will attack almost anything inside it. There hasn't been a male in this area for some time. The storm must have drove him to a new hunting or mating ground."

"Wonderful" Finn groaned, "can there possibly be anything else on this planet that wants to either kill or eat us?"

"Once we found the tracks I pulled all patrols and work details back to within a half mile radius of the fence line." Tayte explained, "we got lucky on this latest supply drop, it included our night vision equipment and three of our heavy weapons, the pulse cannons. I've already assigned a detail to get those weapons charged up and ready for action."

Finn felt a measure of relief with that news. For the most part, supplies and equipment had been packed many months ahead of launch in a very specific order. Since the security element was added after the fact, a lot of their gear had to be spread out and stored wherever space could be found. This meant that they likely wouldn't see all their equipment until the entire ship was offloaded. Having at least a few cannons and their night vision gear in this initial supply drop was a major win in terms of their capabilities. It remained to be seen however if even the added firepower would be enough to hold back an eight-ton killing machine.

They worked their way cautiously back towards the main gate. A hundred yards away they started hearing sounds of work in progress, the long drone of chain saws, clanking of metal on metal and shouted commands along with the occasional expletive.

As they entered the compound they found a hive of activity as workers scrambled about continuing the offloading of gear and equipment from the cargo holds of the two shuttles. Additional work crews crawled over and around various buildings making repairs, adding solar panels or assessing updates and additions.

A trio of heavy-duty ATV's crossed the path in front of them, each vehicle dragging a large piece of freshly cut timber in its wake. They made their way towards the lumber mill where another crew was replacing or repairing equipment as they made the yard ready for use.

"Looks like Phoenix has his people working overtime." Finn observed.

"Oh yeah. As soon as the storm broke he was shaking their racks and had them setting up portable generators and lights to get things rolling." Tayte said approvingly, "he's running things like a military operation, smooth and efficient, happy to be working with him."

As they made their way across the compound, workers would stop and stare at the newcomers.

Reaching the command center, Finn motioned for a pair of security officers and sent them off with instructions to retrieve Phoenix and Dutch to attend a briefing in the next few minutes.

"That reminds me." Tayte offered, "Dutch spent most of the night studying the…" he trailed off as his eyes fell on Marcela and her cybernetic attachments, "…remains we recovered from the firefight the other night. She's got some very interesting updates on that."

After Dutch and Phoenix arrived, Finn had everyone join him around the conference room table as he provided an overview of the events of the last twenty-four hours. He covered everything they had learned up that point about the Revati tribe, the existence of the Creators and the known threat from their extensive slave army.

Finn then turned the briefing over to Phoenix asking him for updates on their unloading and community repair operations.

"Everything's moving right on schedule, as long as the weather holds, we should have both shuttles unloaded by end of the day tomorrow."

"Excellent." Finn exclaimed, it was a pressing issue to get the shuttles unloaded as fast as possible so they could return to the Resolute to prepare for the next landing with additional equipment and personnel. Working around the Resolute's dwindling power supply issue put them on a tight but workable time table.

"Now, what obstacles are you running into in getting to repairs and additions to our outer defenses?"

"Well, our biggest obstacle is going to be our power consumption. As you know, everything from vehicles to hand tools, communications and weapons essentially run on battery powered rechargeable cells. Most of the existing power framework is either damaged or has been removed."

Finn glanced at Marcela who quickly spoke up, "yes, we scavenged what we could over the years. Solar panels, wiring, converters, charge packs, whatever we could get our hands on and easily carry off site."

"Ok, fair enough, and understandable given the circumstances here." Phoenix continued, "that means we need to replace a shit load of power producing infrastructure. We have some solar panel units included in this drop, but only a fraction of what we really need. I've been putting together an extensive list to send back to the Resolute on what supplies should be front loaded for future drops, but it's simply going to take time before we get everything we need down to the surface."

For the first time Finn was starting to feel less like a military commander and more like a civilian administrator. The mission design had called for the basic groundwork of a civilian government to be established by the Discovery mission. While they had a backup plan with an administrative team amongst the colonist on the Resolute, the security situation on the ground had to be solidified first. This pretty much dumped all matters related to governing directly in his lap for the time being.

Phoenix continued his assessment, "In the meantime we will need to ration our energy consumption to the most critical equipment only."

"We can conserve power by diverting it from non-essential areas like the kitchen, housing units and even the medical center when it's not actively in use." Dutch offered.

Finn inwardly sighed at that, it was going to be a kick in the ass to morale for the entire security and work force to suddenly switch to cold rations and showers. He had to admit that the thought of a hot meal followed by a steaming shower later that evening had been on top of his own to do list.

"Agreed, security is our top priority and all resources need to be focused there." Finn replied.

Phoenix continued leading the discussion for another hour and a half covering his plans for repairing and improving perimeter security. He wrapped things up with an overview of how he wanted to allocate his work force by splitting them into three teams, security, infrastructure and agriculture.

After Phoenix was finished, Finn turned to Dutch who was nearly climbing the walls to have her contribution heard.

"Since I pretty much went without sleep last night during that lovely little hurricane." Dutch began. "I spent the night looking over the cybernetics we recovered."

Dutch took control of the view screen with her own tablet bringing up an overhead, top down shot of an eyepiece, chest and spinal attachment.

"A lot of the tech is still well beyond anything I can explain, but I was able to get into the sub routines and figure out the basics of each device."

Focusing on the eyepiece she continued, "this piece alone is simply an amazing piece of work. It's actually a two parter in that it connects and controls optic nerve functions in addition to a highly advanced microcomputer that interfaces directly with a human brain."

There were muted exclamations around the room as everyone leaned forward in their seats partially sickened and partially amazed with the information.

"From what I can tell the optics provide each individual with some pretty advanced features well beyond our own basic vision. With this attachment each of them has infrared, night vision and telescopic abilities as well as a heads up display that interfaces with both an internal and external database providing targeting and tracking data."

"Jesus." Tayte murmured, "no wonder they were so accurate."

"What do you mean by external database?" Finn asked.

"That goes hand and hand with how all the equipment interfaces with the human host. There is a wireless connection, with both upload and download capabilities, that allows direct access to a central database. In essence, it gives the user access to a ton of on the fly data, while also instantly sharing anything they observe or encounter with that same database."

"So, what one of them knows, they all know?" Tayte asked.

"Pretty much, and it's a super-fast connection too. I couldn't actually clock it with our equipment since its all offline, but from what I found its likely damn near instantaneous."

"Alright, this is a point we need to consider for any future engagements." Finn said, "we can't underestimate these things. They certainly have a tactical advantage with this equipment."

"That's not all." Dutch said as she adjusted the display and focused on the remaining pieces of equipment.

"The chest piece does pretty much exactly what Lauren thought. It seems to have a built-in defibrillator, oxygen regulator and even a processor capable of taking over all functions of the heart. If you consider the healing properties of the planet's atmosphere, my guess is that these devices can keep an individual alive in the face of a traumatic injury long enough for the natural healing process to take over."

Moving on to the spinal attachment, Dutch focused the view on a small fluid filled ampule near on the underside of the device.

"This bad boy is the reason these things are so fast and strong. I ran a sample of this fluid through our own AI and found a close match."

On the screen a string of text appeared showing the chemical breakdown of a familiar substance.

"Epinephrine? Like adrenaline?" Finn asked.

"Yep, only something like a hundred times more potent. I'm not exactly sure what this stuff is, but the capsule feeds an auto-injector that would pump this stuff directly into the spinal receptors. My bet is that it's like a shot of rocket fuel, giving these things incredible speed, strength and endurance."

"It's an army of super soldiers." Tayte exclaimed his face turning red as his frustration and anger built up, "doesn't matter that they were only farmers or workers without any prior military training, this equipment puts them in a league of their own. How the hell do we fight a force of Terminators!?"

Marcela shifted uncomfortably in her chair enduring the occasional misgiving glance from Tayte. Noting the exchange, Finn turned to her and asked.
"What do you know about this?"

"Honestly, it's all news to me." She said with a quivering voice as her hand unconsciously touched the attachment covering her eye, "I mean, I knew it served some purpose, but never fully understood the scope of it all."

"You don't have any kind of x-ray vision with that thing?" Tayte asked as he gestured towards her implant, his voice dripping with suspicion but a glare from Finn told him to tone it down.

"No, of course not. I have no vision at all from my left eye, this thing never worked and as far as I know the one in my chest and back have never served any purpose. I think it was all disabled when we were tossed away."

"Anyway." Dutch raised her voice to continue, "it's an extremely complex system that we have no direct means to circumvent."

"That may not be completely true." Marcela offered, all eyes turned towards her but she kept her voice steady and he head held high as she tried to portray confidence. "I told you that some of our people managed to break into the Creator's communications center and send the warning you received."

Finn nodded recalling the story she had earlier relayed about that ill-fated raid.

"Well, that same facility houses an array of high-tech equipment, most of which was well beyond any of own tech. It's a good bet that if they are broadcasting a beacon across the galaxy from inside there, the same location is being used to transmit data to and from their ground forces."

"A raid like that would cost a lot of lives and we can't even guarantee we'd be able to breach the outer doors." Finn mused. "I don't think the possible gains would be worth the cost in blood."

"You wouldn't necessarily have to get inside." Marcela replied. "I don't know a lot about the tech involved. However, I would assume if that facility is used to send signals over long distances on the planet's surface, as well as into deep space, it probably isn't a hardened site."
Her eyes locked with Dutch's and it was evident the two women were thinking along the same lines.

"Of course!" Dutch quickly caught on, "an EMP outside the facility would fry everything."

Noting the quizzical looks around the room she explained, "an electromagnetic pulse."

"We know what an EMP is Dutch." Tayte growled, "unfortunately we don't happen to have a nuclear weapon to trigger one."

"Don't necessarily need a nuke for something like this." Dutch continued. "The Resolute's power plant is a fusion reactor, right?"

Heads around the table nodded in agreement but no one other than Marcela seemed to pick up on where she was going with this.

"The fusion cores! We can use them to trigger a localized EMP. It would work on the exact same principles as a nuke or solar flare, only minus the radiation."

"Unfortunately, we can't exactly pull any of those cores from service." Phoenix offered, "those last four cores are the only thing keeping the ship operational."

"We don't need the operational cores." Dutch immediately countered her mind already two or three steps ahead in working through the mechanics of the situation.
"The damaged cores still contain their original isotopes. They may no longer be capable of powering the reactor, but they still have the same energy signature. Those are stable isotopes that could be reconfigured into a chain reaction. From the description Marcela gave of the site, two cores set off on opposite sides of the mountain would be more than enough to flood the entire area with electromagnetic waves. If we're lucky, the equipment isn't shielded and the pulse will fry every single component inside the place. We could probably pull the whole thing off without firing a single shot."

Finn drummed his fingers on the table in front of him as he soaked in these new revelations. His experience on the battlefield had taught him that there was a great deal of truth behind the quote, 'the best defense is a good offense'. They had arrived at their new home to find themselves at a near hopeless disadvantage. While they certainly never asked for this fight, it had been thrust onto them and for the few remaining inhabitants of their planet to have any hope for a future, it was a fight they had no choice but to win.

Locking eyes with Dutch he said, "tell me exactly what you need."

~~~~

CHAPTER 11

Humidity hung like a thick curtain in the morning air and Finn's sweat soaked t-shirt clung to him like a second skin as he jogged around the inside of the fence-line. He passed a squad of security officers running in formation offering a curt nod to the squad leader as he called out a steady cadence.

He had to hand it to Tayte, the grizzled First Sergeant understood the value of establishing routines in order to help maintain discipline. Even as they faced a bleak and uncertain future on a new and hostile world, he managed to keep things running like a well-oiled machine. Divided into platoon and squad level elements, Tayte had organized a schedule that included training activities, physical training as well as professional development exercises on top of assigned shift work. It helped keep the men not only physically but mentally fit while instilling a structured environment.

It had been eleven days since the first pair of shuttles had been unloaded and returned to the Resolute, and in that time an impressive amount of work had been completed around the colony. Most of the damaged housing units had undergone repairs and the groundwork for several new buildings laid out.

Farm fields had been cleared and tilled with planting now underway. With winter not far off, this had been deemed the second highest priority after their security concerns. While the supplies in the hold of the Resolute would last them for up to two years, self-sufficiency with a reliable food source was a critical need for their long-term survival.

Nearly three quarters of the fence had been repaired or replaced along with some added improvements. With the wood mill fully operational and an abundance of high-quality timber to work with, Phoenix had designed a system of elevated guard posts every hundred yards or so along the wall. These posts provided the perfect vantage point to keep watch on their surroundings.

There'd been only a single encounter with a handful of cyborgs several days earlier. They were spotted by a sentry in the early morning hours skulking about in the nearby forest. A brief exchange of gunfire on both sides resulted in no friendly causalities and the enemy pulled back without pressing the attack.

Finn was convinced that it had been a scouting mission with the intent of gathering details on their disposition and strength. He also believed it pointed to the very real possibility that a large-scale attack would be forthcoming, sooner rather than later. Any reservations he'd once held about striking first with Dutch's plan to use an EMP device had melted away following that encounter.

As he approached the wooden bridge crossing over the stream he spotted a small group of off duty workers kicking back with homemade fishing gear along the water's edge. Fishing had become a favored past time for most of them and it provided a welcome change to the bland, pre-packaged meals they were forced to endure while the kitchen was shut down to conserve power. A fire pit in the central square served as a community barbecue where fish and the occasional deer or wild boar were roasted and served.

The men lining the bank offered Finn a friendly wave as he jogged on by following the path towards the rear gate.

A voice crackled over the radio on his PDA, "Base this is unit Charlie Six, requesting clearance to enter the perimeter."

Finn immediately quickened his pace and changed direction towards the main gate. The speaker had been one of the guards left behind with Lauren at the Revati settlement. His presence could only mean that Lauren and the rest of the crew had finally returned.

Standing at the main gate, Finn watched as a line of people emerged from the forest and slowly marched towards him. It came as a surprise to see the very man Lauren had remained behind to care for leading the group. It had only been a little more than a week when he was knocking on deaths door with his intestines spilling out and now here he was looking physically fit and no worse for wear.

Lauren was near the front of the column. Her eyes were downcast and she looked dirty and tired but once she glanced up and spotted Finn her eyes lit up, her pace quickened and a broad smile spread across her face.

"Oh you are a sight for sore eyes!" Lauren gushed as she drew close and then surprised him with spirited hug that nearly knocked them both from their feet.

Caught off guard by the sudden and unexpected display of affection, Finn tentatively returned the hug while casting a wary glance towards the nearest security personnel. He saw in each and every one of their faces that not a single person seemed caught off guard or surprised by the coupling. Finn had to wonder how long the rumor mill had been churning out speculation about the two of them.

"We weren't expecting you this morning or I would have rolled out the welcome wagon with food and drinks."

Reluctantly pulling back from the embrace, Lauren replied, "to be honest, I'll settle for a hot shower and a few hours' sleep. I'm so out of shape, trudging through the woods while dodging dinosaurs all morning really isn't my thing."

"Well, I hate to be the bearer of bad news." Finn fretted, "its cold showers and rations for the time being."

As they entered the gate and made their way across the settlement towards her quarters, he gave her a quick rundown on their power rationing as well as their upcoming plans to shut down the Creators communications and jamming center.

"As much as I deplore violence, I have to admit this is something we have to do and I'm so glad that it might be done without bloodshed."

She indicated that she had news of her own, but they had reached the front porch of her building and she was anxious to hose herself down, brush her teeth and grab a fresh change of clothing. They agreed to meet back up at the pavilion outside the dining area in an hour. Before disappearing inside she turned back and said.

"Oh, and have Marcela join us if you don't mind, some of what I found pertains to her and I have some questions."

For their part, Marcela, Linc and Rune had remained at the colony and quickly ingratiated themselves with the work crews. The pair of Revati had become something of a novelty within the ranks, their sheer size, unexpected intelligence and quick wit won over pretty much anyone they encountered. Finn had been surprised to note a tight bond forming between Linc and Tayte with the towering Revati hunter eager to sit in on training exercises and learn everything he could about military tactics and the way they fought. In return for taking him under his wing, Linc had constructed a long bow for Tayte and was showing him the benefits of the silent hunt. The pair were personally responsible for providing an impressive quantity of fresh meat into their diet.

Rune, had been spending a great deal of her time working side by side with the crews assigned to preparing farming operations. She was fascinated with how quickly and efficient the fields were made ready with their tracked and wheeled vehicles. The agricultural foreman took a little time to show her how each vehicle operated and before long she was pulling shifts on the detail operating plows and backhoes as though she'd done it her whole life.

Meanwhile Marcela had been keeping herself busy shadowing Dutch. Their combined skill set in both engineering and IT made them a natural team and it was seldom one was ever seen without the other. They had already started working on an alternate power source modeled after the hydro system in use at the Revati village. The final pieces of equipment they needed were expected on the next supply ship due at any time. Finn had picked up on some subtle cues that there might be a budding relationship of another kind developing between the two of them and found himself inwardly rooting for them.

The better part of half a boar roasted lazily on a spit over a smoldering fire in the center of the village. After filling a plate with a generous portion of the savory meat, Finn joined Lauren, Dutch and Marcela at a shaded picnic table along the edge of the bustling common area.

"Oh my god. This is so good." Dutch squealed as she ignored her silverware and fed long strips of the tender meat into her mouth by hand.

"Try dipping it in this." A voice called from over her shoulder. Tayte appeared seemingly from nowhere and offered a small plastic cup with an amber sauce.

Dutch stabbed a piece of pork into the sauce and everyone watched with amusement as her eyes first lit up with excitement and then squeezed shut in utter contentment as she made a show of relishing each individual chew.

"Spicy barbecue sauce?" she cooed approvingly, "where the hell did this come from?"

Sliding into a seat at their table, Tayte replied, "enjoy it while it lasts. My own secret stash, I've got three more bottles. I can only hope and pray someone learns how to make something similar before I run out."

"I take it we have you to thank for lunch?" Finn asked as he shoveled in another mouthful of the tender meat.

"Linc and I both." Tayte replied, "I've never seen anywhere with such plentiful game. This sucker much have tipped the scales at eight or nine hundred pounds" he said holding up a chunk of meat from a plate of his own, "had to call for a front-end loader to help us get it through the gate."

For several minutes they all sat and enjoyed a satisfying meal and casual conversation before Finn finally asked Lauren for an update on her latest findings.

"After learning how certain people are simply 'cast aside' when captured by the Creators. I started to ask myself, what it was that made them different and if there was any way we could possible use that information in the future."

"Let me guess." Dutch interjected, "you found something?"

"I think so." Lauren replied, "over the past week I have gathered blood and tissue samples from all of the former prisoners now living with the Revati. The salvaged equipment in their medical center had everything I needed to run a genome analysis and I found a single common trait each of them share. They each have a mutation in the gene known as MC1R."

"Mutations?" Marcela cried, "That's not possible. Everyone was medically screened for this mission; any genetic anomaly or mutation would have disqualified them."

"I know. I was part of that screening process for the Resolute." Lauren countered, "I'm familiar with the criteria for a medical disqualification. However, this is a recessive gene and one that would never have been considered as a disqualifying factor. You probably know it better as 'the red head gene'.

"You've got to be shitting me." Tayte nearly exploded with laughter, "the almighty and powerful Creators kicked these people out of their exclusive club because they're all red heads? Now that's almost funny."

"Given what we know about the Creators, it actually makes sense." Lauren explained. "It's called the red head gene, but in reality, there's more to it than simply hair color. The gene itself is what's known as a receptor and it plays an important role in pigmentation of the skin, eyes and hair. It's the reason that red heads tend to have much lighter skin and, in many cases, light sensitivity in their eyes. Those factors mean that extended exposure to sunlight has a greater risk not only for severe sunburns but several forms of related skin cancers."

"I don't understand." Dutch replied, "What would the Creators care about things like skin tone and hair color?"

"That's where things get interesting." Lauren said, "from what I learned during the autopsies of the dead cyborgs, it's clear that their DNA had not only been substantially altered but there were also indicators that quantities of genetic material had been removed over a long period of time. I believe the Creators aren't capable of living on the planet's surface. It could be something about their own DNA that might make them susceptible to the limited background radiation from the sun, something that actually benefits us could be deadly to them. I'm still not 100% on that part, but it does fit with the rest of my findings."

"So, you think they are stealing genetic material from our people and using it as a form of protection against harmful sun rays?" Finn asked.

"In a nutshell, yes. But it's not as simple as that. I believe that what we're dealing with is a race of being's intent of forcing an evolutionary change of some type. It may explain why they live underground and why the Revati have never encountered anything other than their cyborg army. The entire process would take generations, I'm talking thousands of years, but in theory, if their science is advanced enough, it's possible they could eventually force a mutation that would allow them to one day move to the planet's surface. By rejecting those with the red head gene, I think it tells us a great deal about conditions that may be threatening to them, specifically, atmospheric conditions here on the planet's surface."

"But what about Marcela?" Dutch asked, "I mean she's Hispanic, dark haired and with olive skin, she's not exactly a candidate for the red head gene."

During the entire exchange, Marcela had quietly sat alongside Dutch picking at the plate of food in front of her and listening intently. As all eyes now fell on her she met their stares with a lowered head and drooping shoulders.

"She's right, I do have the gene." She replied weakly. "My grandfather was an Irishman and my grandmother Latino from Puerto Rico. It was a source of embarrassment in our family. We were always concerned while living in Puerto Rico about having a red headed, fair skinned child. They would have been brutally bullied because of it."

"I'll be damned, way to go professor, seems you've cracked the case." Tayte quipped, "but how does this help us in the long run? Can we actually use this information to fight them?"

"It's something we didn't know before." Finn said, "it also gives us a little insight into their motivation and what it is they might be after."

"Exactly." Lauren added, "as far as using it to help fight them. If we can assume the surface conditions, be it direct sunlight, the atmosphere or oxygen levels, are a threat to them, I would assume there is a way to use that against them if need be."

The crack of a thunderous boom high in the sky overhead interrupted the lunch conversation as all eyes turned skyward.

"Excellent!" Dutch exclaimed, "the supply drop is early."

CHAPTER 12

The two fusion cores and a crate of electronics requested by Dutch were the first items unloaded from the shuttle's cargo bay. The cores loosely resembled large propane tanks, constructed of a corrosive resistant tungsten alloy. The fissile material itself was housed in the slender neck of each core with the reactive components and electronics contained in the lower tank. Each core was painted a bright yellow along with a stenciled identification number and associated information along the side as well as an external control pad with connecting ports near the top. Weighing nearly 250 pounds each, they were carefully manhandled onto cargo trailers behind waiting ATV's and then taken directly to the mechanic shop where Dutch and Marcela were standing by to work their magic.

"I held something back in the briefing." Lauren started as stood alongside Finn and watched the flurry of activity around the shuttle.

"Oh?" Finn asked curiously.

"I talked to many of the former detainees in the Revati camp about life on their planets and what made them turn to space. Some talked of natural disasters like plagues, asteroid impacts and climate change similar to our own. Of course, a few spoke of manmade calamities like wars and overpopulation. They talked about their home worlds and comparatively speaking it was amazing how alike all of our planets actually are but with unexpected and unusual variations.

Elvis Presley died of old age on one planet JFK was never assassinated and served out his complete term. In one case the Beatles never even became a band and the 9-11 attacks never took place."

"Yeah, the whole deal with multiple Earths scattered all around the galaxy is still something I haven't completely come to terms with." Finn replied.

"Well, one thing that I did learn is that in some cases the difference in our worlds are somewhat alarming. In one case the Roman empire was never defeated, another the Chinese maintained rule over all other nations stemming from the Qing Dynasty in the 1800's."

Lauren's voice caught in her throat as she continued.

"I spoke with one man where, in his world, the Nazi's won World War II and eventually became the single leading superpower. Their space program wasn't intended to find a new home for an ailing planet. To hear him tell it, their planet was actually in relatively excellent shape, no wars, no climate crisis, other than the whole Nazi way of life, no major problems to speak of. They set out into the stars with the intent of conquering new worlds and extending their reign across the galaxy."

"Jesus. As though we didn't have enough on our plates already." Finn muttered as he glanced around making sure no one else was within earshot. "I'm actually glad you held back on that little gem. That's going to push a lot of buttons and likely stir up certain levels of suspicion in our new allies." His eyes remained glued on the workers clambering in and out of the shuttle's cargo bay as he chewed the information over in his head.

"It's something we need to look into and address, but right now, one thing at a time and I need everyone focused on tomorrow before we start looking at next week and beyond."

Rows of workers and the first group of colonists; farm workers in this case, streamed out of the shuttle where they were directed to an impromptu in-processing area to be assigned billeting and a work schedule. It was hard to miss the darting eyes and nervous looks of the new arrivals especially when they spotted armed guards standing watch in elevated towers along the imposing outer wall. While word of the dangers awaiting them on the planet's surface had now been included in their pre-departure briefing, actually having feet on the ground in the thick of it made it all suddenly very real.

"This really isn't how we dreamed it would all turn out, is it?" Lauren offered as studied the anxious faces of settlers as they got their first look at their new forever home.

Finn considered that for a few moments before replying, "we knew there would be challenges, but no, nothing like this."

"Is this what it was like being stationed in a war zone back home?"

"Not exactly." Finn said, "back there we knew it was only for a brief period of time, a year, maybe eighteen months for some. But we always knew we would ultimately ship back home where it was safe. That's simply not the case here. This time there's nowhere to run, no reinforcements are coming, it's all or nothing. We are fighting for our very existence."

"It's a lot to shoulder." Lauren said as she watched the new arrivals shuffle quickly past.

Next to emerge from the cavernous cargo hold was a long, rectangular wooden container. The ceiling mounted crane slowly moved the container from the hold and off to one side behind the shuttle. As it settled into the grass, a team of workers immediately began removing the cargo straps and plying the external casing loose.

Inside the crate, a skillfully packed rigid hull inflatable boat (RIB) along with supporting equipment and a powerful air pump waited final assembly. Measuring twenty-three feet long and equipped with a pair of 20 horsepower electric outboard motors, it could carry up to 15 personnel and several hundred pounds of gear. They had a total of four such boats and for the plan to cripple the Creators jamming and communications facility, they would need two.

Watching as the unloading moved ahead, Finn distantly replied, "that's exactly why we're going on the offensive. This is our home now and we're damn well going to fight to keep it."

Finn had thought that paper maps were a thing of the past, however, without GPS mapping and satellite aided renderings, they were forced to make do with the only tools at their disposal.

Linc and Rune had spent painstaking hours committing every detail of the terrain surrounding their objective to paper.

"This is impressive." Tayte observed as he studied the fine details on the map. "All this from memory?"

"Yes. Remember, we have lived, hunted and walked these lands for nearly three of your own lifetimes." Linc advised.

There was a total of twenty of them inside the operations center conference room. Along with Finn, Tayte, Linc, Rune, Dutch and Marcela, they had a small contingent of security personnel as well as the shuttle's three-man flight crew. The plan was to keep the raid as small as possible with speed and stealth being the operative strategy.

"This will work." Finn added as he reviewed the map. "We'll shuttle in to this small island."

He tapped a spot on the map several miles shy of their objective. Addressing the flight crew, he continued, "Were going in an hour before dawn. We need to keep the shuttle low and slow on the approach, night vision only, no external lights. If they see or hear us coming it's all going to fall apart before it even begins."

Tracing his finger along the map he said, "the shuttle will drop both RIBS right here along the banks of the river and then set down in this clearing. We'll need to get the boats loaded and ready to go before daybreak. From here, we'll keep to the shallows as much as possible. According to Linc and Rune there are some nasty creatures in the deeper waters, we certainly want to avoid any encounters with wildlife on this trip."

He continued tracing a path following the outline of the river until he reached a point two hundred yards short of their objective.

"Once we reach this point, we'll tie off on the shore and break into two teams. I'll be leading team Alpha, we'll make our way to this point on the northern edge of the mountain. Team Bravo, led by Tayte, will come up on the southern approach."

Timing would be key; however, it was suspected that close to the jamming equipment their comms would be next to useless. Finn had drawn up a timetable for each team to follow.

"Dutch and Marcela will be in charge of setting the timers for detonations, Dutch will be with me and Marcela with team Bravo. The Resolute will be making a course adjustment to put it in orbit directly overhead. It's important to note that the ship doesn't have the power to perform this maneuver again, so no pressure on us." Finn said adding a little levity while ensuring they all understood the stakes at hand.

"Commander Tilley has relayed that come hell or high water the Resolute will be on station and ready at exactly 1000 hours local time. Now, without any direct comms with the ship, there's zero room for error on our part. We need to be in position and ready well before the deadline. I've given us four hours from the time we're dropped off for both teams to get into position."

Turning to the pair of Revati he continued, "while I hate to throw around stereotypes, it comes down to the fact that you two are the only ones physically capable of handling the cores once we leave the boats. I want Rune with me and Linc with Tayte's team, any objections?"

Neither offered an objection and Finn continued the briefing going over specific details with every member until it was evident they had the plan memorized.

"One last issue, and this is important." Finn stressed, "after we set the timers and make our way back to the RIBS, we will have plenty of time to get clear of the blast but we'll still be within the effective range of the EMP. Ten minutes before detonation, everyone needs to pull the power supplies from their PDA's, weapons and anything else with sensitive circuitry or it will be fried."

Checking his PDA, he announced, "Ok, its almost 1900 now. Grab some chow and get some rest. I want an equipment check at 0400 and we are wheels up by 0430. Any last minute questions? Comments? Jokes?"

~~~~

CHAPTER 13

The steady drone of the shuttle's engines vibrating through the metal decking under their feet felt almost soothing as the ship eased over the forest at treetop level.

They ran with black out lights only inside the cargo bay where the two teams were assembled and riding alongside their assigned RIB, the red lighting cast ghostly shadows on the walls of the expansive bay. Both inflatable crafts were fully assembled with all their gear carefully stowed aboard and attached to the ceiling mounted crane system. No one spoke as the minutes and miles ticked by as they continually ran over their individual rolls in their heads.

"One minute." The pilot announced over the intercom as they approached the landing zone.

Near the front of the bay, the shuttles crew chief clambered down the ladder from the cockpit and approached a control panel near the rear hatch and waited. Forward momentum slowed and then stopped as the pilot guided them into position.

"Go, go, go." The pilot called out.

The crew chief tapped a button on the panel the floor plating under the RIBS dropped and parted outward. Twenty feet below the shuttle the surface of the water frosted under the downdraft of the ship's engines.

The hydraulic lifts whirred into action as they slowly lowered the RIBS. As the boats reached floor level, the crews clambered aboard their assigned crafts and hurried to their individual stations. Seconds later both inflatables touched gently down and settled on the water as the last of the slack was released from the lift lines.

The sun was just starting to rise in the distant skyline but a low hanging layer of fog over the river promised to provide a little cover as they made their way upstream.

"Sir. There's a lot of activity on the depth finder here." The boats pilot called out.

Finn stepped forward to the small wheelhouse where a depth finder on the instrument panel gave an overview of what was happening in the waters around them. Grey shapes of all sizes slipped past as the boat cruised along at a steady fifteen knots. The sounding directly under the keel of the boat registered a depth of six feet but quickly dropped off only a short distance away into deeper waters. Within those depths the depth finder highlighted shapes that easily dwarfed the boat in size.

"Keep hugging the shoreline. Last thing we need is to tangle with some underwater monster that could swallow us whole."

They continued up the stream until reaching a fork where a smaller stream fed into the larger river, Linc held up a hand from the second boat signaling a halt.

"This is where we stop. Tie the boats off here." He said as he motioned towards a twisted knot of trees with an intricately exposed root structure stretching from the shore into the shallows of the river.

They tied off and scrambled into the surrounding woods. The instant their feet touched the ground they were assaulted by clouds of stinging and buzzing insects nipping and biting at every inch of exposed skin.

"What the hell!" Cried out one of the officers as he swatted something resembling a mosquito but was the size of a small bird from his forehead. A rivulet of blood flowed steadily down the bridge of his nose as he turned his attention to a second and then a third giant blood sucker attracted to the warm, coppery scent of fresh blood.

Reaching down into the ankle-deep mud sucking at their feet, Rune made a show of scooping up a handful of the foul-smelling muck and spreading it like lotion across her arms and face.

"It will stop the bugs and hide us from predators." She explained as she continued smearing the substance over her body.

"Do it." Finn ordered sharply as he followed Rune's lead and slathered on a thick layer of the putrid slime.

Despite the odor, the reprieve from the clouds of bugs was nearly instant and he had to admit that he'd much rather deal with a rank stench then battle a constant army of super-sized bugs.

The two teams separated at the bank of the river and Rune took off into the brush leading them at an impressive pace as they fought their way through low hanging branches, enormous fern bushes and imposing tangles of calf deep vines and roots.

~~~~

Thirty minutes into their trek the forest began to thin until it faded into the background and they emerged in a rock-strewn valley at the base of a craggy highland stretching off into the distance.

Finn checked his watch and noted they had made better time than he'd anticipated. Even with the heavy burden of a Fusion Core strapped over her back, Rune had proven herself a true trailblazer in the way she had moved effortlessly through even the most imposing brush.

"Spread out in a perimeter. Everyone take ten; drink water and double check your gear." Finn called out.

"It's not far now." Rune said as she sipped from the animal hide canteen she kept in a pouch at her side. Motioning towards a cleft in the rock ahead she said, "we climb from here, maybe an hour, maybe less and we reach the location."

"Good lord. What the hell is that stench?" A security officer gagged as a change in the breeze carried the foul stink of rot directly into their faces. Even the pungent muck covering their bodies couldn't help against this new and more powerful assault on their senses.

Finn recoiled as he recognized the smell, it was an odor from his days in a warzone, one that you never forget and hope to never encounter again. It was the smell of death and decay, a smell that only a rotting corpse was capable of giving off. Judging by the sheer magnitude of the stink, he knew immediately that several corpses had to be the cause, and they were close by.

"Rune, with me. Everyone else, hold tight and keep alert." Finn said motioning for Rune to lead the way up a path opposite the one they intended to follow. Easing her burden from over her shoulder, she pulled her bow lose and nocked an arrow into position as she headed off.

The path in the rocky ground was well worn, a clear indication of heavy use. While the recent rains had wiped away any trace of footprints, Finn knew right away the trail had been created by people and not animals. He kept his body low, his rifle pressed to his shoulder and his head constantly scanning from side to side as they picked their way cautiously up the rise.

Reaching a crest of boulders overlooking the open expanse of a cavernous gorge, Finn and Rune pulled themselves up to eye level at the top of the boulders freezing in shock at the sight that lay before them.

The gorge appeared to be man-made, the remnant of some type of mining operation. Stretching three or four hundred feet wide, it dropped another two hundred feet below the boulder strewn surface with several smaller tunnels disappearing deep into the rocky walls below. Dotting the entire area at the base of the gorge were hundreds of rotting human corpses. Large, carrion feeding birds and dense clouds of insects filled the air within the chasm. Packs of lizard like animals the size of large dogs roamed throughout the mess of bodies picking off chunks of flesh and the occasional limb. Tracks in the ground showed indications of larger predators passing through and grabbing a snack from the horrifying buffet of flesh and meat.

The bodies all showed a wide range of decay and animal activity with some already stripped to nothing but skeletons and others appearing fresher, maybe a matter of days or even hours old. The layering of the bodies indicated that this had been used as a dumping ground for quite some time. Even from a distance it was clear that every one of them bore the electronic implants of the Creators force of cyborgs.

"My god." Finn muttered, his hand pressing against his mouth as he fought back the urge to vomit, "why?"

Appearing unaffected by the horrors below, Rune studied the bodies before offering an opinion, "many are missing arms and legs, some appear old and maybe had grown feeble. I would guess this is how the Creators dispose of those that are no longer useful to them."

"I've never seen anything like this." Finn replied, "it's the most horrible thing I could have imagined. It's like picture I remember of German concentration camps."

"Even in our darkest times when war comes between our clans we honor our dead and respect the sanctity of life." Rune said with a cool and detached voice. "this is not honorable."

"Alright." Finn said, "I've seen enough. Let's get back to the others and press on. There's nothing we can do here."

~~~

A little over an hour later they crested a rise and spread out along a plateau overlooking a wide valley with a pyramid shaped structure rising from the ground and soaring hundreds of feet into the sky. Jutting out from the sides of the pyramid's base was what could only be described as a vast warehouse of some type. The single story, metal sided building was a bleak, windowless complex with spacious doors on three sides that stood open and seemed to be the only way in or out of the structure.

The valley floor surrounding the pyramid and warehouse was covered end to end with a dismal and bleak shanty town. The mismatch collection of buildings assembled from scavenged materials along with palm fronds, tree branches, twigs, hunks of grass, stone, animal hides and mud, filled nearly every inch of space. The ramshackle deluge of dwellings and other featureless buildings housed thousands maybe even tens of thousands of cyborgs many of whom were visible from their vantage point.

Carrying tools such as shovels, picks, axes, sledgehammers and others, they filled in and out of the central valley from any number of caverns or neighboring canyons.

Beasts of burden, hundreds of them, pulled crude wooden carts stacked high with chunks of chiseled rock and raw minerals. The creatures looked vaguely familiar, although that recognition came only from his knowledge of dinosaurs. Standing anywhere from ten to twelve feet tall, the creatures walked for the most part on four legs but at times were seen rising up on their muscular hind legs and scratching at themselves or eating with their narrow forelegs. Their most distinguishing feature was the flat, wide head crest that swept back from the top of their skulls. They appeared docile in nature, likely a non-aggressive breed that was easy to conquer and turn into a workforce.

The creatures were all constrained with sturdy leather harnesses over the back of their shoulders and crossing under their wide chests, bridle bits were forced into their mouths. Each beast had a handler nearby brandishing a whip that they seemed to use at indiscriminate intervals simply to remind the creatures who was in charge. Even from a distance, cruel and bloody wounds were visible on many of the animals from the lashings.

"Wow." Dutch breathed in awe as she crept up alongside Finn and peered cautiously over the rocky rim into the valley below. "I think we're in the right spot."

"Yeah. Sure looks like it." Finn mused as he panned a pair of high-powered binoculars back and forth taking in all the details. "This is a hell of a lot more than we anticipated though."

"It's like a confusing Disney land. No one seems to be in charge and there doesn't look like a lot of organization." Dutch observed as she took in the activity below.

"More importantly, they don't seem to be taking any serious security measures." Finn added, "no fencing, no guard posts, no patrols and I can only see a handful of them with weapons. For the most part those few seem to be more concerned with keep an eye on the workers than watching for intruders."

"Ummm, I don't know a lot about guns, but what are those big black things lined up outside the south exit of that warehouse?" Dutch asked.

Finn adjusted his binoculars and focused on the area until he exclaimed, "Shit! Those are old school cannons! Looks like about thirty of them, a mix of twelve pounders and Napoleons. That's not good. Those bastards could really spell trouble for us."

Glancing down at the ground around them, Dutch pointed out layers in the rock gleaming with a silvery substance that appeared similar to the rock being mined below.

"This looks a little like quartz or maybe silica, but I suspect it's something different." She offered as she examined the surrounding rock.

Using the flat edge of her knife, she pried a few fist sized stones free and dropped them in her pack for later study.

Dutch added, "I'd sure like to get a look inside those warehouses. I suspect the minerals they are mining are being used for weapon and tool production but I'd really like to know how they do it."

"Put a pin in that for another day." Finn replied, "for now, let's concentrate on the comm center. Once we get satellite capabilities, we can get a better picture of what's going on out here."

Directing their attention to the Pyramid they eyeballed the towering structure from top to bottom familiarizing themselves with its design and searching for telltale signs indicating the presence of sophisticated electronics and communications.

"This is incredible. I mean, it looks nearly identical to the great pyramids in Egypt." Dutch breathed in awe.

"Not quite identical" Finn replied as he closely studied the structure. "Those indents near the top, it looks like they house some kind of antenna array. I'd say this is what we've been looking for."

Glancing at his watch he said to the entire squad, "Ok, it's 0915, we've got forty-five minutes. Everyone keep their heads down and eyes open, last thing we need is to alert that encampment to our presence. Dutch, go ahead and do your magic. As soon as you start the timer we're going to hightail it the hell out of here."

~~~~

With the countdown underway, they backtracked at a brisk pace towards the river and the waiting boats. Every few minutes Finn would steal a quick glance at his watch as time melted away towards detonation. They were within half a mile from the boats when he held up a hand for everyone to stop.

"Alright, we're getting close to kick off. Pull the power packs from your weapons, PDA's and any other electronics you don't want getting fried. Take a minute to drink some water and check your gear again."

Moments later the crackle of rifle and machine gun fire echoed off the backdrop of an otherwise still and quiet forest setting.

"That's south of us." Finn exclaimed turning his head towards the sound, "Tayte's patrol must have run into trouble."

The timing couldn't be worse. With scant minutes before the blasts triggering the EMP, their weapons were powered down and useless.

A long burst of machine gun fire was followed by excited curses and yells that drew closer with each passing second.

Drawing the Kbar knife from his vest, Finn gestured towards the nearby brush and ordered, "everyone spread out, get down and be ready for contact."

"Dutch." Finn called, "how long after the blast until the EMP passes by?"

Crouched low in the bushes behind him she replied, "Instantly, sound travels slower than the actual pulse. By the time we hear the blast it would have already passed us by."

Another burst of weapons fire, much closer this time was followed by the sound of heavy footfalls as the patrol drew near coming in at a full sprint.

"Go, go…" Tayte's voice cried out as he urged his men on.

Finn spotted a blur of motion between the trees as first one and then a second and a third security officer charged past. Gun fire behind them blasted through the forest, a stream of bullets impacted the trunk of a nearby tree sending a spray of bark and pulp in all directions.

Crashing into the clearing, Tayte and Marcela appeared, their arms wrapped tightly around a bloodied figure as they half carried and half dragged him along. The guard was slumped over, unconscious, the color drained from his face as blood poured from bullet wounds stitched across his abdomen.

Following a short distance behind, Linc appeared. The bulky Revati ran a few paces into the clearing, turned and loosed an arrow towards a target in the woods behind him. An instant later he was rewarded with a wet smack and the thump of a body hitting the ground as the arrow found purchase. In a blur of motion, he fired off two more arrows before turning and charging ahead to catch up with the rest of the patrol. A flurry of leaves and branches danced along behind him as return fire chased after him.

With an arrow at the ready Rune began to rise and take aim into the forest when Finn waved her down and indicted for her to remain hidden. Reluctantly she ducked her head back down and turned to look in the direction Linc had vanished.

The sound of splintering branches and pounding feet announced the arrival of the pursuing force. Finn counted fifteen cyborgs as they streaked past hot on the heels of the fleeing patrol.

The cyborgs were still making their way out of the clearing when a pair of thundering booms echoed from the hills behind them. At the same instant they heard the blast, the enemy suddenly began stutter stepping, their heads whipping wildly from side to side in confusion. Instead of pressing ahead in a human wave attack, they drifted off into smaller groups with their attention divided between where Tayte and his squad had disappeared into the forest, the sound of the blasts or simply off into space with an empty look on their faces.

The confusion and disorganization caused by the EMP presented an opportunity and Finn intended to capitalize on it.

Slamming a charged cartridge into his rifle he worked the action as he climbed to one knee shouting, "Open fire!!"

Lined up almost perfectly at the enemies back, their sudden and unexpected ambush caught them completely off guard. Their initial volley cut a swath through the unsuspecting cyborgs dropping nearly a third of them right off.

The sound of pulse rifles firing behind them, let Tayte and his own patrol know it was now safe to use their own weapons and in moments the enemy found themselves caught in a raging cross fire between the two squads.

Return fire was sporadic and poorly aimed, but still heavy, forcing Finn and his people to remain behind cover as they laid down suppressing fire. A group of four cyborgs emerged from cover, charging headlong towards them, two of their numbers firing belt fed machine guns from their hips sending a wall of lead into the trees and brush all around the squad.

Despite the volume of incoming fire, Finn remained rock steady on his knee. Taking careful aim, he sent a pulse blast through the forehead of one of the gunners, knocking him off his feet and sending him pinwheeling off to the side as a fountain of blood, brains and electronic parts rained down around him.

Rune sighted her arrow on the second gunner and let loose a shot that through his throat. As he began to fall his finger tightened on the trigger of his weapon and held it back, releasing a wild and uncontrolled spray of bullets that peppered the woods all around them. Finn saw it coming and dove backwards driving his shoulder into Dutch's side as he forced them both flat onto the ground. Rune had been reaching for her next arrow and was a second late in recognizing the danger, a pair of bullets stitched across her unprotected chest driving her backwards against the base of a thick pine tree.

Streams of pulse rounds cut across the field cutting down the remaining two cyborgs as Tayte and his squad pushed forward into the fray.

Finn jumped to his feet and rushed to Rune's side as he pulled a trauma kit from his pack.

Blood soaked the front of her tunic as he used a layer of gauze to probe for the wounds. A frothing slather of blood identified one of the entry wounds and also told him that she had taken at least one round in a lung. The second wound appeared to be more superficial along her side but judging from the discoloration had likely cracked or broken a rib.

"Clear!" Tayte's voice cried out several moments later as his squad completed a sweep of the area for any stragglers they may have missed.

A moment later the burly NCO was kneeling alongside Finn offering a second med kit from his own pack.

"How bad is it?"

"Punctured lung and broken rib, possible internal bleeding." Finn replied. "We need to get her back to the medical center ASAP. How many casualties in your squad?"

"We lost Anderson." Tayte replied stoically his voice cracking and strained, "Miles and Johanson are walking wounded but not critical."

Finn recognized the faltering in his friend's voice and looked up to see Tayte clutching a hand over his stomach, dark blood oozing from between his fingers. Tayte was already turning pale and it was clear he was close to losing consciousness.

"Shit! Medic! Get a medic over here right now!" Finn cried out.

With the fighting now over, the two squads automatically fell into a defensive perimeter. The combat medic from Tayte's element was beside him in an instant and together they helped lay

Tayte prone on his back and then the medic started an IV line.

"He's critical sir." The medic said as he assessed Tayte's injury, "I can stabilize him for now but we need to get him to the medical center right away."

"Captain! Sir." Another officer called from nearby, "Comms are up. I've got the shuttle."

"Thank god, we finally catch a break." Finn exclaimed, "Alright, we need to move. Give the pilots the coordinates for the RIBS, tell them we need immediate pick up. Have them radio ahead and let the med center know we're returning with medical emergencies aboard."

~~~~

CHAPTER 14

Commander Tilley swirled the glass and marveled at the golden liquid at it sloshed lazily from side to side. He sighed to himself as he stared out the view-port window of his private office overlooking the splendid green and blue marble of the planet they had worked so hard to finally reach.

The bottle of single malt Scotch whiskey, was a personal gift from the British admiralty to be opened and enjoyed when the Resolute successfully reached its destination. For years the bottle sat unopened on the corner of his desk, where it served as a talisman urging him on each and every day of their long journey.

Taking a sip of his drink, he cringed as even the tiniest movement of his wrist sent electric bursts of pain radiating along his forearm. The arthritis had gotten much worse in the last year, so much so that he had taken to hoarding a private stock of pain killers. The drugs were only a stop gap though, more often than not they did little to actually help but instead left him groggy and fuzzy in the head.

Reaching down to tug at his tunic he scoffed at the snug fit as he sucked in a little harder and forced his expanding midsection back into place. It had always been a source of immense pride that in all his years of service his uniform measurements had stayed the same as his first day in the academy. As an officer with the Royal Navy, he lived his life by a code that required the highest standard of physical fitness. The ravages of time were now causing those standards to slip and it shamed him to view himself in the mirror every morning.

He found himself spending a great deal of time recently in reflection of the events that led him to this moment. He'd watched his country and for the most part, his world, slowly start to fall apart as one ecological disaster followed the next. Britain and most of western Europe were hit especially hard with long periods of acid rain wiping away farm lands, poisoning water reserves and turning their entire health care system on its head with a flood of sick and dying.

It was a source of national pride that both the Discovery and Resolute were named after famous British sailing ships. Of course, Britain had contributed an enormous amount of capital in terms of supplies, money and expertise in the construction of both vessels. It was therefore only fitting that the crews of both were primarily British naval and air force officers.

The knowledge that the world they left behind was now likely nothing more than a radioactive wasteland hit all them very hard. But it was made worse with the news they had agreed not to share with the rest of the colonists. Even though it was major breach of protocol, as Commander he had been the one to put it to a vote leading to the unanimous agreement that only that one piece of information ever be shared.

For the first several years of their voyage, they had received continuous updates on deteriorating conditions back home. The day they had launched, the world's top experts had estimated somewhere between 50 to 100 years before the Earth was no longer able to sustain human life. Those estimates proved to be way off the mark.

Food production had dwindled faster than thought, clean water was nearly nonexistent and extreme weather conditions had escalated exponentially. They received word that in many nations, cannibalism had been decriminalized and, in some cases, supported by governments, population control measures had been turned over to the armed forces and mass executions even in the most civilized parts of the world had become commonplace. Disease, starvation, faltering government and civil unrest had rapidly consumed the entire planet.

It had actually come as little surprise that the handful of nuclear nations had finally played that final card.

As a crew they had decided to spare the colonists as much of the grim details as possible. While it would be impossible to hide the fact that a nuclear holocaust had befallen their home world, it did nothing for them to know the true horrors that lead up to that fateful conclusion.

Commanding the Resolute had been the greatest achievement of his life. He was both honored and humbled to be part of such a professional and close-knit crew of men and women. In his mind they were more than simply crew mates, they were a family.

As he stood gazing out that view-port and taking in the vastness and beauty of this strange new world he found himself regretting the end of their journey. The time would soon be at hand when he would step from the bridge for the last time. The plan had always been for the crew to entire into a life of retirement in their new home and of course, many dreams had been shared over the years of how wonderful and anticipated that next chapter in their lives would be.

Now they knew that what waited for them on the surface was far from a life that included a peaceful log cabin, quiet walks through the forest and a morning tea along the shoreline. Their new home was a dangerous world, teeming with creatures and enemies nothing had prepared them for. It was a land for the young, strong and brave, not the old, arthritic and tired.

The buzzer on his desk sounded followed a moment later by the excited voice of his 2nd in command, "Commander, jamming has ceased. We now have a clear signal with open relays and are in position for satellite launch."

"Very well, stand by I'll be there in a moment." Commander Tilley replied.

Taking one final swig from the tumbler, he placed the glass on his desk, straightened and adjusted his uniform blouse and stepped from his office onto the ships bridge.

The bridge was unusually crowded with all stations manned and ready for the upcoming launch.

Commander Tilley walked the short distance from his office to his seat in the center of the bustling room.

"Report." He called out as he took his seat.

"Sir, our sensors show surface jamming has ceased around the colony." Lt. Commander Oliver Webb reported. "However, we have identified another two dozen regions emitting strong surface to orbit jamming. At our current velocity, we have a 90-minute window for full deployment before we drift into the next jamming zone."

Sliding a mobile console in front of him, Commander Tilley tapped commands into the keyboard allowing one of his display screens to monitor the individual launches while the other was ready to start receiving telemetry the moment the satellites began sending data.

This was a crunch moment for the crew and tension was running high. Mission planning called for the twelve satellites to be launched one at a time over a period of weeks. They were now crunching that into a nearly impossible time frame.

Glancing around the bridge, he noted that each crew member involved in the launches stood ready and awaiting his orders, "Initiate deployment."

The officer overseeing final launch prep hovered his finger over a button on his console, double checked the readings on his screen and then announced, "Unit one, launch in five…four…three…two…one…".

There was muted clunk and a slight vibration through the floor plating as unit one was jettisoned into space. Each satellite was the size of a small car, weighing in at 2500 pounds with a length of fifteen feet. Jammed packed with sensors, cameras, communication arrays and all measure of scientific gear, each unit was the latest and greatest ever developed back home.

"Clean launch on unit one." The launch officer reported, "ready for ignition sequence."

Intent on not repeating the same mistakes that started their own planet on a downward ecological spiral, they were relying on clean and renewable energy sources for a fresh start on their new home. Their only source of fossil fuel was the 100 pounds carried inside each satellite. Enough for a ten second burn of their external thrusters, the fuel was designed to be exhausted moving the satellites into a precisely calculated orbit.

"Engage." A control officer replied.

On their screens they all watched as the motors fired and the satellite began accelerating away. At the station next to the launch officer, another crew member steered the unit with a small joy stick, his eyes locked on the computer readout providing him the intricate coordinates where the satellite needed to be placed.

"Engine burn complete." The officer replied calmly, "Unit one is in position."

"Extend and deploy solar arrays." The control officer ordered.

At the next station over, another officer stood ready to feed those instructions directly into the satellites onboard computer systems.

"Deploying arrays." The officer advised.

A pair of metal arms began slowly unfolding from their tucked positions along the body of the satellite, when completely unfolded and extended the arms stretched thirty feet to each side of the satellite and over the next several minutes solar panels began extending outward along the entire length of each arm.

As the panels continued unfurling the control officer issued his next order, "Commence full systems checks, run level four diagnostics and cross check."

Commander Tilley stared intently at the blank screen to his right and waited. After what seemed like an eternity the screen suddenly blinked to life as the satellite began transmitting a signal as it went through its checks.

Glancing at the digital timer he'd started the moment the unit was launched, he grumbled to himself as he looked up towards the ships navigation officer and issued an order.

"Helm, engines all back, full reverse."

"Sir?" The helmsman replied with a puzzled look.

Normally he wouldn't explain an order he'd given and it was rare for any his bridge crew to offer such a challenge. In this case he felt compelled to explain his motives for all to understand.

"No choice. We need to buy another 90 minutes in a jamming free orbit or we will not get all these satellites in position."

"Aye Sir." The helmsman replied.

Another shiver ran through the deck plating under their feet as the thrusters fired and their forward momentum dwindled.

Monitoring their progress on his console, Commander Tilley carefully clocked their position until finally he called out, "All stop. Engines ahead, maneuvering speed only."

Even at their slowest speed they were still cruising through space at several hundred miles an hour, but the maneuver had bought them the extra time to complete all the launches. No one said, but they knew that they had cut nearly two months from their power reserves. The butcher bill for that expense would eventually be paid in lives.

Throughout the bridge, crewmembers silently ran the math in their heads, while it was still too early to know for certain, it was now a fact that somewhere between thirty and one hundred colonists would never awaken from cryo sleep. Timetables across the board would have to be drastically accelerated in order to unload as many passengers and as much equipment as possible before they were dead in space. Decisions would have to be made and the unfortunate fact was that those decisions would cost lives.

With a nod towards the control officer, Commander Tilley said, "Continue with the launch sequence."

Struggling to keep his posture straight and dignified, he walked purposefully across the bridge towards his office. All he could think about in that moment was the trade off in lives he had made in order to provide satellite coverage. He tried to rationalize it in the knowledge that given the hostile and alien nature of the planet, that coverage was critical for their long term survival. However, deep down inside he knew it would be impossible to ever truly come to terms with what he had done. His goal now was to get to his office, close the door behind him and finish the remainder of the bottle of scotch, in the hope that at least for a few hours he could find some temporary refuge from the internal loathing of his actions.

~~~~

CHAPTER 15

Lauren stepped out into the sunlight and stretched her tired back as she stripped off her blood-soaked surgical gown and gazed wearily at the small crowd waiting outside the medical center. Despite Finn's insistence that everyone who had participated in the raid get some food and hit their rack, to a person not a single one of them was willing to leave while their comrades went under the knife.

Finding Linc near the edge of the group she said, "Rune is going to be fine. The lung will heal in time, she'll be on bed rest for the immediate future and I want to keep her sedated for the time being but I don't expect there to be any permanent damage."

The elation on Linc's face was immediately evident, the massive Revati had spent the entire night pacing throughout the camp, his heavy footfalls and worried expression making most of the workers extremely uneasy.

When Lauren's eyes connected with his own, Finn felt a sinking in the pit of his stomach. He knew that Tayte's injuries were severe. Lauren hadn't pulled any punches over his chances but before disappearing into the surgical ward, she had sworn to do everything in her power to help him pull through.

"He's alive." Lauren offered, her voice doing little to stave off the other shoe that was about to drop. "But his liver was destroyed. I had to put him in a medically induced coma."

While he didn't possess a great deal of medical knowledge, Finn knew enough to understand that a human being could not survive without their liver.

"Let me guess, a transplant is his only option?"

"I'm afraid so." Lauren replied sorrowfully. "I can keep him alive with drugs and machines for a while still. However, at some point…some point in the next few days at least, a decision will need to be made."

Those words were like a kick straight to his gut. Glancing around he saw all eyes on him as everyone knew the decision was now resting squarely on his shoulders.

"I'll review his records. His wishes in a situation like this will be spelled out in his living will." Finn said after a few moments of consideration. "Everyone get some rest, there's nothing more we can do for him now. I'll make an announcement tomorrow evening on where we go from here."

It was lie, he already knew that Tayte had appointed him as guardian and the deciding authority in just such a situation. There was a specific provision that he had no wish to be kept alive artificially in the event no alternative means of resuscitation were available to restore a reasonable quality of life.

He had done the same in giving Tayte the same power for himself. While he knew it was a selfish decision, he justified it to himself that Tayte wasn't suffering at the moment. He would pull that paperwork for review as was required of him, but he also wasn't ready to start that process until he was emotionally and physically ready, and for that to happen, he needed at least a day to sleep on it. Deep down he hoped that Tayte would understand why he wasn't exactly rushing to pull the plug until his head was completely clear.

Both Dutch and Marcela had maintained the night long vigil along with everyone else. As Finn spoke they shared a conspiratorial look and before he finished talking they quietly slinked off towards the mechanical workshop. Without a word between them they had come up with an idea that needed their immediate attention if it had any hope of success.

~~~~

Rainclouds moved in during the morning hours bringing cooling temperatures along with a steady drizzle that seemed intent on hanging out throughout the day. The weather was an eerily appropriate backdrop for the solemn atmosphere hanging like a veil over the colony.

Finn had called for a meeting shortly after the dinner hour, giving everyone a full day of rest and reflection. At least that's what he tried to tell himself, since it was his own thoughts and reflections that were suddenly taking center stage.

Walking into the operations center ten minutes early, he was surprised to note that everyone was already there, seated around the table and clearly waiting anxiously for his arrival.

Given the somber nature of the meeting, Finn was surprised to note casual conversations intermixed with muted laughter and an otherwise jovial spirit shared with Lauren, Dutch and even Marcela. Locking eyes with Lauren for a brief moment, he noted a spark in her eyes along with a suppressed grin that was a far cry from her glum demeanor earlier that morning. For a moment he considered questioning why Marcela was present given her status as an outsider still, but dismissed that thought and decided to move things along.

Before he could speak, Lauren rose and addressed the room with an uncharacteristic confidence that immediately drew everyone's attention.

"We can save him." She said pointedly.

Shaking his head in sudden confusion, Finn faltered, "what?"

Sharing a glance at Dutch and Marcela, Lauren continued, "Tayte, we think we've found a solution, a way to save him."

"I don't understand." Finn faltered, "twelve hours ago you said his only chance was with an organ transplant. Did a matching donor suddenly come forward?"

"Not a donor, but the next best thing." Lauren replied, "it's possible we can develop an artificial liver for him."

"Not possible." Dr. Hughes interjected immediately, "an artificial liver never made it beyond clinical trials, it's never been done before. Besides, we don't have the tools or equipment to replicate anything that complex."

Nodding her head in agreement, Lauren held up a hand and quickly countered, "all excellent points and I agree. An artificial liver transplant has never successful taken place. However, if you recall, in 2024, the prototype for just such a device had cleared all laboratory and clinical testing and was ready for human trials. Unfortunately, the climate crisis and escalating collapse of the world health care system kept it from reaching that final step."

Tapping her data pad, she added. "We have detailed schematics of that very device on file."

"Even so." Dr. Hughes quickly fired back. "While our 4d printing technology is highly advanced for creating a wide assortment of tools and equipment, it's not capable of rendering something so incredibly sophisticated as an artificial human organ.

A prosthetic limb? Sure.

A liver? Not a chance."

With a nod towards Dutch, Lauren replied, "maybe Dutch should explain a little further, since it was really her idea."

Finn was uncomfortable having a meeting go suddenly off the rails like this. He'd walked into the room expecting to make the proclamation that his closest friend was to be removed from life support.

All of a sudden, he found himself on the sidelines of a hearty debate about a far-flung idea on how to save him, he was willing to hear them out and see where this went.

On cue, both Dutch and Marcela stood and walked to the back of the room where they retrieved a pair of leather cases and a small knapsack. They arranged the cases on the table in front of them as Dutch began, "Dr. Hughes, you're 100% correct. The tech toys we have at our disposable are not capable of producing such an intricate device. That's why I'm about to offer a hypothesis about where we may be able to find such technology and how it may be possible to 'borrow' it for our purposes."

Reaching into the knapsack, Dutch retrieved a sample of the rock she'd recovered from their perch overlooking the Creators jamming and communication facility.

Next, she opened the two leather cases and laid out several of the rifles and knives recovered from their first engagement with the Cyborg's along with a collection of the cybernetic implants removed during Lauren's autopsy of their bodies.

"Now, I know this is all going to sound a bit over the top. Maybe even a little crazy." Dutch prefaced as she glanced around the table stopping briefly to hold each individuals confused but somewhat intrigued gaze before continuing, "but please. Hear me out before you outright dismiss everything I'm about to say."

Gesturing to the weapons and cybernetics in front of her she explained, "I ran tests on this equipment and discovered that the weapons and the electronics were all produced from the exact same base compound and I believe that was done through the use of a highly advanced fabrication method."

"How can you possibly tell something like that from such a small sample?" Dr. Hughes scoffed.

"That's a good question." Dutch replied, having clearly anticipated exactly that line of questioning.

Gesturing towards the rifles she pointed to a deep scratch above the trigger guard, a similar marking appeared on each weapon.

"Typically, in any manufactured goods there are going to be subtle differences, slight variations in tool markings, maybe even calibration errors at the nanometer level. What I found here was the exact opposite. In the case of each piece of equipment, they are exactly similar in every aspect. What really tipped me off was this scratch in the rifles trigger guard. That exact same scratch appears in every single rifle we recovered, depth, length and shape, down to the cellular level."

Dr. Hughes settled back in his chair, his eyebrows steepled in thought as he allowed Dutch to continue.

"This got me thinking, so I went ahead and conducted a mineralogical analysis of the material from the weapons and implants. I discovered that both were constructed of the exact same material but wasn't able to figure out what it was until this morning when I was finally able to link with the Resolute's main frame."

Hefting one of the rock samples she said, "the mineral inside this rock is what we know as Tanzanite."

"Wow." Phoenix exclaimed as his eyes grew wide and he sat up straight in his chair.

"You've heard of it?" Dutch asked surprised.

"Oh yeah. It's the rarest mineral on earth." Phoenix explained, "if I'm not mistaken, only a few pounds of it had ever been discovered. Its 100's of times more valuable than gold or diamonds."

"That's all well and good. Pretty shiny rocks, diamonds and gold." Finn said as he grew restless with the ongoing debate that to him still seemed unrelated to the issue at hand, "but how exactly does any of this pertain to Tayte's situation?"

"2400 degrees." Dr. Hughes said with a sudden look of clarity and understanding.

"Exactly!" Dutch replied, "Tanzanite has a melting point of 2400 degrees. When smelted into liquid, the raw ore becomes pliable and can be used as a manufacturing precursor."

"Incredible." Dr. Hughes continued, "The quality of that ore would be much higher than anything we've ever seen in manufacturing, it would be the perfect material for extremely complicated adaptive materials."

"Like artificial organs." Lauren added.

"Like artificial organs." Dr. Hughes replied, "I stand humbly corrected in my assertion that it was impossible."

"If their manufacturing is so high tech, then why are they producing weapons that by our standards are nothing but antiques?" Phoenix asked gesturing towards the rifles on the table. "I mean why not pulse weapons or some alien ray guns?"

"Actually, it's quite brilliant." Finn offered, "while these particular weapons are certainly outdated from our point of view, they are perfect for equipping an otherwise untrained army. They are easy to fire and maintain with the added benefit of being extremely rugged and durable. Even the cannons we spotted make perfect sense in that regard, just point and shoot, little to no training needed. When you get into more complex equipment, the level of necessary training rises exponentially."

"I think we've only brushed the surface on their overall capabilities." Lauren added. "The cybernetics alone show not only highly advanced technical abilities but also an evolved understanding of human physiology. It stands to reason that they possess the tools necessary to fashion a functioning artificial human organ."

Finn was finally starting to catch on and felling the first initial ray of hope that Tayte may stand a chance. "So, we melt these rocks down and what? Feed the resulting goop into our 4d printers? Is that how it works?"

Dutch, Lauren and Marcela shared a look and Finn suddenly realized they had walked him down the path and were now about to let the other shoe drop.

"Not quite." Dutch said, "our tech is still way behind in terms of capabilities. Even with the right precursor, we'd never be able to construct anything so intricate."

The light went off in his head and he finally understood.
"You're out of your mind." He scoffed, "if you're really thinking what I think you are."

"Hang on Finn. Let her finish." Lauren interjected.

Opening a datapad, Dutch connected the device to the display screen in the front of the room. An overview of the planet's surface surrounding the Creator's jamming and communication apparatus appeared.

"Now that we finally have satellite coverage, I was able to do a little snooping around that warehouse." With a tap of the keypad the view zoomed in until the screen was filled from end to end with the sprawling warehouse facility.
The shanty town appeared as it had when they observed it live and in person. Although it was somewhat obscured in heavy rainfall, they could make out workers going about their activities throughout the valley. Carts overflowing with raw ore, pulled by beastly dinosaurs streamed in and out of the warehouse.

"We know they are mining Tanzanite and other ores from the surrounding area and depositing it into the warehouse. The mineral goes in and then completed tools and equipment come out the other end. The question stands, what happens in the middle of that process."
With a few more taps of the keys the view changed to show a wire model of the warehouse along with what appeared to be multiple stories of large underground facilities directly underneath it.

"With thermal scanning I was able to piece some of that picture together." Dutch said, "this entire structure, the warehouse and the sublevels are nothing more than an enormous fabrication unit. Heat signatures on the lowest levels are conducive to a smelting operation. From there, the refined ore is used to produce pretty much anything they want."

Cyborgs now appeared on the screen as featureless white blobs as the thermal scans registered their body heat. They could see the heavy concentration of workers around the outside of the building with less than a hundred scattered around the inside of the structure and only a handful on any of the sub levels.

"Wait a minute. I thought we shut that entire operation down with the EMP?"

"Not in the least." Dutch replied, "the production facilities are all deep underground as you can see from the imagery. The EMP only impacted electronics above surface level, anything below the surface was naturally shielded under tons of dirt and rock."

"Your suggesting we break in and what? Steal that equipment?" Finn scoffed.

"No, she's not." Marcela offered, "She's suggesting we break in and 'use' the equipment."

"That's right." Dutch continued, "we have the schematics, we upload them into their computer system and direct their equipment to produce an artificial liver for us. Based on the level of detail in the cybernetic implants, a liver should be no problem for their tech."

"How much of this is guess work?" Finn asked.

"A lot." Lauren agreed, "granted, it's a long shot. But it's the only chance Tayte has and we thought you'd like all options on the table before making a final decision."

Finn had to admit that she had him over a barrel with that argument, as ridiculous and audacious as their plan might have been, it was more than they had little more than an hour ago.

"How long can he survive on the machines?" Finn asked.

"Technically, indefinitely." Lauren replied, "However, according to the charter we drafted for this mission. Each and every one of us is allotted a percentage of our overall expendable medical resources. Going by the book, he would have eight days from today before he reached that threshold."

Seeing that Finn was on the fence with a decision, Dutch pushed ahead with her findings.
"We found something else when we were mapping the terrain."
Using a laser pointer, she highlighted an area on the map some distance away from the valley.
"This tunnel appears to have been mined out some time ago and is now partially flooded. The entrance is about two miles west of the valley and thermal scans show that it comes back up at the base of the valley only a few dozen feet from the side of the warehouse."

Tracking the tunnel on the display, Finn noted that Dutch's summary was right on the money and that the tunnel appeared to offer an avenue of approach that would bring them right where they needed to be, completely undetected. He found himself impressed with the detail that had gone into their planning, the work rivaled military intelligence he'd dealt with in his past.

Finn stood, ran a hand through his cropped hair and paced to the front of the room where he stood facing the projected display of the production facility.

With his back to the table he said, "If we do this. Its key personnel only, myself and Dutch. I won't ask anyone else to put their lives at risk."

"Afraid that's not good enough." Lauren replied, "I have to be there, if this is too work, I'll have to take precise measurements once the rendering is complete. An artificial organ has to conform to exact specifications or it simply won't work."

~~~~

CHAPTER 16

The following morning found Finn wandering aimlessly throughout the compound. He'd spent a restless night tossing and turning, with any hope of restful sleep eluding him as his mind refused to shut down even for a few minutes.

After enjoying a light breakfast of instant oatmeal and powdered orange juice, he decided to take a stroll through the compound and wrestle with his thoughts. With an accelerated timetable to offload the remaining colonists and so much still to do, Phoenix had his crews working around the clock. Construction on a number of essential buildings was really taking shape and Finn found it fascinating to see the progress made in such a short time.

Passing the wood shop, he watched as workers fed sections of tree trunks into the mill where each went through a number of stations before eventually transforming them into lengths of usable lumber. The constant buzz of the cutting blades, the fog of sawdust and the comforting smell of freshly cut timber gave the entire scene a familiar and homey feel.

Workers smiled, shared jokes and small talk as they went about their duties. Finn could see a real sense of belonging and community starting to develop.

He continued walking by exchanging waves and friendly nods with the work crews as he passed. A block further on he came upon the framed outline of a new structure he'd not seen before. The building was set off a distance from the others around it and featured a wide middle section with narrow hallways branching off each side. Etched into a piece of wood hanging over the entry the words "city hall" helped clarify its intended purpose.

Finn knew that Phoenix had his crews working off a long list of building requirements ranging from housing, storage, manufacturing, agricultural, military, cultural, and community use. He hadn't realized that government type buildings had been included, although in retrospect it made sense. At some point they would hold elections and establish a democratic civilian leadership, that governing body would need a building of their own.

As he approached the front of the building he spotted a lone figure standing in front of a large piece of tree bark tacked to a section of exterior wall. The woman was tall, thin and lanky, dressed in greasy coveralls with a tool belt wrapped around her waist. Her back was to him as she hunched over the piece of bark and carefully worked at it with a carving knife.

Drawing closer and from over the woman's shoulder, Finn could see that columns of words had been scratched, carved and even burned into the wood and it was clear it had been hung as a makeshift bulletin board:

New Hope
Babylon
Sherwood
Mount Hood
Brookport

Finn eventually understood the meaning, it was list of suggested names for their new home. There were easily fifty names already included with room for many more. Some of the names didn't seem to make sense, but he figured they held special meaning to their authors, others were names or variations of names of familiar cities back home:

New Boston
New London
Bonn
Vienna

He smiled as he read some of the more sarcastic suggestions, some stolen from popular literature or movies, but interesting ideas all the same even if they were unlikely to be taken seriously:

Hogwarts
Racoon City
Mos Eisley
Gotham City

Sensing his presence, the woman glanced back over her shoulder and offered him a friendly and acknowledging nod before returning to attention back to the board.

She was nearly finished with her contribution and Finn read her carefully scrawled words:
Fort Redding

Not recognizing the name, he asked, "Does that have any special significance?"

Continuing her carving she replied softly, "Its Dutch, it means 'Salvation'."

She spoke with a soothing accent that presented the words and their meaning in such a reverent manner that it struck a chord with him.

"That's perfect. I couldn't think of a better name."

She finished the carving a few moments later and carefully wiped away a layer of sawdust before standing and admiring her work. With one final glance in his direction, she offered a fleeting smile before disappearing back inside the building.

Further down what was starting to turn into main street, a wide, heavily traveled path where the dirt was now compacted into something nearly resembling pavement, he heard the excited screech of an animal followed by howls of human laughter.

Following the path to the edge of town, he came to clearing behind two bunkhouses and a future cafeteria where there was a row of buildings dedicated for farming needs. Silos, barns, chicken coops, sheds, stables, greenhouses, milking sheds, pigpens and others all in various stages of construction. Most notable was the brooding house and agriculture center where thousands of stored animal embryos would eventually be thawed and nurtured into herds of livestock and beasts of burden.

The fields beyond the structures showed great progress in clearing and preparations for planting. A lone tractor puttered along in the distance pulling a plow behind it and making quick work of the soft soil.

A group of around twenty workers were all clustered together taking a break in the shade.

Their voices intermixed into an unintelligible gaggle, but from time to time they roared in mutual laughter. Finn stood back and watched for a minute, not wanting to approach and interrupt their downtime.

One of the workers reached down towards his feet and stood back up holding a large roll of duct tape in one hand. Looking off to his left he mocked throwing the roll a few times before finally hefting it high into the air straight out in front of him.

A small monkey like animal, with a long curled bushy tail, brown fur and marble like eyes that extended almost comically from its face, darted suddenly into view. The creature leapt onto the edge of a table, shot into the air and caught the roll of tape like a frisbee. As nimble as a cat the small creature touched down on its hind legs and walked a few feet towards the crowd of workers where it proudly presented the tape back to worker who'd tossed it. A roar of laughter along with a round of applause exploded from the crowd. The creature and several of its companions howled and chirped back at them with an excited reply.

"Harmless fun." Phoenix commented as he appeared from behind a nearby bunkhouse.

"What is it?" Finn asked as he watched several more of the small monkeys appear from within the tall weeds as the workers offered scraps of food.

"Doc Hughes says they are one of the oldest known species of primates. He called them, Arhicebus." Phoenix explained as they stood together and watched the work crew as they continued to feed and play with the animals.

"There's a couple families of them living in the trees just beyond the fields. That one..." Phoenix said gesturing towards the larger one that had caught and returned the roll of tape, "he's the friendliest of the bunch, comes out every day and watches the work. The guys named him Archie, a play on the species type I believe, and he seems to be an innocent distraction. They even put aside a bed for him in the bunkhouse and I understand he's spent a few nights sleeping with the crew."

The radio on his PDA crackled as the group started breaking up as break time ended. Finn felt the hairs on the back of his neck start to stand up as an excited voice announced a new sighting of a T-Rex along the western perimeter.

~~~~

Finn clambered up the wooden ladder where he joined Jenna in one of the observation posts on the western wall. She already had a pair of binoculars pressed to her face as she swung them back and forth across the distant tree line.

With Tayte down and out, she was next in the chain of command and had taken charge of in-house security issues. She'd been out conducting her own perimeter inspections when the alarm had sounded.

"There!" She exclaimed gesturing to a spot near a clearing where the stream cut a break through the trees.

It was his first actually sighting of one of the massive creatures and he sucked in a halting breath as he took in the true size and power of the beast. The Rex was standing in the open, nearly two hundred yards into the forest on the grassy bank along the edge of the stream. Towering to a height of at least twenty-five feet, to call it impressive was hardly doing it justice. Standing fully erect it would almost reach the very top of their defensive wall, Finn suddenly felt that even their heaviest hitting weapons might not be enough to withstand a full-on attack from one or more such creatures.

"What do you think it's doing?" Jenna asked as she studied the creature through her binos.

"Not sure, but it doesn't seem interested in us at the moment." Finn replied.

He'd barely finished the sentence when the Rex's head shot forward into the brush with surprising speed where it disappeared from view for a few moments. Seconds later it stood back up, the bloodied and struggling carcass of a bulbous headed dinosaur twitching and screeching in pain dangling from its jaws. With a violent shake of its head the Rex shook its prey from side to side, the sickening crack of the snapped neck carrying over the distance like a gunshot.

With the limp and now very dead creature dangling from either side of its mouth, the Rex nimbly stomped its way back into the dense foliage and quickly disappeared from view.

"Damn! Wonder why it didn't just eat the thing right there on the spot." Jenna pondered aloud.

"I think I know why, but we need to make sure." Finn offered as he tilted his PDA to his mouth and said, "Dutch, I hope you're online and ready to move, that thing it moving away pretty fast."

"Good to go." The reply came back immediately.

Finn turned and gazed back over the colony until he spotted movement on the roof of a particular building near the center of the complex.

Dutch had set up one of her drones on the roof of her shop where it sat ready to launch as a surveillance platform for any sightings of cyborgs or dangerous wildlife anywhere close to the fence line.

A moment later he watched as the suitcase size device lifted into the air and then moved off towards the forest in pursuit of the giant Rex.

The live feed was beamed directly to the PDA network enabling Finn and Jenna to monitor the drones progress as it raced to catch up with the fleeing creature.

"Come on, come on." Finn breathed excitedly as they watched the forest whip by under the drone. Seconds turned to minutes and he started thinking the Rex had simply vanished when Dutch cried out excitedly over the radio.

"Gotcha, you big bastard!" Dutch sounded out before adding, "change your view to thermal. Can't pick him out on video through the thick cover."

Finn made the adjustment on his PDA and was rewarded with a view that showed a white and red blob moving rapidly through the forest almost directly under the drone.

"I thought these things were cold blooded? How are we picking it up on thermal?" Jenna asked as she watched the action on her own screen.

"They are." Dutch replied, "but even when a cold bloodied creature exerts itself like that, their heart, lungs and organs warm up enough to register on thermals. You're actually watching its innards moving through the woods."

"Damn, pretty sharp." Jenna replied.

"It's really moving." Finn said, "are these readings accurate Dutch? My PDA says twenty-five miles per hour."

"That's what I'm showing as well, the sensors on the drone are precisely calibrated, that guy is really moving out." Dutch responded, "the drone maxes out at thirty mph, so if he speeds up too much more we could lose him."

Despite its size the massive Rex moved with a surprising grace and ease through the thick vegetation.
Nearly ten minutes later it finally began to slow as it drew near a stretch of marsh covered ground deep within the forest.

"Might have something here." Dutch called out. "I'm seeing a few more heat sources about fifty yards north of the big guy, they must hear him coming but aren't making any effort to move out of the way."

"Ok, I see them too." Finn replied, "He's slowing and heading directly towards them. I count seven more contacts, that seem right to you?"

"Roget that." Dutch responded, "looks like another large animal and six much smaller ones."

"Oh shit!" Finn replied as realization struck home. "It's a nest! It's a damn T-Rex nest. That must be the momma waiting at home with the babies."

"Try switching back to live video." Dutch said, "the canopy is a little broken up around here and I'm going to try dropping the drone down a bit to give us a better picture of what's going on."

Adjusting their views accordingly, Finn and Jenna watched their screens as Dutch deftly piloted the drone down through a layer of leaves, expertly dodging branches as she moved it into a stationary position around a hundred feet over the ground.

There was a slight depression in the bog, thick moss and wide palm fronds covered the ground in a relaxing display of brilliant dark green and blues. It took a few moments to spot the second adult Rex as it was nearly directly under the drone, but they saw movement as it turned its head towards its approaching mate. The female was larger than the male, both in height and weight, this one easily topping thirty feet. It was partially hidden in the foliage, almost as though by design. In the moss several feet to the right of the mother, they could make out two smaller creatures, while their overall body shape appeared similar to the adults, the similarities seemed to stop at that point. Covered head to toe in a brilliant display of multicolored feathers along with a softy downy coat of fur topping the crown of their heads and narrow faces, the babies resembled birds more than lizard like predators.

"Incredible!" A new voice chimed in over the airwaves as Dr. Hughes offered his unsolicited insights in the discovery. "It's always been a source of debate and speculation that many dinosaurs actually evolved from birds. I have to say that even I had my doubts."

The male T-Rex came into frame at that point. With the corpse of the bulbous headed dinosaur still dangling from the sides of its mouth, it walked slowly up to its mate and allowed the female to sniff and nudge the bloody offering before turning its head away seemingly in a sign of approval.

Dropping the body into the moss near the female's feet, the male bowed its head down near the ground where it gently nuzzled and guided its offspring towards the prize.

The moss was dense and made it difficult to ascertain details, but they could see enough of the smaller Rex's as they bound in and out of view their tiny snouts tearing and shredding into the flesh and meat of the offering. Soon their feathers and downy fur were coated in a rich lather of blood and ooze as the feeding took on a frenzied pace.

"Ok Dutch, I think we got the point." Finn said after a few minutes of watching the gruesome feeding. "Map that location and bring the drone on home."

"That nest is only about three and half miles out." Jenna noted, "if those things keep eating like that, it won't be long until we've got real issues with the local wildlife."

"Yeah, but at least we know where the nest is." Finn replied, "All we can do for now is keep an eye on them and keep our people well clear of that region."

~~~~

CHAPTER 17

Evening was giving way to night as Finn and Jenna found their way into the Operations Center where they found Dutch, Marcela and Dr. Hughes hunched over computer terminals and exchanging excited bits of conversation.

"What's up?" Finn asked, automatically suspecting the worse.

"We just got the first satellite update." Dutch replied without turning away from her monitor. "The mapping software is going to take a while to give us an overview of the planet but we've now got a better picture of the continent were currently calling home."

With the entire satellite array now fully deployed in orbit, they would start receiving detailed telemetry and sensor data for the entire planet. The initial run would take at least a week or more, but once complete, they would have access to real time imagery including weather data, terrain mapping, geological formations and most importantly, thermal readings from any living creature anywhere on or below the surface.

"We've got a lot of company." Marcela added.

Three known locations were prominently marked on the computerized map currently displayed on the overhead screens. Their colony, the Revati cave complex and the cyborg production facility. Using these three locations as reference points, the imagery radiated outwards in increments of ten-mile grids that now showed nearly the entirety of the continent. All together it was a land mass twice the size of what they had known as North America back home.

Thermal markers were showing nearly a hundred individual concentration of returns, each representing thousands of humanoid life forms.

"Damn." Dutch mused, "there goes the neighborhood."

"I know that place!" Marcela exclaimed excitedly as she stabbed a finger at the screen.

She was gesturing towards a location roughly five miles west of the production facility. Tucked away in a deep rocky gorge, at first glance it appeared nothing more than a barren chunk of land at the edge of the forest. Thermal scans however showed there was much more to the location.

A subterranean complex running under the surface was crowded with hundreds of individual heat signatures. The scans could only penetrate a few hundred feet below the surface, but it was evident that whatever was down there continued on well beyond that limit.

"That's where they first took us after we were captured." Dutch continued, "I'm pretty sure they drugged us shortly after we arrived because I can't remember much of anything about the layout inside. I do remember being forced down a narrow path in that gorge. We had to move single file and two or three people lost their footing and fell over the edge."

Marcela stopped for a moment, the unpleasant memories churning up long forgotten emotions.

"It's ok." Dutch offered as she draped a comforting arm around Marcela's shoulder and pulled her tight.

"This is a new twist to an already complex situation." Finn added, "Can you determine the range from the colony to the next closest concentration of cyborgs?"

"It's going to take a little time to finish compiling the data." Dutch replied, "but a quick estimate is something like two groupings within thirty to forty miles. I'd say somewhere in the neighborhood of ten thousand individuals each."

"And each of them is sitting right on top of some kind of subterranean complex." Dr. Hughes interjected.

"More production facilities?" Finn asked as he studied the display trying to make heads or tails of the confusing imagery.

"I don't think so." Dutch replied, "there's no independent heat signature to indicate a foundry or any significant industrial activity. It's hard to tell, but judging from these readings, I would guess it might be more along the lines of an underground city."

The lights in the Operation Center dimmed suddenly, flickered and then winked out casting the entire room into darkness.

"Shit!" Dutch exclaimed as she fumbled in a tool kit for a flashlight. "I was afraid of that."

"What's going on Dutch?" Finn asked.

"Overloaded circuits." Dutch explained, "We've been steadily adding infrastructure to the grid; solar panels and windmills, but we're limited on the number of available regulators and power distributors. We've only had a handful in the last few drops, other than that we're running through what was left in the colony and many of those were pretty torn up. Give it a minute, the backup generator should pick up the load."

An anxious minute passed before a generator finally kicked on lighting a handful of overhead bulbs.

"This isn't acceptable Dutch." Finn groaned, "we're surrounded by hostile creatures on all sides day and night, we need continuous access to those satellite feeds."

"You're going to have to talk to Commander Tilley about that I'm afraid." Dutch fired back, "I can only work with the equipment I have on hand and the way the gear is packed on the ship is the way we are receiving it."

Finn realized she was right and regretted snapping at her, the frustrations of command and issues outside his control were weighing on him.
"You're right, I'm sorry, I know it's not your fault." He offered.

The doors to the room opened and Lauren stepped in and offered abruptly, "If we have another power outage in the medical center, we're going to lose Tayte."

"I'll go over the entire system top to bottom once again." Dutch responded defensively, "But until we get the replacement parts from the ship, I can't guarantee we won't have more outages like that."

"We can move him to the Revati complex." Marcela chimed in.

Everyone stopped and looked at her as she continued, "We have a reliable power source and our medical center is comparable to the one here. Plus, we already have a staff of nurses on hand."

"That's not a bad idea." Lauren replied after a few moments' consideration. "Rune's been climbing the walls to return home, this could be a good compromise for her as well. We'll need to use a shuttle though."

"The next shuttle run is two days from now." Finn replied, "Once you get Tayte and Rune settled in the Revati med center, we can use the shuttle to ferry us for our little raid."

~~~~~

"Finn, you have a minute?" Phoenix asked as they filled out of the operations center.

Lauren had been hanging back waiting to walk with him but as he offered her a friendly wave and a disappointed shrug, she nodded in understanding, presented him with a broad smile that quickened his pulse and continued on into the night. Finn turned back to face the big German.

"Of course, what's on your mind?" Finn said as he gestured towards a table and adjoining bench under a nearby tree.

"I'm pretty sure you've made up your mind and are going to press ahead with this raid." Phoenix began.

"I think I know where you're going with this." Finn replied, "but let me ask you this, what would you do if you were in my shoes?"

Phoenix remained silent for a moment as he considered the question, "I don't think I'd go through with it." He finally answered, "there are less than 3,000 of us now, that's all that remains from our world. Can we really afford the lives of three people in a long shot to save one? Not just three people mind you, but three people who each hold critical positions."

Finn understood where he was coming from with this. In fact, it was a continually nagging thought that played out over and over in the back of his mind but he was able to draw on certain experiences from his past to help him reconcile the decision.

"Let me share something with you that might help put things in perspective." Finn began, "First, you're right. Our numbers are depressingly small and that's all that remains of life from our own planet."

Phoenix nodded in understand as he sat back and quietly listened.

"The way I see it, that fact alone means every single one of us are our most valuable commodity if we expect to have any future at all. I believe that makes it even more critical that we must fight with everything we have to protect every individual life."

"But risking three lives to save one? Isn't that an unwise investment in that same future?" Phoenix countered.

"Years ago, when I was a platoon leader on my first tour in Afghanistan. Our second trip outside the wire we ran into an ambush. Twelve of us against an enemy force of nearly a hundred. It was a brutal slug match and we took some casualties. One of the injured was a 20-year-old female truck driver, she was only two months out of basic training, a single mother who was trying to turn her life around following an abusive relationship."

Finn stared off into the distance as the memories and emotions came flooding back.

"She lost a leg right off the bat, it was just gone from the thigh down. If that wasn't bad enough she also caught some shrapnel in her neck. It was amazing she survived the initial shock, but she did. Our medic did what he could for her, but the injuries were critical and she needed to get to a hospital within the hour if there was any chance of saving her life. I called it in, requested extraction by medical helicopter.

That request was denied.

Do you know why it was denied?"

Phoenix shook his head in a silent reply.

"It was denied because we were still locked in a fight and the higher ups wouldn't risk the lives of three crewman on a helicopter just to save one 20-year-old soldier. For them it was simple math, the same math you're trying to apply with me right now."

Finn paused letting his words hang in the air for a moment.

"I watched that poor girl die. I was holding her hand and looking into her eyes. I've never felt so helpless or defeated in my entire life. She was my responsibility and she'd put her trust and confidence in myself and the Army as a whole to take care of her.

152

We not only abused that trust, but in doing so we failed her miserably.

The following day, I sat down to write the letter to her family, I used those exact words as I apologized for allowing the system to fail their daughter."

"Look Finn, I know things were rough over there. I served a few compulsory years in the German Army, but never deployed to a combat zone. I can't imagine how hard that was for you. But that was a different time, a different place and under completely different circumstances. We have a second chance now to make better decisions."

"That's where your wrong." Finn replied, "I mean you are correct about us having a second chance and making better decisions this time. But it's how those decisions are guided that I believe our views may differ. The way I see it, every single life among us is not only priceless, but it's also worth fighting for."

Phoenix's brow furled as he let Finn's words soak in.

"We can't simply let someone slip away just because the math doesn't work. That's the old way of the thinking. From here on out, at least if I have any say in it, every single person will know that if it comes down to it, we will stop at nothing to preserve their lives."

It was evident that Finn's words were having an impact on the big German, his shoulders slumped slightly as he registered a deeper understanding of what their second chance truly meant. Simply surviving could no longer be their goal, they had to reconsider their entire belief and value systems and that started with the preservation of a single life, no matter the cost.

"I'll be the first to admit when I make a mistake. You're right, we have to move beyond the old way of thinking. I apologize for questioning you on this and of course, you have my full support."

The two men stood and shook hands, after which Finn grasped him firmly on the bicep.

"We have a long road ahead of us, and it's going to take a lot of blood, sweat and tears to get there, but I know, deep down in my gut, that we WILL get there."

~~~~~

Commander Tilley studied the energy consumption readings and mentally calculated how that broke down in terms of the Resolute's remaining endurance. Even though those same figures were easily available on an adjoining readout, the mental exercise was something he could never shake.

"1850" he muttered to himself before finally allowing his gaze to drift and compare his math against the computers which read '1825 hours remaining until core shut down'.

It was close, but borrowing a phrase he'd learned in his dealings with Americans, close only counted in horseshoes and grenades. In his youth he would have nailed those calculations to the nearest second and given the computer a run for its money. He realized that it was more than his health that was slipping with the ravages of time, his mental acuity was waning more and more all the time.

"Sir, the next pair of shuttles are away." A bridge officer reported.

"Very well."

Activity aboard the ship had reached a fevered pace of late. Losing nearly a full month of power reserves by maneuvering to complete the satellite launches had been a big gamble. Every able-bodied colonist was being pressed into service as soon as they recovered from cryo sleep. Most safety measures were now being overlooked and corners were being cut at every turn, but they simply had no other options.

Tons of carefully packed cargo remained stored throughout the ship and every scrap of it needed to be moved to the hangar bay and prepped for loading on the shuttles.

Even the cryo schedule had been dangerously modified to the point that they were now waking dozens of colonists every other instead of the recommended max of one group every other week.

No matter how many corners were cut and how much they pushed the schedule, they would still fall short in reviving every last colonist. Projections now showed that at least 75 individuals would be left behind in cryo sleep by the time they were forced to abandon ship. Commander Tilley could no longer bring himself to visit the cryo deck, each chamber suddenly appearing more like a coffin than a sleeping pod. His every waking moment now filled with the faces of those he'd condemned to death with his order. He slept in restless fits, only a few minutes at a time before waking in a cold sweat from one of several nightmares that threatened to torture his soul for all of eternity.

"Commander, I'm reading some unusual solar activity." A technician reported.

The man's voice was strained, fatigue registering heavily on his face. They were all fighting exhaustion, back to back eighteen hour shifts with little to no rest in between was wearing on them.

Punching in the command to mirror the technicians screen on his own, Commander Tilley studied the telemetry and data.

Viewed through a sensitive filter, the sun appeared as roiling orange, red and black ball against an intensely jet-black background. As he watched, large tendrils of liquid magma snaked away from the star's surface in large sweeping arcs reaching thousands of miles into surrounding space.

"It looks like solar flare activity." He said aloud. "What's the status of our radiation shield?"

"Fully deployed and intact sir." The technician replied, "We shouldn't have any trouble aboard the Resolute, but the shuttles are another story."

He uttered a silent curse as he searched the fog that had been filling his memory lately for the technical details of the shuttles. Information he should have been able to instantly recall but now found himself struggling to retrieve. Finally, he simply let it go, the specifics weren't exactly important anyway. The shuttles simply couldn't be caught in transit when the solar activities reached them or their crews would risk extreme radiation exposure.

"How long until the flare overtakes our position?"

"Fifteen hours sir and with a duration of seven to nine days."

"Very well, transmit that data to the surface. Inform Captain Finnegan that we need both shuttles back on board within twelve hours."

~~~~~

CHAPTER 18

It took nearly two hours to get both Tayte and Rune safely to the medical ward in the Revati cave complex. Another two hours for Lauren to fully brief the pair of Revati nurses who would watch after them and to gear up.

Finn knew they were cutting it close with the approaching solar storm, but while he would have preferred to wait at least a few more hours and move out in the dead of night, time was short and they needed to move quickly.

It was growing dark outside as the shuttle skirted low over the trees following a carefully mapped flight plan that would keep them well away from any significant concentration of cyborg activities.

"Captain, we're approaching the drop zone, two minutes out." The pilot reported.

Positioning himself at the controls to the loading ramp, the crew chief pressed a button on the panel casting the entire cargo bay in a dim red glow.

Finn stood and adjusted the pack on his back while making one final adjustment to the sling attached to his rifle as he felt their forward momentum slowly bleed off into a hover.

The shuttle touched down gently and the crew chief lowered the ramp giving them their first view of the barren and rocky landscape.

With his rifle raised and at the ready, Finn led the way down the ramp and rushed across the open ground until he reached a large boulder where he stopped and dropped to one knee. Sliding a pair of night vision goggles over his eyes, Finn switched them on and watched as the blackness of night turned suddenly to day. Tinged in a greenish hue, the light amplification of the goggles allowed him to see effortlessly up to a hundred yards in all directions. Motioning to both Lauren and Dutch, he silently directed both of them to put their own goggles in place.

The three of them remained still as statues and waited silently while the shuttle's engines spooled up and the craft eased skyward where it disappeared into the night.

Finn had instructed the pilot to maintain a high, energy conserving orbit and wait for their call. He gave them a total of six hours, if they weren't back by then, they were to be assumed lost and the shuttle should return to the Resolute as planned.

They remained in place for nearly ten minutes after the sound of the departing shuttle gave way to the chirping of bugs and soft rustling of an evening breeze.

Linking his PDA to the viewfinder of his goggles, Finn was presented with a small window in the upper right of his vision where he could now see a detailed topographical map of the surrounding terrain. With a direct link to an overhead satellite, he would have real time coverage of their surroundings at all times. Their target was highlighted with a small red dot, pulling his rifle tight against his shoulder he oriented himself in that direction.

"Ok, keep close, keep quiet, let's go." He said as he led the way across the rock-strewn landscape.

A mile further on and Finn signaled for a halt as several heat signatures bobbed into view in his goggles. They lowered themselves into a rocky crevice, pressed their bodies flat against the rock walls to either side and waited.

Finn could make out at least fifteen individual signatures, they appeared in his goggles as spectral blobs of green and white moving diagonally across their path.

"Patrol?" Lauren quietly asked as she watched the moving blobs through her own display.

"Maybe. There seems to be constant activity around here. Their mining operation runs around the clock." Finn whispered back.

They remained in the crevice and watched as the heat signatures moved off into the distance and faded from view. Finn allowed another two minutes to pass before signaling for them to start moving again.

Thirty minutes later and they slid down a narrow embankment to the entrance of the mining tunnel.

"Ok, a mile through this tunnel and we'll be right next to the warehouse. Keep close and call out if you start falling behind."

For the first hundred or so yards it was easy going as the ground was straight, dry and flat with clear indications of heavy wear along the ground and surrounding walls from mining operations. That quickly changed when they reached a bend winding off to the right. Rounding the turn, they stopped short as they were confronted with a pile of rock and debris.

"Looks like a cave in." Dutch muttered.

Studying the pile of rock through her goggles, Dutch leaned closer to view what she first thought was the handle of a shovel or axe protruding from the base of the mound only to suddenly rear back when she realized it was human bone.

"Jesus Christ." She exclaimed and then quickly chided herself for the outburst.

"You said it." Lauren added as she bent closer and examined the remains. "It's the leg bone from an adult male." She offered with a clinical indifference.

"There's more." Finn added as he gestured further down the mound of rock. The skeletal remains of additional limbs, ribs and even a pair of skulls were visible further into the passage.

"It doesn't look like they even tried to pull them free. Not a single rock appears disturbed." Lauren observed.

Cybernetic implants were scattered within the remains. The eye pieces were the most ominous looking of the relics, even more so than when affixed to the face of a living specimen. Those dark, black voids seemed capable of looking right into your soul even as they lay discarded within the pile of old bones. Lauren shivered at the thought.

"I'm starting to suspect the cyborgs are nothing more than semi useful tools in the eyes of the Creators. They don't seem to see any need to expend any resources or energy saving them." Finn said.

"Either way, we need to keep moving."

The passage became narrow at that point with the walls on both sides constricting keeping them moving in a single file line. Several yards beyond the start of the cave-in the ground began a gradual slope downwards and after a few moments of walking Finn's feet came down with a splash as they ran into the start of the flooded chamber.

"Ok, here's where the fun begins." Finn noted.

Continuing on, their pace slowed some as Finn probed ahead cautiously with each successful foot fall searching for drop offs or other obstacles hidden beneath the dark waters.

"Wow, it smells like raw shit down here." Dutch moaned with an exaggerated sniffle.

"Stagnant water." Finn explained, "There's probably just enough run off from the rains to keep the chamber flooded but not enough to circulate it. It's likely that it's also mixed with all sorts of unsavory crud; dead animals, plant matter, and other…things."

"Yeah, it's those *other things* that I'm having trouble not thinking about at the moment." Dutch lamented.

The water rose to their stomachs before the floor finally leveled out, slowing their progress as they sloshed ahead.

"Check this out." Dutch said suddenly as she studied a chunk of rock jutting from the wall at shoulder height. The rock was dark and smoothed around its edges, standing out as noticeably different from the lighter colored stone and bits of ore around it.

"I think this is obsidian."

Exchanging a befuddled look with Lauren, Finn finally shrugged and said, "Ok, enlighten us, what is obsidian?"

"Volcanic glass. Its formed from the passage of lava. It's an incredible find, this stuff cuts finer than a surgeon's scalpel when its refined."

"Good to know." Finn replied as he continued on, "one thing about this planet, its sure turning out to be rich in useful ores. Hopefully we'll all live long enough to benefit from it someday."

Several minutes later and the floor began a gradual upwards climb. Finn was the first to notice that the darkness inside the tunnel was giving way to light and he called for a halt indicating that they should remove their goggles and allow their vision time to adjust naturally to the increasing light. A short distance later and they relished the feeling of stepping from the putrid waters back onto dry land.

At a bend in the tunnel he called for another stop as he crouched and peered around the corner.

"We're here." He whispered as he ducked back behind the corner. "Another twenty-five feet ahead is the exit. Slow and easy from here on out, no noise."

Creeping ahead, Finn eased up towards the tunnel's exit keeping his body pressed against the rocky wall behind him and side stepping one foot over the other.

The exit was nothing more than a narrow slit in the rock wall near the center of the canyon. Remaining cloaked in the shadows Finn could see that it was only a stones throw from the side of the nearby warehouse. Seeing it close up for the first time, he was astonished at the size of the building as it filled their view, blotting out the opposite end of the canyon. To his right he saw the outer fringes of the shanty town a short distance away, flimsy and shabby looking structures dotting the landscape as far as he could see. Open fires burned in a number of locations casting dancing shadows across the warehouse walls.

Studying the near side of the warehouse, Finn was relieved to spot what looked like a seldom used service entrance tucked away some distance further along its side.

"Stay right on my heels." Finn instructed.

Taking one final glance around he kept his body low to the ground and darted across the open ground. Reaching the side of the warehouse, the three of them pressed their backs against the wall and shimmied sideways towards the doorway.

In place of a handle the door had only a small metal push plate which Finn pressed gently with the palm of his hand and breathed a sigh of relief when it swung freely without resistance or noise. Opening the door a small crack, he glanced inside to see that the door led into a dark and deserted hallway. Holding the door open only as wide as needed for the three of them to slip inside, he pulled it shut behind them as they quickly darted inside.

The hallway was short, stretching only thirty feet from end to end and its sole purpose appeared to be to house an array of pipes, wiring and electric conduits running haphazardly up and down the length of the corridor. There was no door on the far end of the hall, only an opening in the wall leading directly out into the main section of the warehouse.

They could hear the sounds of heavy equipment along with the occasional loud scuff and scrape of rock and ore being manhandled about as the mining operation continued around the clock. The intermittent hiss of a whip followed by the excited shriek of an injured animal sent shivers of anger down their spines.

Moving down the hall until they were a few feet short of entering the warehouse. Finn took in their surroundings and calculated their next move. The interior was sectioned off into segments, bland metal walls blocked his view of the adjoining rooms, but it seemed they were entering the largest section where most of the activity was centered.

A steady flow of cyborgs and their beasts entered through the cavernous opening pulling wagons heaped high with rock and minerals. Each wagon was pulled onto a metal platform in the floor where the contents were dumped in rough piles. Several feet over from the platform an equally sized section of floor was missing entirely revealing a gaping black cavity.

They watched the activity for several minutes as the heaps of rock steadily grew. Eventually there was a rumbling sensation under their feet followed the hiss of escaping steam and a shrill whistle. The missing section of floor slowly rose back into place with a metallic clank and seconds later the other section of floor, packed high with rock and minerals slowly began dropping into the ground and out of sight.

"It's a steam operated elevator system." Finn whispered. "They fill the platform with ore and it lowers down to the refining level underneath the building while the empty platform takes its place allowing for continuous deliveries. Pretty simple and efficient system, I'll bet they can process several tons of ore a day at this pace."

"Yeah, well, that's where we need to go." Dutch replied, "but I don't see how we're going to catch a ride on that platform without a hundred workers spotting us."

Crude wooden animal pens were lined up along the wall directly outside the hallway. Finn could make out three distinct breeds of dinosaurs corralled inside the various pens. Harnesses, whips and bridal bits were draped over the rails of each enclosure. Most of the creatures appeared to be sleeping, all showed horrific signs of abuse, gaping wounds, slash marks and chunks of missing flesh. From his position Finn could even see that their claws and teeth had been forcibly removed leaving behind bloodied and swollen limbs and mouths. The enclosures offered nothing in terms of bedding, worn, bare dirt lined the floors and shallow holes had been dug and filled with putrid brown water for drinking. A few of the animals looked close to death, their glassy eyes staring off into the distance, bony bodies nearly completely devoid of muscle as starvation and abuse took their toll.

While the sights were bad, the smells made it even worse. The entire warehouse stunk of a fetid mix of animal waste, rotting meat, and human body odor all mingling together with several other unidentified scents that made the flooded tunnel seem like a field of lavender potpourri.

"Im gonna be sick." Dutch gagged choking back a mouthful of bile. "This is the most disgusting place I've ever seen or smelled in my entire life."

"Look, over there." Lauren chimed in gesturing towards a corner of the warehouse off to their right. A guard rail surrounded a dark opening in the floor. "That looks like a stairwell."

"Excellent." Finn replied. "Follow me."

Keeping to the shadows in the darkest recess of the structure, Finn led them behind the rows of animal pens keeping the structures between them and the workers. They covered the distance to the top of the stairwell without incident, the few creatures that did note their passing, seemed either uninterested or simply physically incapable of raising any kind of ruckus with their presence.

Taking the first few metal plated steps two at a time, Finn descended quickly to a deserted landing where they paused to catch their breath and listen for any sign of pursuit.

"Ok, so far so good. Hopefully that was the toughest spot we had to cross."

With his rifle up and at the ready, Finn led them down the winding stairwell. Every fifteen steps they reached another landing and turned a corner as the stairwell spiraled along into the depths. The stairwell was dimly lit with a bluish glow emitting from the underside of every third or fourth step, the source of which remained a mystery they didn't care to investigate. At each landing a nondescript metal doorway sat recessed into the rock wall. With their objective at the lowest level, they passed each door without bothering to check behind it.

Ten stories down, the stairwell ended and they stood facing another metal door. Standing off to one side, Finn cautiously pressed against the push plate on the face of the door and inched it slowly open.

The door opened into a brightly lit corridor bathed in a bluish tinted light that seemed to come from everywhere and nowhere all at the same time. The walls, floor and ceiling were a perfect shade of pure white, pristine and nearly sterile in appearance. Leading off a hundred or so feet into the distance, the hallway was empty, no cyborgs, no doorways, no exposed plumbing, pipes or wires, nothing, just a bright and empty passage. At the end of the passage, the hallway ran straight into a blank wall where it simply dead-ended.

"Well, this is unexpected." Finn noted as he took in the empty and seemingly pointless hallway.

Pushing the door fully open he took one tentative step across the threshold when he was met with a blast of warm, steamy air that sent him scrambling back into the stairwell in a blind panic as he raised his rifle and readied himself for a fight.

When nothing else happened after a few moments he leaned forward and examined the door frame. Tiny nozzles were recessed into the wall and floor inside a paper-thin gap around the entire frame. Finn offered a shrug of his shoulders, pushed the door open again and stepped inside. The blast of air encapsulated him on all sides, it was odorless and appeared harmless so he kept moving until he was several feet into the corridor.

"I think it a disinfecting system." Lauren offered and then when she noted Finn's blank expression she explained, "It's a way to kill germs and infectious agents. Judging by the condition of this wing, it looks like they may be trying really hard to keep it sterile."

"Yeah, well, they could have posted a warning sign or something." Finn quipped.

Both Lauren and Dutch followed him into the corridor one at a time, each passing in turn through the blast of air.

"It sure doesn't help with the stench." Dutch said as she wrinkled her nostrils at the vile odor rising from her damp clothing.

Drawing his pistol, Finn allowed his rifle to drop free and hang against his body from its harness. With his left hand now free he began feeling his way cautiously along the wall and down the hall until he reached the end. Turning he did the same on the opposite wall until he was back at the other end where Lauren and Dutch waited and watched.

"Nothing, not a seam, a crack or any kind of mechanism. It's just an empty hallway to nowhere, makes zero sense."

Dutch turned her attention to her PDA and began entering commands. Studying the readout, she walked several feet down the hall, stopped and then turned to face a section of wall almost halfway down the corridor.

"Satellite scans are showing two human size heat signatures only a few feet directly in front of me." Reaching up she placed the palm of her hand against the door and added, "right behind this wall. There's a large room here, maybe 1000 square feet in total."

Standing to either side of her, Finn and Lauren studied the wall, ran their hands over the smooth surface from top to bottom.

"Maybe if we knock?" Lauren offered.

"Or I could just blow a hole in the damn thing." Finn exclaimed his frustration growing with each passing minute. "We sure as hell don't have time to stand here wagging our dicks all night."

He was raising his pistol when Dutch waved her hands and excitedly exclaimed, "Wait, wait, one of the figures is moving towards the opposite side of the wall." Holding her PDA up to eye level she motioned with her other hand to a spot several feet back down the hallway.

Moments later a faded blue light formed a spectral outline on a section of wall the size and shape of a doorway, the section suddenly dematerialized leaving an open doorway behind. A figure in a white lab coat stepped through, a coffee mug in one hand raised to his lips as his eyes fell on the three strangers all with pistols raised and pointed directly at his head.

The mug of coffee dropped from the man's hand and smashed onto the floor. His right eye grew wide and his lips trembled as he haltingly took a step back into the open doorway. The implant over his right eye identified him as a cyborg, but they could all see that something was different with this one.

He appeared a little past middle age, somewhere in his mid to late 50's. He was white, around average height for a man but with a large midsection and an all-around chubby face. His graying hair had receded off to the sides of his scalp leaving a shiny and exposed dome in its place. Dressed in a crisp, white lab coat he appeared clean, well fed and in remarkable shape for a cyborg.

"Wh...whoo...who...are you?" He stammered, he spoke English but mixed with a thick accent that Finn vaguely recognized as Greek or even ancient Roman.

Finn's finger remained against the trigger but he held his fire, the man was unarmed and clearly terrified, he posed no immediate threat.

"Shut your mouth." Finn ordered, pressing the barrel of his pistol against the side of the man's temple he guided him backwards and further into the hallway until his back was pressed firmly against the far wall.

In a well-practiced maneuver, Finn ran his free hand up the length of the man's legs, around his waist and patted under and down both arms. Satisfied that he wasn't concealing any obvious weapons he glanced back to Dutch and said "keep him covered."

Stepping to the open doorway, he darted across the threshold swinging the barrel of his weapon along with the angle of his gaze. The room was large, rectangular, covering nearly the entire distance of the adjoining hallway from end to end. It appeared stark and utilitarian. Furnished only with a handful of toadstool looking white tables evenly spaced across the middle of the room from one end to the other. The room's purpose was puzzling but not immediately important. A lone figure stood at a bench near the back of the room, the woman had her back to the door but upon hearing Finn's footsteps turned towards him. Their eyes met and she froze in her tracks as her right eye locked onto the barrel of his pistol which was aiming directly at her forehead.

Like her companion in the hallway she was adorned with cyborg tech and also decked out in a clean white lab coat. She was blonde, her shoulder length hair slowly giving way to gray streaks. Finn thought she was close in age to man, somewhere in her fifties, also like the man she was clean, well-groomed and in seemingly good health.

"Don't shoot! Please, don't hurt me!" She cried, her arms stretched out protectively in front of her face.

"Don't move and keep your hands where I can see them." Finn commanded as he swept the room and moved rapidly to her side. Quickly frisking her and finding her unarmed he called out.

"Clear! Bring him in here." Grabbing the backs of two chairs from their places at one of the toadstool stations, Finn dragged the chairs across the room placing them against the wall. With a wag of his pistol's barrel he gestured for both the woman and man to take a seat.

Standing a few inches directly in front of them the business end of his pistol alternating back and forth between the pair, Finn forcefully demanded "Who the hell are you?"

"I...I'm Sallustia. This is my wife, Helena. We're technicians, not fighters, I promise, we are no threat to any of you." Sallustia replied, his voice shaking and quivering, panic registering on both their faces as they likely contemplated their impending demise.

"You can speak?" Dutch asked, the surprise evident in her voice, "I didn't think cyborgs could communicate in any form."

Exchanging a confused look with his wife, Sallustia said, "Cyborgs? I don't understand."

"It's the term we've been using when referring to your people, the ones enslaved by the Creators." Lauren explained while gesturing towards the implant on his face. "The implants, they are cybernetic in nature, at least that's how we see them."

"You're talking about the thralls, aren't you? The fighters and workers on the surface. You've not encountered actual slaves like us before, have you?" Sallustia replied.

"Thralls?" Lauren responded.

"You don't know the term?" Helena asked, her voice steadier than her husbands.

"I do, I'm just not sure how your using it in this context. You just referred to yourself as slaves, what's the difference?"

"It's actually how the Creators categorize all of us. There are slaves, like us, who work as skilled laborers in laboratories and factories below the surface. There are very few of us, maybe several thousand around the entire planet. Then there are the thralls. The mindless robots who serve as soldiers, workers and test subjects for medical experiments. They are on the surface and they number in the millions all over the planet." Helena offered. She seemed genuinely perplexed at having to offer such an explanation as though it should be common knowledge.

"Wait a minute, are you saying you actually work for the Creators? Of your own free will?" Finn asked.

"Not at first." Sallustia replied, his voice steadier now that it appeared they wouldn't simply be killed outright. "Everyone comes into the fold as a thrall to begin with. A select few are chosen as slaves, we are given certain freedoms, fair accommodations and privileges. We're allowed to marry, have families and live a life of relative peace. In exchange we serve at the will of the Creators. My wife and I are part of the technical staff, we oversee the equipment in this facility and ensure production moves along as directed."

"You mean your collaborators." Finn retorted, the disgust evident in his words.

"I guess that's a fair way of looking at it." Sallustia shrugged, "It's the way of things here. Some of us, a select few, are given a choice, live a life of relative freedom as a slave or languish as a mindless thrall. We made that choice."

Addressing both Sallustia and Helena he continued, "you said this is the production facility, what is this room? There is nothing here."

"Yes, this is the control room. The actual process is automated, it's an incredible work of technology. From this room we direct the machinery to create anything that is needed, from weapons, tools, building supplies, clothing, furniture, pretty much anything."

Gesturing around the room Finn demanded, "explain how this works. There's nothing here but a handful of tables. I don't see any controls, monitors or equipment to run such a facility."

Helena nodded towards a nearby toadstool table and asked, "may I stand and approach that station? I can show you."

"Go ahead." Finn offered with a wave of his pistol.

Helena stood and approached the table. Standing inside the curve portion she waved her hands across the surface and they watched in stunned amazement as a multitude of floating controls and view screens suddenly appeared all around here. Two screens were filled from top to bottom with data while others contained a variety of controls and keyboards.

"Holy shit!" Dutch exclaimed, her eyes going wide in excitement, "Its a haptic four-dimensional system! I've read theories about such things but the tech was never there to put it in practice anywhere on our planet."

"Very good." Helena responded, "Except it's actually a five-dimensional interface."

Helena demonstrated by moving around the table in a slow circle, the floating, virtual controls followed along with her maintaining their relative location in precise correlation to her body's position.

Following her example, Dutch moved into position at another table, waved the palm over the tables surface and was instantly rewarded with a slew of floating controls and empty screens hovering precisely at eye level.

"This is so cool!" Dutch exclaimed as she reached her hands out and began experimenting with the controls and getting a feel for the system.

"Dutch, can you make it work?" Finn asked skeptically.

Dutch continued manipulating the controls for several moments as she considered her answer, "probably. The underlying architecture seems pretty straight forward. There's a menu of options and from there I can enter the specifications for any object I'd like. But it might take a little while for me to get accustomed to these controls."

"I can help." Helena offered eagerly.

"Like hell." Finn exploded and then stopped short when he noted Lauren motioning for him to step off to one side and speak privately with her.

"This is a little more than we bargained for." Lauren explained, "I'm sure Dutch could eventually figure it out, but do we really have the time? If they are willing to help, I can keep a close eye on how the schematics are programed and ensure it meets the right specifications. I think we need to trust them."

Finn exhaled loudly as he glanced back to see Helena walking Dutch through the use of the controls while pointing out various system settings. She seemed genuinely interested in helping and was offering information readily without any apparent reservations. For his part, Sallustia remained seated in a chair several feet away, his eyes darting back and forth from his wife to Finn, unease and fear registered in his face. It was clear that he was trying to decide if the two of them would be walking out of this situation alive or not.
"Ok, but you and Dutch need to watch her like a pair of hawks."

Helena helped Lauren establish a link with the data storage on her PDA and they were able to upload the detailed plans for the artificial liver and were instantly rewarded with a rendered likeness of the liver floating in the air before them.

"A human liver." Helena mused as she studied the likeness, "intriguing."

With a gentle flick of her wrist, Helena spun the image from top to bottom marveling at the intricate design.

"Can the machine produce it?" Lauren asked.

"Oh yes, absolutely. It will turn out exactly to the letter of the specifications you provided." Helena replied, "Shall I begin?"

Finn had moved to the open doorway where he took a position keeping watch down the outer hallway. Lauren locked eyes with him for a moment and he offered a small nod of approval.

"Do it." Lauren exclaimed.

"Very well." Helena acknowledged and began stabbing at the floating controls with a well-practiced grace while both Lauren and Dutch oversaw her every move.

"It should take no longer than twenty minutes once the rendering begins. These controls also allow us to direct the flow of completed products, many are returned to the surface while others are directed into a subterranean supply chain. I am programing the system to send the completed product directly to this room."

Gesturing to a section of wall several feet to the right of her husband she continued, "there is a conveyor belt running behind the wall there, when the liver is deposited, a portion of the wall will automatically open."

"What can you tell us about the Creators?" Lauren asked Helena as she kept close watch on the work in progress.

"Not much really. We've never seen them in person. They communicate with us only when necessary and it's all done through our neural processor." Helena replied as she tapped gently on the metal frame on the side of her face.

"Never seen them in person?" Dutch asked in surprise, "how long have you been here?"

"That's actually hard to say." The reply came from Sallustia as he appeared to begin relaxing somewhat believing that they may actually survive this encounter, "we have no real concept of the passage of time here. We've estimated that it's been something like 200 years since our arrival, but with how our biology is affected by the planet's atmosphere, we're aging at a much slower rate, one that has proved almost impossible to accurately track."

"200 years!" Lauren declared. "That's incredible."

"In all that time, you've not once met the Creators? How can that be?" Dutch asked.

"I can't exactly explain it." Sallustia replied, "they provide for us but ultimately leave us to live out our lives as we see fit as long as we continue managing the equipment for them. From time to time they sort of 'deposit' messages in our minds, instructions really, telling us what they want us to do. We don't ask questions, we just do as we are told."

"The floors overhead." Finn probed from his position across the room, "what's up there?"

"The next floor up is a supply area, spare parts and equipment for the lab. Above that the next several floors are our living quarters. The top two floors house equipment for the structure on the surface."

"How many others like you are on those floors?" Finn asked skeptically.

"There are fifty of us total in this facility." Helena replied before sensing Finn's apprehension and quickly adding, "all unarmed technical staff, no fighters."

"Should we expect any company? How long until your relieved by another crew?" Finn continued prodding.

Helena and Sallustia exchanged confused looks as though they weren't exactly sure how to process the question. After a few moments of awkward silence Sallustia offered, "we won't be relieved. Once we start working we remain here until finished."

Gesturing towards a spot on the wall he explained. "There are cots inside the wall there and a washroom and kitchen area directly across the hall. We stay until all our assigned work is completed. It could be days or even weeks, we never know or even realize how long to be perfectly honest."

"It's ready to submit." Helena interrupted and addressed Lauren, "would you care to inspect the design first?"

Lauren took Helena's place in the center of the table and carefully reviewed the template she had assembled. For several long minutes she meticulously compared every centimeter of the design against data stored in her PDA. Finally satisfied she stepped back and nodded for Helena to continue.

Helena's hands flew across the air as she manipulated a series of controls.

"Done." She proclaimed a few moments later, "its processing now."

Finn craned his ears in anticipation of hearing something that would confirm a mechanical process was underway. The room remained still, there was no sound of machinery, no sensation of moving parts simply nothing that would outwardly indicate the design was actually under construction. Glancing towards Dutch who had taken note of his apparent skepticism, she held up a reassuring thumbs up and nodded knowingly towards the floating view screen where she was monitoring the construction process.

With nothing more to do now but monitor the process and wait, Lauren took a chance in probing for more information. "There's a great deal we still don't understand about this world and those that have traveled here from other planets."

"Planets?" Sallustia questioned, confusion in his tone. "You're from Earth, just like us, aren't you?"

Now it was Lauren's turn to express a level of confusion in her reply, "We're from Earth, yes, but a different planet than your own of course. Our Earth is in what we call the Milky Way galaxy."

Helena's eyes grew wide as she glanced at her husband, "they don't know."

"Know what?" Finn exclaimed, a suspicious note in his tone.

"We're all from the same planet here. It's our time lines that differ." Sallustia replied.

"What the hell are you talking about?" Finn demanded. "That's the most ridiculous thing I've ever heard."

"No, actually it's not." Dutch interjected as she addressed Sallustia, "you're talking about the parallel universe theory, aren't you?"
Noting his blank and questioning expression she explained, "a hypothetical theory that our reality is only one of an infinite number of varying possibilities. The theory holds that within the fabric of space and time, countless variations of our universe exist side by side while remaining unseen and unaware of each other."

"Yes, yes, that's a reasonable way of explaining it." Sallustia replied, "one planet, countless alternate dimensions. All pulled together into the same reality by passing through the dimensional gateway."

"Dimensional gateway?"

Pausing for a moment as if trying to find the best words to explain, Sallustia finally said, "you passed through a storm in space, your ship was likely damaged, yes?"

"Yeah! An ion storm of some type is how the crew described it. Our ship's reactor suffered severe damage. It basically stranded us here." Dutch explained.

"That storm is actually a gateway that bridges all our realities together." Helena explained, "we don't know the specifics but we do know that it was designed long ago by the Creators to bring us all together in this place on the same plane of existence."

"This unbelievable and incredible all at the same time." Dutch gushed, "it's right off the pages of a fantastic science fiction novel."

"Rendering complete." Helena exclaimed as a light flashed momentarily across the screen floating in front of her.

There was a muted clunk behind the wall near Sallustia, a moment later a panel the size of a shoe box slid open and a rectangular plate extended several inches into the room. Resting on top of the plate was the completed artificial liver.

Lauren approached tentatively and carefully examined the liver. Snapping on a pair of surgical gloves, she lifted it from the plate and turned it around on all sides comparing the final product to the information displayed on her PDA.

After several minutes she finally exclaimed, "It looks perfect."

Pulling a small carbon coated container from her pack, she opened the box and carefully placed the liver into the sterile compartment before snapping it shut.

"Ok, we've got what we came for."

As they made their way towards the door, Lauren turned back unexpectedly and offered, "Come with us."

"Oh my dear." Helena replied, clearly touched by the gesture, "we're actually quite happy and content here. I know it may be hard to understand, but this is the only life we've known for so long. The world above is a strange and dangerous place, we could never make such an adjustment."

With that, they offered brief words of thanks and goodbye before hurrying their way back to the stairwell where they retraced their steps and disappeared into the night.

~~~~

CHAPTER 19

Pacing mindlessly back and forth in a circle around the medical center, Finn had actually worn a smooth track in the dirt surface. His neck was starting to hurt from absently glancing down at the time on his PDA every few minutes.

"How long?" Dutch asked as she appeared suddenly in front of him holding out a cup of steaming coffee and a clay dish heaped high with fresh fruits.

Accepting the offered drink and snack, Finn replied, "Sixteen hours and counting."

"Wow!"

"Exactly." Finn replied as he took a seat on a nearby bench. "One of the nurses stepped out a few hours ago and said everything was going well, but since then, nothing."

"I'm guessing you haven't slept much since we got back." Dutch said as she helped herself to a few pieces of fruit.

"A few hours after we got back, but that's it."

They sat together in silence for several minutes, listening to the gentle pounding of the waterfall outside the cave entrance. The ever-present roar of the flowing water had a tranquil effect that Finn found both relaxing and reassuring in its ability to keep them hidden from the outside world.

A short time later the door to the med center creaked open and Lauren stepped outside. Her surgical gown was caked in blood and dried sweat but the smile plastered across her lips when her eyes met Finn's quickly lifted his spirits.

"Everything went well."

"Oh thank god." Finn exclaimed with an exaggerated release of air.

"There were a few minor complications, but the Revati nurses are top notch and were right there when I needed them." She explained, "the next few days will be the most critical. It's now a matter of whether or not his body accepts or rejects the transplant. But I have to say it was a genius design and I'm very optimistic that he will be just fine."

They were interrupted by a crackling on their radios as Marcela's excited voice boomed out, "Hey. You guys all need to come out to the cave entrance, there's something you're gonna want to see."

Following the winding dirt path to the mouth of the cave, they rounded the final bend to find Marcela and a small crowd gathered under the misting spray of the falls and peering out to either side of the mountain pass towards the night sky above.

Dancing and twisting lights, greens, yellows and reds spiraled their way across the heavens in a stunning display that put any fireworks show to shame. As it struck the planets outer atmosphere, the solar flares rendered a mesmerizing Borealis display several times more intense than that of the northern lights back home.

Finn felt a warm weight leaning into his shoulder and he glanced down to see Lauren resting her head against him as she took in the remarkable display of nature. Her eyes hung in bare slits and she blinked repeatedly as the combined effects of the waterfall along with the ebb and flow of the light show played on her exhaustion.

"I think we need to get you to bed." Finn said as he stared down at her.

Grinning mischievously, she replied, "Why Captain, are you considering taking advantage of me in my weakened state?"

Finn started to pull away in dismay at the accusation but she hooked her arm into his and pulled him back tightly offering a playful grin.

"Just enjoy the moment. Ten more minutes and you can put me to bed."

~~~~

Dr. Hughes' mouth hung open and Finn couldn't swear by it but at one point he even thought he actually spotted a line of drool running from the corner of his mouth before disappearing into the mop of hair he was developing into a ragged beard.

As it turned out, Dutch had a flair for not only the dramatic but her attention to the smallest detail made her the ideal story teller in recounting their experiences inside the Creator's facility. It was her retelling of their conversations with Helena and Sallustia that riveted Dr. Hughes and kept him glued to every detail in Dutch's rehash of their encounter. In particular, their explanation of how the Ion storm the Resolute passed through was actually a portal of some type allowing movement between an infinite number of alternate realities back all emanating from their Earth.

They had gathered in the Revati meeting hall where Marcela and Dutch had commandeered a corner table and turned it into a mini command center complete with computer interfaces and satellite unlinks. Their goal was to eventually link the two communities sharing not only material resources but information technology and intelligence gathering. Plans were already underway to construct a building dedicated specifically to that end, for the time being, they made due with what they had.

"It explains so much." Dr. Hughes exploded with excitement, "Why didn't you bring them back? There is so much we could have learned from them!"

"Doctor, while I'm sure these revelations hold scientific importance to you. It should be made clear that these people are not our friends or allies, they are collaborators who as far I'm concerned have sold out their race for their own personal comforts and gains." Finn fired back.

"Dr. Hughes, I'm not completely clear on the whole 'multiple dimension' thing. Dutch has tried explaining it from a science fiction point of view, but, if you don't mind, can you fill in some of the blanks from your own perspective." Asked Marcela.

Always eager to impart his knowledge on others, Dr. Hughes was nearly gushing as he started, "Its a scenario that supposes that an infinite number of worlds exist in parallel to ours. While these other worlds occupy the same space and time as our own they are both separate and undetectable to each other. For example, in our world you are a computer tech who was selected to join the crew of the Discovery and travel to his distant planet to escape a dying planet. According to the Many Worlds Interpretation, another world exists where you might be a school teacher in a society without a global crisis. In still another one you might be a homeless veteran living on the streets of Los Angeles. Such scenarios can go on and on forever."

"Why'd you have to make her homeless?" Dutch interjected, "couldn't she be a CEO of some large corporation instead?"

"Of course, the possibilities are simply endless." Dr. Hughes continued, "there were always competing schools of thought on the subject. Many in the scientific community considered the Many Worlds Theory nothing more than pseudo-science and completely fictional. I was one of the handful that actually felt that the possibility of alternate realities, given our limited understanding of the universe, was credible."

Finn pulled up a chair and plopped down, not often a fan of scientific discussions, he was starting to find this particular topic interesting.

"The Ion storm is actually a multidimensional gateway." Dr. Hughes noted, "that is such an incredible notion that had I simply heard it in any other setting I would have laughed it off as pure nonsense. However, given what we now know and in hindsight of our own experiences, it makes perfect sense."

? peaked

"What exactly would such a gateway do?" Lauren asked, her own interest peeked as she sat down next to Finn and listened intently to the ongoing discussion.

Dr. Hughes arranged a number of bowls on the table around a central fruit filled platter. One additional bowl he moved far off towards the very end of the table.

"It actually solves a couple problems." He explained as he gestured towards the central platter. "First, let's imagine this platter is Earth 2.0."

With a bowl in each hand, he raised one a few inches above the table while dropping the other an equal distance below the tables edge while a third remained flat on the table and even with the platter.

"Even this planet exists in its own individual dimension. In that reality, only a single one of our own Earth's can also exist at the same time. These other Earth's, ones we would consider alternate realities to our own, are on different planes of existence."

Moving the bowl floating above the table towards the platter, he kept it steadily moving forward along the same path until it pass over and beyond the central platter.

"There would be no way to travel from one of those dimensions to this one. The gateway is therefore a portal where the Creators have figured out a method of funneling matter from one dimension directly into this one. In a manner of speaking, it's a like a bridge connecting two ends over a bottomless chasm."

"That's simply incredible." Dutch exclaimed, "can you imagine the level of technology involved in creating such a gateway? If this is all true, just the ability to realize those alternate worlds is so far beyond anything humans would be capable of. I'm starting to wonder if these Creators aren't actually from some highly advanced alien society."

"It's quite possible." Dr. Hughes proposed, "considering their own self-titled, slaves, have never even laid eyes on them in the centuries they have served them. It does make you wonder."

"Doctor, you said the gateway solved a couple problems." Marcela interjected, "other than serving as a bridge, what else does it do?"

"Ahh yes, thank you for bringing us back on track." Dr. Hughes continued, "I had always found it quite interesting that after so many decades of studying the solar system with long range telescopes and deep space probes, our own species only managed to discover the existence of this planet in recent years. In terms of our interstellar neighborhood, a habitable planet only from fifteen light years of our own should have been noted a long time ago."

"Meaning? What exactly?" Marcela prodded him to continue when he ended his statement without offering a complete explanation.

Finn could tell by the exasperation in her voice that even Marcela was starting to grow weary of Dr. Hughes annoying habit with verbal theatrics. The man seemed to almost take pleasure in forcing others to drag important details out of him.

"I believe that Earth 2.0 is actually much further from our home world than we believe. I think the gateway not only allows us to pass between dimensions but it also moves us spatially over a great distance at the same time."

"That kind of makes sense." Dutch chimed in, "the distance we are capable of traveling through space is limited by our technology. If the Creators truly desired to draw us here, they had to find a way to make it feasible within those same limits."

"That might actually be the point." Dr. Hughes said, "it's conceivable the Creators wanted to draw people here from our Earth, from multiple time lines, but only at a specific level of technical advancement. They may not have wanted to deal with us a century down the road when we were much more capable."

"Not that we would still be around in another century." Finn joined in.

"That's true, at least in our case as well as some of the other worlds that have traveled here in the face of extinction level events. But I think those events are simply a means to an end. Something that hastened our willingness to risk sending manned missions into deep space."

"Wait a minute." Dutch said, "do you think they had anything to do with our home world falling apart? Are they orchestrating cataclysmic events simply to draw people to their world?"

"It's possible. We know that various tragedies have befallen many other worlds that ended up traveling here. I certainly wouldn't rule that out."

"But why?" Marcela asked, "why are they drawing us here in the first place? What is it they want from us?"

"I think they're dying." Lauren interjected, all eyes suddenly shifted in her direction waiting for her to continue, "I've studied the autopsies of the, what did you call them? Thralls? That we recovered early on. They all showed signs of not just medical experimentation, but very specific genetic level manipulation."

"Interesting." Dr. Hughes mumbled as his mind quickly churned over the possibilities, "if the Creators suffer from some type of genetic deficiency then it's conceivable that they are trying to force either a genetic mutation or even an evolution in our people that they could then introduce to their own population."

"Nothing about that makes me feel any better about them or this planet." Dutch added.

A series of alarming beeps began emitting from one of the nearby computer stations. Marcela slid her chair over and tapped several keys on a keyboard before saying, "something's going on. We just received an automated alert from the Resolute that one of our satellites has picked up some unusual activity around the Creator's industrial complex."

"Can you transfer the feed to one these screens." Finn asked as he and Lauren stood nearby.

Dutch joined Marcela at their station and immediately began tinkering with the controls and rapidly keying in commands. "There's a lot of interference, the solar storm is really mucking things up. Voice communication with the Resolute is still out for the moment but our data uplinks are operational."

The screen filled with a high-altitude image giving them an overview of the land surrounding the production facility.

"Can't really make anything out from this view. Can you zoom in on that Dutch?" Finn asked as he studied the screen.

Making incremental adjustments Dutch zoomed in until they were viewing the surface from slightly below tree top level. They were looking at a top down view of a void and rocky crevice. Hundreds if not thousands of thralls were working their way steadily up a worn dirt path to conjugate in one large mob at the very top of a sheer cliff overlooking a rock-strewn valley several hundred feet below.

"What the hell are they doing?" Finn wondered aloud.

"Look, there, on the upper left of the screen, see those individuals in blue? Those look like the same lab coats Sallustia and Helena were wearing." Lauren noted.

"Yeah but now there's a bunch more of them." Finn replied.

"Look there, off to the side of the larger group, see those two individuals off to themselves." Lauren exclaimed as she stabbed at the screen, "Dutch can you tighten it up a little more on those two?"

Dutch's fingers danced across the keyboard and in seconds the view snapped in tighter on the two solitary figures. Even though the resolution was starting to get fuzzy at that magnification along with interference from the solar storm, enough detail was present that they recognized the figures.

"That's them, Sallustia and Helena." Lauren exclaimed, "but what are they doing?"

The two slaves were standing several feet apart from the main crowd with their heads tilted back and their faces looking directly into the camera lens of a satellite orbiting so far overhead that they had no possible way of spotting from the ground.

"Oh my god." Finn exclaimed, "their waiting to make sure we're watching."

As if his words were the catalyst for the coming event, the mixed mob of both thralls and slaves began marching almost in rhythm towards the cliff edge. Without so much as a pause or second thought, they began spilling over the precipice like some kind of sickening waterfall. Behind the active jumpers a steady procession of moving flesh continued making its way steadily up the pass feeding into the advancing crowd as they poured over the edge.

They watched in silent horror as a virtual sea of human beings flung themselves onto the jagged rocks at the base of the canyon. All the while the pair of slaves who had helped them construct a new liver for Tayte stared smiling up into the clouds above as if they knew they were being watched and by whom.

One minute passed into two and the crush of bodies slowly began tapering off as the column of thralls coming up the rock passage finally reached the end of the line. When the last few slaves and thralls tumbled from sight over the edge only Sallustia and Helena remained standing at the top of the cliff face.

Despite the degraded resolution, everyone in the room could see both their faces beaming in broad smiles as they stared upwards and directly into the distant camera lens. Reaching out and grasping hands, the couple finally looked away and turned towards the edge of the cliff. Walking hand in hand they strolled across the lip of the rocky edge as though they were meandering peacefully down a garden path. Their bodies twisted and intertwined as they dropped, picking up speed they quickly became nothing more than a convoluted blur of motion before falling from view into a sea of battered and broken carcasses.

"I...I...I can't believe that just happened." Lauren stammered as she fought to hold back a flood of tears.

A thought occurred to him and Finn suddenly exclaimed, "Dutch, show us the complex."

With a few taps of the keyboard Dutch adjusted the view until the camera showed a top down view over the canyon housing the industrial complex.

"Any thermal readings?" Finn asked.

Dutch studied the readout for several moments and then replied, "Nothing, not a single heat source above or below ground. Not even the foundry is registering."

"Wait a minute." Marcela said as she moved closer to the screen, "what's that?"
She was pointing to the ground near the entrance to the warehouse, several odd shape lumps appeared at the entrance and fanning out in an arc towards the now abandoned shanty town.
Dutch once again adjusted the view and zoomed a little closer revealing a scene of additional carnage.

"Oh no." Lauren shuddered.

The dinosaurs used as beasts of burden for the complex had been led out of their pens and slain in mass. The bodies of hundreds of the tortured beasts were laying in the blood-soaked dirt.

"They moved them out into the open so we would be sure to notice." Finn snarled, his voice thick with a growing rage, "the sick bastards."

"WHY?" Lauren exclaimed, "I don't understand the point to any of this."

"It's a message. They clearly didn't care for our recent visit and they are putting us on notice of how little they value any human life." Finn hissed.

"I've seen enough. Turn it off Dutch."

Finn stood and began pacing the room as his mind raced, considering the implications. Finally, he stopped and looked back to see everyone watching him and waiting for him to say something.

"I don't like this, I don't like it all. I think somethings coming our way and we need to prepare. I'm going to get with Linc and have him and as many of the Revati warriors as they can spare return to our settlement with me. Lauren, Dr. Hughes, I want you to remain here."

Before either of them could offer an objection, Finn held up a hand and said, "We know the Creators, for the most part at least, have left the Revati alone. This is likely one of the safest places you can be for the time being."

CHAPTER 20

Finn was impressed with the amount of work completed during his short absence. Structures that were nothing more than skeletal wooden frames were now fully formed and functional parts of the community. Additional bunk style housing continued appearing along with support facilities for artisans and craftsman alike. A blacksmith shop, tannery and even a bakery had taken shape and were almost ready for operations. Similar shops would soon come; leather-workers, tannery, cobblers, quilters, a long list of shops where skilled specialists would soon begin plying their trades.

They entered the main gate in three staggered columns. Although the Revati had offered to send a few hundred of their best men to help augment the colonies defenses against an attack that Finn was sure was soon to come. He had resisted pulling so many resources from their home. In the end he had settled on a handpicked group of ninety warriors, divided into three, thirty-man platoons. With Linc appointed as overall commander of the Revati forces Finn knew they had at least a fighting chance in a defensive operation against even a sizable enemy force.

They were approaching the main square and Finn noted a pleasant and familiar odor carried along on a warm afternoon breeze. Smoke twisted skyward from atop a clay over behind the bakery. The small shop was already hard at work pumping out a stock of freshly baked bread. With supplies donated from the Revati and an abundance of locally sourced edible plants, colonists were becoming creative in augmenting their otherwise bland menu options.

The heavenly aroma brought back a flood of fond memories of his time stationed in Germany where such bakeries dotted nearly every street corner. Of course, that was a long time ago, and only a few years after he rotated back to the states, most of Germany and its famous bakeries were reduced to little more than ash under roving clouds of acid rain.

Phoenix and Jenna sauntered across the main square to meet them.

Turning to Linc, Finn said, "Why don't you dismiss the men, have them grab some chow and find whatever bunk space might be available. I want you on hand to hear whatever is coming."

Judging by the rapid approach of both Jenna and Phoenix along with their down turned expressions, he knew bad news was coming.

"Your gonna want to see this." Jenna said without preamble.

She led them across the commons to the command center where two security officers were manning the shop and monitoring the equipment.

Gesturing towards a large monitor in the center of the room, Jenna explained, "satellite imagery picked this up about an hour ago."

The thermal view came from an altitude several hundred feet above the jungle canopy. Stretching from one end of the monitor to the next, they could see thousands of individual heat sources moving steadily across the forest floor, an army of thralls.

The imagery was suddenly replaced by a burst of static and bright colors. Shooing the guards away, Dutch took control of the station and began working the controls like a finally tuned musical instrument.

"Interference from the solar storm." Dutch explained, "give me a minute to adjust feeds to a different satellite."

A moment later the image returned, "ok, we can keep this view for another few minutes but I will have to keep jumping satellites when the interference gets too bad."

"We're estimating somewhere north of 8,000 troops along with at least three hundred pack animals, pulling not only supply wagons but nearly forty wheeled cannons." Jenna explained as she gestured towards the monitor and each point of interest.

"Let me guess, heading straight for us?" Finn exclaimed.

"Sure looks that way. They're still about fifty miles out, coming in from our north west. At their current rate of advance, I'd say we have three, maybe four days before they get here."

Linc carefully studied the monitor and then said, "I know this area. The terrain is rough and there are several spots along the way where we can set up ambushes to help slow them."

Finn considered that for a moment and then dismissed it outright, "No, it would only be a pinprick and not worth the possible loss of life and material on our side. They're coming, that's a fact, we need to use the time we have left to buckle down and fortify our defenses. We have the advantage of being on the defensive."

"But they have the numbers and firepower." Jenna added. "We can't hold them off indefinitely. With cannon support, they can punch holes in our perimeter from a considerable range and then hit us with a human wave attack."

"Then we need to find a way to keep them from massing." Finn mused. "If we can draw them into the open in smaller numbers, we can pick them off from our elevated positions along the wall. With the supporting Revati platoons mixed in with our own troops, I think we can hold them back if we can keep them spread out along a wide front."

Other than taking control of the video feed, Dutch had remained uncharacteristically quiet and restrained ever since leaving the Revati village. Finn knew she was upset that Marcela had elected to remain behind, citing a need to implement some long overdue maintenance on their electrical grid. Up to that point the two women had been virtually inseparable and made an ideal team working through both engineering and technical issues. While Finn hated separating the two he needed Dutch with them and it wasn't long before she demonstrated exactly why she was such a valuable asset.

"I think I have an idea."

For several minutes Dutch outlined a plan so crazy and off the beaten path of any tactical training or military strategy he'd ever known that he actually found himself considering it.

"Ok, first and foremost. Phoenix, I need your people to devote all resources on shoring up our defensive positions. I want at least twenty additional observation and firing posts put up along the north, west and southern walls. With the river and rugged terrain to the east, I can't see them attempting to maneuver either cannon or large numbers of personnel for a mass assault on that front. We'll assign our reactionary force to that sector, they will be responsible for filling in any gaps along the main front or reinforcing anywhere it looks like we could be hit with a massed attack."

Phoenix nodded his understanding followed by a few minutes of back and forth as he clarified certain points with both Finn and Jenna.

There was a knock on the door and a moment later three colonists appeared carrying trays of fresh baked bread and jams produced from wild berries along with a basket heaped high with fruits and pitchers of coffee, juice and water.

It was a welcome break and after the long trek back from the Revati village the food and drinks were descended on with the eagerness of a pack of ravenous animals.

It was in that act, that Finn truly understood that a sense of family was starting to blossom within their community. There were few things in life he truly felt worthy of laying his life down for but in that moment, he knew that if came to it, he would put his own personal safety on the line in order to protect what they had here.

As they drank and ate, he pressed ahead with the briefing.

"Jenna. With Tayte out of action, I'm looking to you to take personal charge of our own forces. I want you to break them into squads, ensuring that each has a stable and reliable leader. We're going to spread them out along the north, west and southern walls where every man will have an assigned field of fire overlapping with the position to either side of them. Every inch of ground leading up to the wall needs to be saturated with coverage. We'll be heavily outnumbered, but with the high ground and defensive fortifications, we can hold them back."

Jenna nodded as she furiously jotted notes and Finn felt a growing confidence that if he wasn't able to have Tayte by his side for the looming fight, she was more than capable of filling those shoes. He continued.

"Starting now, I want you to personally ensure energy packs for every weapon are fully charged. We're going to be relying heavily on our pulse cannons to break up any massed assault. Ensure that every position with a cannon has a portable recharger on hand, those weapons need to remain fully operational at all times."

The atmosphere around the colony had changed from one of nervous excitement and hope for a second chance at life to one of despair and fear as the time for battle drew near. Those colonists not directly involved with work on fortifications were restricted to working in the southern fields or the immediate area of their barracks.

It had been decided that when the fighting began, all noncombatants would seek shelter in the agricultural buildings. With those facilities furthest from the front walls, it was hoped they would remain safely out of reach from the longer-range weapons. In the event the walls were breached and it looked like they colony would fall; the colonists would make a run for the south gate where ten Revati fighters were detailed to guide them to the cave sanctuary.

~~~~

Finn finally forced himself to grab a few hours of sleep late the evening before and as the sun rose on a new day, he felt energized and recharged. His time was divided between inspecting their defenses and wandering in and out of the command center to watch in real time as the enemy drew ever closer.

"Despite everything we've learned about them, we still have barely scratched the surface." Dutch lamented as she sat at her station monitoring incoming satellite feeds. The overhead screen to her left remained focused on the approaching thrall army and she gestured towards it as she continued speaking.

"Other than a few short patches, they haven t stopped to sleep or rest. I think the only thing they actually slowed for was to feed and water their animals, otherwise, it's been nonstop progress."

"How far out are they now?" Finn asked as he stared at the screen.

"Around twenty miles, I'd say no more than ten hours give or take."

"Ok, then its crunch time." Finn noted as waved to another officer and directed him to take over for Dutch. "Grab your toys and meet me at the west gate in fifteen."

~~~~~

The early morning sun was beating down on them through clear skies as Finn, Linc and Dutch gathered together and made their way out the gate and into the surrounding forest. Their first stop was at a mud bank along the edge of a nearby stream.

"I really hate this part." Dutch cried as she closed her eyes and slathered a handful of the rank muck onto her face.

"Think of it as a new wave beauty product." Finn said as he scooped up a handful of the damp mud, held it to his nose and mimed breathing in the pungent stench. "Ahhhh, it's the Chanel and Axe body spray of a brand-new world."

With their entire bodies covered in the slimy muck, Linc produced a pair of clay pots from a pack on his back and the three of them spent the next few minutes filling each container to the rim with the fragrant mud. Once filled, they sealed the tops and secured them in Linc's pack, giving him a few moments to situate the heavy burden over his broad shoulders.

Returning to the forest they moved quickly and steadily with Linc leading the way. Finn found it inconceivable how someone so large was able to move so effortless through even the densest undergrowth while remaining nearly silent at the same time.

Forty-five minutes later Linc raised a balled fist over his head, calling for a halt. Crouching low, Finn eased up alongside him and took stock of their surroundings.

Linc gestured with his right hand towards a rise in the ground about a hundred feet further on and whispered.

"We stop here."

Dropping her pack Dutch immediately set to work readying a small hand-held drone for action.

Once the unit was ready she sent it flying upwards until it was a ways into the overhead canopy and then, with the controls on her PDA steered it carefully through the trees as the camera beamed back live footage of the ground underneath.

Several anxious minutes later and they spotted their objective.

"There she is." Dutch breathed softly a clear warbling in her voice.

The female T-Rex was on the far western side of the oblong shaped depression. The nearly hundred-foot dip in the forest floor made for the perfect nest as the babies were now at an age where they were roaming freely but not quite nimble enough to negotiate the ridge surrounding their home.

"The male is gone, just like we thought." Finn whispered.

"Hunting." Linc replied as he turned his head in all directions before adding, "could be back at any moment."

"I can't believe this is actually my idea." Dutch moaned as she stared at the image of the monstrous beast resting only a few hundred feet away.

"I certainly give it a solid nine on the Richter scale of crazy ideas." Finn said, "but we're here, let's just get it done. Linc, you're up."

Dropping the pack from his shoulders, Linc heft his bow and notched an arrow before slipping off into the underbrush. He was unnervingly quiet as he disappeared from view, but that stealth was soon to be put to the test as he made a beeline directly towards the giant Rex.

Reaching into his own pack, Finn withdrew a specially outfitted tranquilizer pistol. Each of the six high pressure darts loaded in the magazine were filled with a substance developed for animals the size and weight of full grown cattle back home. He was gambling that the same compound would be as effective on toddler T-Rex's. The alternative was to kill the babies, but that was a line Finn wasn't ready to cross even in the face of an overwhelming assault.

Cocking the pistol, he crouched low in the brush and waited.

"I got him. He's coming up behind Momma Rex, fifty feet and closing." Dutch said before adding, "Damn he's like a huge, hairy, Ninja, I can't believe she can't see or hear him yet."

They watched as Linc pulled back the string on his bow and let loose with an expertly aimed shot directly into the soft flesh of the creature's neck. A half a second later the tranquil quiet of the forest erupted with a thick, throaty roar that could not only be heard but also shook the ground under their feet like a minor earthquake.

Linc was already moving by the time the Rex turned her head searching for the source of the sudden attack. His super human speed rapidly put distance between him and the now extremely pissed off dinosaur, but it was about to come down to a battle of wills as the Rex bounded forward hot on his heels in a fit of rage.

"Alright, we're on." Finn exclaimed as he caught a glimpse of the Rex plowing headlong into the forest on a chase that would hopefully keep it busy for the next ten to fifteen minutes.

As the pounding of its foot falls and spine jarring vibrations of its roars faded into the distance, the sounds of the tiny Rex's filled the void.

Startled by their mothers' angry cries and alarmed to suddenly find themselves alone, all four of the toddlers wailed and shrieked in surprise and grief.

Dutch moved the drone until it was hovering a bare ten feet over the head of the closest infant. A high gain microphone on the underside of the device was already active as it recorded the cries and moans of the frightened babies.

While Dutch worked her magic with the drone, Finn moved up to the edge of the depression until he had a clear field of view on the four birdlike creatures. He took a moment to marvel at how unlike their parents the babies appeared, despite their current size at close to two hundred or more pounds, the smaller dinosaurs acted and looked almost helpless and pitiful at that moment. He knew it wouldn't be long however until that helplessness was far behind them as they grew to become some of the most fearsome land creatures this world had to offer.

Finn did a quick mental calculation to determine the order of his shots and then sighted the dart gun on his first target and waited.

"How we looking Dutch?"

"Just a few more seconds." She replied as she whirled the drone from side to side trying to catch as much variety of the wailing cries as possible. "Not exactly sure what they're saying but they don't sound happy."

Ten seconds turned to fifteen and Finn felt tendrils of cold sweat running down the back of his neck, patience in a tense situation was not his best virtue.

"Ok, that should be enough." Dutch exclaimed as she piloted the drone back towards her and landed it gently at her feet.

Time slowed for Finn as he focused along the sights and concentrated on his target. In his head he accounted for distance, a slight wind and the downward trajectory of the shot. With a pull of the trigger there was a slight pop of escaping air as the dart was fired. A fraction of a second later he was rewarded with the sight of a feathery blossom appeared in the soft underbelly of the first baby Rex.

The tranquilizer was instantly released into the creature's blood stream and its wails became gargled as it began staggering in a wide circle before collapsing in a heap near the center of its nest.

Finn targeted the remaining three dinosaurs in rapid succession. In less than two minutes all four babies were sleeping soundly.

"Ok, we've got to move." Finn exclaimed as he hurriedly secured the dart gun back in his pack.

Clambering down the side of the depression, they raced to the nearest baby dinosaur.

"Shit this is thing is a lot bigger up close than I had imagined." Dutch said as they crouched in the tall grass next to the slumbering Rex.

"Heavier too." Finn exclaimed as he grasped the babe under its shoulders and struggled with all his weight to move it a few inches further into the densest part of the nest. "Grab its damn legs, we just need to get it about twenty feet further into the brush where it can't be seen."

"Ok, that's good." Finn stammered after they had struggled to move the beast into a thicket of brush, "go grab the first mud jug while I fill the pee jar."

Dutch clambered back up the side of the nest as Finn dug into his pack and withdrew a large syringe, a tube and a half gallon specimen jar.

Fitting the tube into place on the end of the syringe, he studied the baby Rex's body for a moment trying to remember the diagram one of their veterinarians had sketched out for him. Finding the spot he was looking for low and to the left side of the creatures belly, he pressed the needle into the soft flesh and eased it gently into its abdomen until he felt a bit of pressure followed by a slight pop.

With the opposite end of the tube inside the jar, he slowly pulled back on the plunger until a steady flow of dark yellow urine began moving through to tube and into the jar.

Behind him he heard a curse and a rustling in the brush as Dutch struggled to maneuver the heavy jug of muck across the uneven terrain, "Linc sure made it look a lot easier." She huffed as she stutter stepped the jug the last few feet until it was alongside the slumbering Rex.

"Think we got enough?"

"Don't know, but I sure hope so. This thing is bigger than I thought." Finn replied, "you get started on this jug and I'll grab the other. Be careful not to bump the pee tube though, we need every drop."

As Finn rushed back to retrieve the second jug, Dutch scooped out handfuls of the vile goop and starting with the head, began slathering it into the feathery hide of the baby Rex.

Two minutes later, Finn reappeared half carrying and half dragging the second jug of mud. They worked fast, ensuring every inch of the creature was covered in the slimy mess.

A distant roar along with a soft rumble under the feet caused them to stop as they cocked their ears and listened.

"That came from south of here." Dutch cried.

"It's the male." Finn said, "we need to hurry."

While Dutch continued layering the mud onto the creature, Finn pinched off the tube and withdrew the syringe from its belly. Sealing the top as tight as he could, he withdrew a roll of duct tape and wrapped several layers around the lid and top of the bottle. Finally, he scooped out a generous handful of mud and coated the bottle from top to bottom before carefully securing it in a foam lined container in the bottom of his pack.

Another angry roar rattled tree branches and shook the ground at their feet, the male was close and moving quickly towards the nest.

"We need to move." Finn exclaimed as he swung his pack over his shoulder, grasped Dutch by the arm and directed her back towards the far edge of the nest.

They had just finished clawing their way over the lip of the rise when a blur of movement off to his left caught Finn's eye and caused him to drop to one knee and swing his pulse rifle off his back and into the ready position.

Linc suddenly broke from cover, soaked in sweat and battered with scratches and small cuts across his arms, legs and torso, he stopped when he spotted Finn and Dutch, pausing to catch to his breath.

"We must go. The male is returning and the female is not far behind me. She is very unhappy."

Almost to emphasis his point, another ground shaking roar sounded from deep in the woods behind Linc followed the by the distant crackle of splintering tree limbs as the beast drew closer.

With a sweeping gesture back the way they'd come, Finn said, "Lead on."

~~~~

CHAPTER 21

As darkness descended on the colony, a light drizzle began to fall. Finn strained his eyes in the night vision goggles willing himself to see deeper into the forest. Despite the light magnification of the goggles, all he could only make out was the occasional fleeting shape as it darted between the distant trees.

The thrall army had arrived a few minutes earlier and began spreading out along an expanding line several dozen yards into the wood line. With continued interference from the solar storm, their satellite imagery was spotty at best making it difficult to get a clear picture of how or where the enemy was massing.

"I think they're just going to hit us up and down the line." Jenna offered as she gazed over the sights of her rifle waiting for a viable target to present itself.

"Massing on one particular area would make more sense and give them the best chance for a breakthrough, but I don't believe they think that way."

"One thing I've learned about them, they don't show any regard for standard military tactics. So you're guess is as good as mine." Finn replied.

"Maybe not, but they're pretty smart. I mean is it a coincidence they picked the exact timing of a solar storm when our eyes and ears in the sky are compromised? Or that their force march put them right on our front steps just after dark?"

"Well, I don't think it will be long before you can ask them in person." Finn replied as he spied a group of thralls probing closer to the edge of the forest.

The crack of a single rifle from inside the forest was immediately followed by a long burst of machine gun fire further down the line. Through the goggles the twinkle of muzzle flashes stood out like signal flares against the darkened background of the hazy woods. Additional gunfire rang out in sporadic locations up and down the line. The defenders continued holding their fire as they watched and waited for enemy targets to appear.

The bark of gun fire and several machine guns opening up directly to their front sent pieces of flying bark and shrapnel spraying across their position forcing both of them down into cover.

"Here we go!" Finn shouted.

As the patter of impacting rounds stitched their way further down the wall, they clambered to their feet and began sending return fire back into the woods. Up and down the line beams of light stabbed out into the night as pulse rifles opened fire. Although they couldn't see it, the night air also came alive with volleys of arrows rippling across the open field in search of fleshy targets as Revati warriors joined the fray.

Moments later the first volley of cannon fire opened up, the reverberating booms of the shot followed an instant later by heavy thuds as both solid shot and exploding metal canisters found purchase on the wall.

"Medic! Medic!"

Finn and Jenna exchanged knowing looks as the cries rang out from two locations inside their perimeter.

Pulse cannons added fiery basketball sized meteorites to the mix as gunners concentrated their fire on the cannons as those positions were identified. Fountaining geysers of fire, smoke, dirt, leaves and limbs flared into view through their goggles as the heavy weapons found their mark.

A spectral image moved across Finn's field of view at the edge of the forest, he fired off a double tap and let out a curse as both blasts went wide and the figure disappeared from view behind the bulk of a thick tree.

"They're staying right at the edge of our effective range." He shouted as Jenna pumped several blasts into the trees at another figure.

"As I said, they may not know tactics but they're not stupid. Their rifles and machine guns aren't as accurate, but the amount of firepower they can bring to bear is going to whittle us down over time." Jenna cried back.

Into his PDA Finn called out, "Keep pouring on the fire. Try to prevent them from massing in any one location. Gunners, get those damn cannons knocked out as soon as you identify them, that's the number one threat at the moment."

Another volley of cannon fire, nearly thirty pieces this time, launched a thunderous wall of shells exploding up and down the wall. At least four of the solid shot rounds punched through the outer wall and Finn cringed when he saw impacts on buildings further back inside the colony. The explosive rounds carved out large chunks of bark and filled the air with a blizzard of deadly shrapnel resulting in more cries for medics and the loss of at least one pulse cannon and its crew.

"Dutch! You there?" Finn cried out as he drew down on a pair of thralls and fired a succession of shots dropping one in their tracks while the other disappeared into the darkness.

"Ready for operation Jurassic Park?" Dutch called back.

While he winced at her picking that moment for jokes, he refrained from commenting as he realized that she wasn't a soldier and if humor helped her deal with the fear she must be experiencing, then he wasn't about to make an issue of it.

"We need to get those cannons out of service ASAP. Try and drop the payload right over their heads."

"You got it boss." Dutch replied. Despite her shaken and rattled voice her steadfast determination came through loud and clear.

~~~~~

Tayte rubbed at his eyes as he squinted against the harshness of the overhead light. He tried taking a mental inventory of the rest of his body but judging by the warm sense of floating he was experiencing, he realized he was pumped full of pain killers making it next to impossible to tell if anything else was actually hurting.

An oxygen tube running to a nasal cannula fitted in his nose providing a steady and refreshing supply of crisp and cool oxygen into his lungs. The soft and rythmatic hum of the flow meter and nearby humidifier nearly lulled him back to sleep.

"There he is." Lauren cooed softly as she eased up alongside the bed.

"You really got me flying high, don't you doc?" His own voice sounded slurred and far off as though he talking through a long, winding tunnel.

"Trust me, three days out of transplant surgery, you don't want to go without the good stuff." Lauren smiled down at him as she leaned over and inspected the instrument readings from several devices connected by various wires to different parts of his body.

As Lauren bent down, another figure behind her came into focus. The Revati nurse was a tall woman, several inches taller than himself even. Her facial features were similar to the other women of her species, rugged, with a domed forehead and exaggerated cheekbones that gave them all a somewhat animal like appearance. He'd never really given any of them a second look, once the initial shock of their actual existence wore off, he'd started seeing them as allies and friends, while the physical differences had no bearing on how he viewed them.

In that moment however, there was something different about this particular nurse, a kindness in her oversize brown eyes, a tenderness in how she offered him a genuine smile and an electric buzz when her fingers brushed against his forearm as she reached out to check his pulse.

"What's your name, beautiful?" Tayte mumbled.

With a glowing smile the nurse met his gaze as she replied, "Bew"

"Easy, big fella." Lauren scolded as she noted his pulse rate starting to rise.

Raised voices somewhere outside the medical center caught their attention. A pair of gunshots echoed through the building followed by shouting and cries of alarm.

"Lock the doors! Lock the doors!" Lauren called out as she gestured frantically towards another nurse near the clinic's main doors.

Before the nurse could start to move, one of the doors cracked open a sliver and a metallic cannister skittered with a clang across the floor and under a cart loaded with medical supplies. There was a slight pop and then a hiss of escaping air as a yellow mist escaped from under the cart and began filling the room.

Two nurses caught in the expanding smoke cloud coughed and then dropped almost instantly to the floor.

"Gas!" Lauren cried, grabbing a thick handful of gauze and pressing it to her face.

Bew coughed and staggered forward as she reached a hand towards a nearby cart grasping for a box of disposable masks. She had a mask in her hand and was raising it towards her face when her eyes suddenly rolled back in her head and she collapsed face first onto the ground.

Recognizing the threat, Tayte fought through the haze in his head and began ripping monitor leads from his bare chest as he sat up in bed and searched around him for anything he could use as a weapon.

His eyes fell on the bottom shelf of a nearby equipment cart where he spotted his folded uniform, utility belt and the butt of his pulse pistol extending from its holster.

Lauren had backed herself up until she was nearly leaning against his bed as she listened to yells and the sounds of scuffling in the med center lobby. Glancing back towards Tayte she saw him eying the pistol and quickly bent down to grab the weapon.

The doors to the center flung open and Lauren raised the pistol ready to fire. With her finger pressed to the trigger she suddenly froze in her tracks as Marcela entered, a mask pressed to her face, her eyes glazed and odd as they anxiously darted around the room.

Their eyes meet and for a moment Lauren felt a wave of relief thinking that whatever had happened was over. She lowered the pistol and took half a step towards Marcela when two more figures entered the room right behind her. Both of the newcomers bore the facial cybernetics of thralls, a common sight in the Revati village. However, these two were different, they were covered head to toe in a strange reflective cloth, their mouths and noses covered in filtered gas masks and they were each brandishing rifles that they used to sweep across the room as they moved.

Marcela nodded in Lauren's direction and then pointed directly at her before stepping off to one side and allowing both thralls to move past her. They covered the distance from the doorway to either side of Lauren in only a few steps. In that time Lauren's mind raced as she tried to understand what was happening. When it finally dawned on her that something was wrong and the warning bells in her head sounded an alarm it was too late.

The first thrall to reach her grabbed her wrist and wrenched it hard to the side causing her to cry out in pain as she opened her hand and dropped the pistol on the bed alongside Tayte. At almost the exact same moment the second thrall snatched her other hand away her mouth and nose. Exasperated and in near shock, she breathed deeply only to find her vision growing blurry and her head swimming in a confused jumble of thoughts and images. Lauren's body grew limp and she began to drop before one of the thralls reached out and guided her carefully down to the floor.

In his weakened state, Tayte was slow to react, but the moment the thralls descended on Lauren he recognized the threat and moved to action. Scooping up the pistol he pressed the barrel directly against the side of the head of one of the thralls and squeezed the trigger. The energy blast ripped a nickel sized hole at the entry point before filling the entire cranial cavity with its concussive force. The far side of the thrall's head exploded outward like a rotten melon sending a splash of blood, brain and bone fragments across the room.

The second thrall side stepped to the left and began raising his rifle towards Tayte, both fired at nearly the same instant. The thralls bullet grazed across Tayte's right bicep, leaving a shallow, bloody trail in the skin but otherwise causing little damage. The energy pulse from Tayte's shot hit the thrall in the upper left side of his chest and pushed him backwards into the next bed where he stumbled and fell onto the mattress. A second shot caught the thrall square in the throat nearly removing his head as his lifeless body sprawled sideways across the mattress in a tangled bloody mess.

Tayte crouched down and verified that both Lauren and Bew were merely unconscious and not in immediate danger, although there was a puddle of blood under Bew's face where her nose had smacked against the ground.

He was still bent over when the doors to the med center crashed open again, this time a group of five thralls stormed across the threshold, rifles up and ready. Tayte started raising his but three of the thralls fired first. The first bullet went wide, striking and exploding the instrument panel of a heart rate monitor. The second round caught him in his right shoulder and sent him tumbling backwards, ripping the oxygen tube from his nostrils, while the third round carved out a deep furrow in the side of his head sending a spray of blood over his sheets and mattress. Without the oxygen flowing into his nose, Tayte breathed in a lungful of gas in response to the pain of two sudden gunshot wounds. There was a sensation of vertigo and he felt himself falling. His body slumped against the side of his bed and onto the floor into a seated position as the darkness washed over him.

~~~~~

Finn ducked as a machine gun zeroed in on their position with a long and sustained burst of fire that hammered into the wooden supports right outside their firing port. Rounds buzzed past only a few inches over their head with a crackle of subsonic disturbances in the air around them.

A round of cannon fire shook the ground as the big guns continued a sporadic and unpredictable pattern of shells flying into or over the perimeter walls. The flickering of fire lights now burned in several locations along the perimeter and in a handful of interior buildings as the onslaught raged.

"Dutch!" Finn shouted into his PDA, "Anytime now."

"I've got the drone on station directly over their cannons." She replied.

"Let it fly!"

A hundred yards behind the wall, Dutch crouched down behind an overturned workbench fighting against a growing panic as explosions lit up the night and shells rained down all around her. Focusing her attention on the hand-held control pad, she guided the drone into position.

A hundred feet over the heads of the barking cannons the drone hovered completely undetected within the cover of leaves and branches. The glass container of baby T-Rex urine was suspended from its belly by a pair of retractable arms. At Dutch's command, the payload was released.

Dutch watched with satisfaction as the glass jar shattered against a thick low hanging branch sending a shower of urine raining over the heads of the thralls below.
"Yes!" Dutch exclaimed to herself. "Hope you bastards enjoy that little piss shower."

Steering the drone higher into the forest canopy she turned it to north west ensuring the high gain speakers were properly oriented before hitting the play button on her control panel.
Over the crashing of explosions, gunfire and bursts of pulse weapons the pitiful cries of terrified baby T-Rexes echoed into the forest targeting a distant and very specific audience of one.

"Ok, payload on target and I've got the music playing." Dutch reported. Her call remained unanswered as both Finn and Jenna had their hands full playing some music of their own but to a much larger audience.

Finn's shoulder bucked slightly under the recoil of another shot as he successfully tracked and targeted a fleeting form. The figure dropped to the ground for a moment only to reappear a second later and disappear into cover.

"Shit! These bastards are hard to kill." Finn called out over the crashing din of battle.

The counter on the side of his rifle indicated a low charge and he took a moment to replace the expended cartridge while taking a moment to inventory his remaining packs.

"Five charges left." He announced as he returned to his firing position and scanned for additional targets.

"Same here." Jenna added.

"We run dry and we're in trouble." Finn added before announcing over his radio. "Pick your shots people, only shoot at what you can hit. Slow and easy while they're still in cover. I don't want to hear any automatic firing unless they make a rush for the wall."

A bullet struck the corner of the firing port showering him with a cloud of wood scraps and shrapnel. Feeling a searing burn on his cheek, he brushed his hand at the spot only to draw it back and see a smear of blood across his palm.

"You're hit!" Jenna called out in alarm as she reached for the med pack in her fanny pack.

"It's a scratch, stay put over there, I'm fine."

His voice was nearly drowned out by a follow up volley of cannon fire. The shells from this round pummeled the wall all around them knocking both of them from their feet and flat on their backs on the floor of the firing post.

"You ok?" Finn asked as he scrambled to his knees, his ears ringing and his head pounding with the concussion of the blasts.

"I think so!" Jenna shouted, "I think I'm deaf though."

"It'll pass." Finn replied as he grasped the edge of the view port and took stock of the latest damage.

Whether by luck or design, the thrall gunners seemed to have gotten their act together and concentrated all their rounds on a single point on the wall some hundred and fifty feet beyond Finn and Jenna's post. A smoking hole large enough to drive an eighteen-wheeler through now presented the enemy with easy access into the heart of the colony. The next firing port down, along with four troopers and another one of their precious cannons had been completely obliterated in the attack.

"Breach! Breach in the wall north of my location!" Finn yelled into the radio. "Everyone stand ready for these assholes to make a rush for it."

Resuming their position, both Finn and Jenna ignored the ringing in their ears and their fog filled brains as they stared intently down the sights of their weapons searching for targets.

It started deep in the pit of his stomach, as first Finn though it was a strange time for his stomach to start growling. Then he felt the slightest of vibrations reverberating up his legs and spine as the wooden decking under his feet trembled ever so slightly.
The pounding slowly grew in intensity with each passing second.
"You feel that?" Jenna asked. "That's not cannon fire."

"No." Finn said as a knowing grin crossed his lips, "it sure as hell isn't."

A short burst of cannon fire rocked the woods from the south as ten of the heavy guns let loose a murderous barrage on another section of wall. An explosion from inside the compound was followed an instant later by screams of pain and desperate cries for help.

"We're getting out asses kicked." Jenna screamed and she angrily bit the inside of her cheek and fired at fleeting shadows dancing between trees in the distant forest.

Then they heard it, a deep, menacing roar. The resounding bellow of a massive creature, enraged, desperate and murderous drowning out the sounds of the battle. The floor under their feet now pounded as several tons of T-Rex battered its way from the depths of the forest headlong into the rows of cannons and their unsuspecting crews.

Obscure shapes darted in and out of view, even with the aid of their night vision goggles it was impossible to get a clear picture of the true carnage happening beyond the vale of trees and brush. One thing was immediately clear though, the level of incoming fire, specifically from the cannon batteries, had dropped off to almost nothing as the thralls found themselves in a desperate battle with a more pressing threat.

The thunderous bellow of the T-Rex filled the night air as the creature smashed, slashed and stomped its way through the enemy ranks. Attracted by the sounds and scents of its missing offspring the frenzied father pummeled the thralls vulnerable rear flank.

"Holy crap!" Dutch called out over the airwaves, "are you guys seeing this? That thing is kicking wholesale ass!"

The turning of the tides should have filled him with hope and a renewed sense of optimism but instead Finn felt a nagging thought picking at the back of his brain.

"Why haven't they rushed the breach?" he asked allowed, "their cannons did the job, they've got an entry point and they've got the numbers to overrun us. What are they doing?"

The demolition of the rampaging T-Rex were all they could hear now and Finn realized that all firing, even from points further up and down the wall had suddenly ceased.

"Section leaders report contact." Finn queried as a thought occurred to him.

One after another different section leaders reported back each with a similar update, incoming fire had ceased and all visual contact with the enemy had been lost. It was as though the entire attack had abruptly ceased and the attackers had faded away into the night.

"Dutch, take the concert on the road." Finn ordered.

Several minutes later the thrashing and crashing of the T-Rex began to fade into the distance as Dutch lured it away with the recorded sounds of its terrified offspring. With the urine covered thralls and equipment already pulverized to dust, the male dinosaur was left with only its sense of hearing to continue tracking its wayward child, at least until the baby awoke from its slumber in the next few hours and cried out to alert its parents to its actual location.

Finn stood and gazed into the surrounding forest searching for the slightest sign of movement. The crackle of burning wood, the occasional moan and cry of the wounded were now the prominent sounds of the night.

"This is wrong." He said after several long moments of gazing into the stillness of the forest. "They came in force. They had us ten to one and breached the wall. Even with the Rex they still had the upper hand."

"What are you thinking?" Jenna asked.

"I'm thinking we're missing something. That maybe this was nothing more than a diversion." As he spoke the words he felt a cold chill moving down his spine.
"Lauren, can you hear me." He called out into the radio.
The airwaves remained silent.
"Marcela, do you copy?"
"Anyone at the Revati compound that can hear me please respond."
The silence was ominous.

Nearly a full minute later Dutch's came back, "I've checked our radio signal strength, the solar storm is still limiting our range to only about two or three miles. They won't be able to hear us at the caves right now."

"Can you get satellite imagery up? I want to see where the thrall army suddenly moved off to as well as any activity near the caves. I need that information yesterday Dutch."

He was close to screaming into the microphone as his pulse rate escalated with every passing second and his mind started playing over the events of the last few hours. He knew something was wrong, he'd missed something in the lead up to this fight. There was a larger picture here but he just couldn't see it yet.

"Give me a few, it's a mess over here."

Turning back to Jenna he said, "Take over here. Get all our people accounted for and get me a count of casualties as soon as possible. I'll be in the control room, I have a bad feeling we're missing something here."

~~~~

Finn arrived at the control room only moments after Dutch, both of them relieved to see the nerve center of their electronics operations untouched from the battle.

"Ok, we still have a boat load of interference." Dutch exclaimed, her frayed nerves now calmed and under control. Her fingers danced across a keyboard in a blur of motion as she fed rapid fire commands into the system.
"I'm compensation by combining the imagery of three satellites for a composite overview."

A few moments later the screen sprang to life with footage of the colony and surrounding forest.
"I can't get much more than thermal imaging; real time video is nothing but static."

"I'll take whatever I can get. Show me what you got."

Hot spots from ongoing fires stood out like a sore thumb as Dutch used the colony as a reference point to expand the search outward to the north and western regions.
"There." She called out gesturing towards hundreds of individual white blobs fanning out in a confused pattern deeper into the forest.

"They're scattering like wild rabbits." Finn observed, "no command or control, they're just running in random directions. This makes zero sense. I mean look at them all, they still outnumber us nearly ten to one. We're sitting ducks for a massed assault, why suddenly break contact and run for the hills?"

"I'd like to think our friendly neighborhood T-Red daddy had a little something to do with it." Dutch replied with a toothy grin.

"Not likely." Finn quickly burst her bubble, "they don't experience fear or other emotions anymore. The whole time that thing was tearing them up there wasn't a single cry of pain or concern from the woods, they just took the beating. No, there's something else to all this. Show me the cave complex."

Beads of sweat were forming on his brow as he continued running ever worsening scenarios through his head struggling to put the pieces together and find that one thing that he overlooked.

"This is odd." Dutch barked as she leaned closer to the screen and studied the thermal picture over the cliff face leading into the Revati camp.
"Look at these heat signatures on the trail behind the falls." She pointed to a line of white blobs, some appearing almost stacked on top of each other and stretching out from a point half way up the trail until the view disappeared into the cave mouth.
"No movement, they're just sitting there."

"Because they're either dead or incapacitated." Finn exclaimed, his worst nightmare suddenly realized.

"The attack was a diversion. Their real target was the caves!"

~~~~

They found the first two bodies a third of the way up the dirt trail behind the falls, both of the Revati warriors were riddled with bullet wounds. A few feet further on was the first thrall body, a female who took a total of five arrows, with the fatal shot piercing her right eye.

Linc and several of the surviving Revati had accompanied both Finn and Dutch on the return trip to the caves. Fear of what they would find grew with every passing moment along the way and as their radio calls were answered with silence.

"Look at this." Dutch said as she knelt alongside the woman's body and studied her unusual clothing.

The material was stiff and unyielding as she grasped it in her hand and worked it back and forth. Constructed of a patchwork of dull silver squares, the material was formed into a cloak that could easily be pulled over the head to form a veil over the rest of the body.

"No wonder we didn't spot them. This material is designed to dissipate body heat and the reflective nature of the panels would make the wearer virtually invisible even from satellite video." Dutch explained.

"So the whole thing was a set up." Finn spat, "they made sure we saw the attack against the colony coming knowing we would concentrate the majority of our forces in a defensive action."

"Meanwhile a smaller force was able to sneak out here virtually unopposed." Dutch finished the thought for him.

Glancing up towards the cave opening, Dutch's face grew pale as she noted several more bodies of both Revati and thralls leading directly into the colony.

"Dutch wait!" Finn shouted as she suddenly bolted ahead heedless of any potential danger.

The carnage continued into the mouth of the cavern but once they reached the main chamber they breathed a sigh of relief when they found the village intact and most of the occupants alive and well as they slowly recovered from the gas attack. It was later learned to their surprise that the thralls had made use of a non-lethal and fast acting sleeping agent intended to incapacitate and not otherwise harm the Revati population. While a handful of armed skirmishes did result in dead and wounded on both sides, it was to remain another mystery why the thralls failed to take full advantage of a successfully executed surprise raid on the complex.

Finn's first stop was the medical center where he found nearly every bed occupied as Revati nurses raced between patients rendering aid to the wounded.

He glanced around searching for Lauren but judging by the tempo of operations and with a constant flow of personnel in and out of the medical center, he assumed she was out rendering aid somewhere.

"You missed the party." A familiar voice drunkenly called out from the midst of the carnage.

Finn found Tayte propped up in bed, fresh bandages covering both his head and shoulder wounds. Judging by the dilated pupils and perpetual smile on his face, he deduced that his old friend was flying high on pain meds.

"You look like shit." Tayte snickered as he approached the foot of the bed.

Finn's hand unconsciously brushed the line of fresh stitches in his cheek.

"Just a scratch." Finn replied, "you sure as hell have a habit of getting into trouble, don't you?"

Tayte's head lolled backwards and his eyes squeezed shut as the pain meds began dragging him off towards dreamland. Looking to the nurse Finn asked, "he going to be ok?"

"Oh yes, he'll be fine. No vital organs hit this time. Two more scars to add to an otherwise impressive collection."

"I tried...I tried to stop them Finn, I swear I did. I tried...." His words were slurred and weak as he fought a losing battle against the drugs but it was clear he needed to get those words out and make his case before he would allow himself to nod off.

Grasping his hand and squeezing it tight Finn leaned over and said, "I know you did old man, you nailed two of the bastards. I couldn't have asked for more. Now get some rest, you've had your ass kicked all over again and I need you back at 100% as soon as possible."

"Captain Finnegan!" Dutch's distressed voice called out over the radio. "There's something here you need to see."

Finn immediately suspected the worse, referring to him by his rank and last name was not something he was accustomed to from Dutch.

Tayte had already slipped into a deep slumber so Finn looked back to the Revati nurse and said, "Take care of him."

Before double timing it back outside and threading his way down narrow paths and between buildings to the large meeting hall near the center of the village.

Dutch was inside standing behind the array of tech equipment in the front corner of the massive room. As Finn approached he noted that a figure was situated in one of the wheeled chairs in front of the controls and slumped forward with their forehead resting on the table.

"Is she ok?" Finn asked recognizing Marcela as the unconscious figure in the chair.

Linc and Dutch were standing side by side staring up at one of the screens, it was Linc who replied, "as far we can see. She's either sleeping or offline at the moment."

"Offline?" Finn asked confused, "What the hell is going on?"

Linc stepped off to the side giving Finn a clear view of the main monitor directly in front of them. The screen was filled with several pieces of information, in the upper left corner, Lauren's service image along with columns of personal and professional data. Next to that, the same information and image for Dr. Hughes was displayed. In the bottom center of the screen, Finn's own service image and personal data stared back at him.

"What the hell is this?" Finn exclaimed, his confusion now starting to give way to anger.

Dutch's eyes fell from the screen and down to the floor at her feet as she sheepishly replied, "Both Lauren and Dr. Hughes were taken by the thralls. From what we can tell so far, Marcela was their inside man. She led them directly to the medical center and pointed Lauren out."

Finn felt a sudden rush of heat coursing through his body, he clenched his fist and began pounding them against his thighs as he struggled to keep a rapidly growing rage in check. "How.do.you.know?"

Instead of responding, Dutch tapped a command into the keyboard. A second monitor sprang to life, on it they watched a detailed recording of the assault inside the medical center. The imagery was coming from the point of view of an individual as though they were seeing the world through someone's eye.

The playback came in distorted segments as Finn's mind struggled to process the images. A gas canister exploded, a pair of thralls darted past, nurses began dropping to the ground, the thralls reached Lauren and there was a struggle, she went down dropping from view, there was the exchange of fire, Tayte was hit and went down. It was like he was watching pieces of a movie stitched together and rewound at a quarter speed minus the soundtrack.

A mirror came into view, a face flashed past. Dutch paused the image and then backed it up a few frames, Marcela stared back at them, her right eye glassy and distant, an amber glow reflecting back from the mirrored surface from the cybernetic implant on the left side of her face.

"There's more. Hours of recordings stored on a partitioned drive. We only glanced at a few clips, it looks as though her ocular viewfinder has not only been active this entire time, but it's also been live streaming the video to a remote source."

"She was included on all our mission briefs." Finn roared, "Everything! They knew every move we made!"

"There's also this." Dutch fretted as she gestured to a small text box at the bottom of the screen directly under Finn's personal data.

Dutch selected the box and expanded the text. It read: '*Alone, dusk, five days from now, they will be safe*' followed by a string of letters of numbers.

"They're coordinates." Dutch offered, "They lead to the center of an open prairie, twenty miles due west."

CHAPTER 22

Finn paced nervously back and forth through the knee-high grass, something about the meadow was off, in his bones he could feel the barest tingles of energy crackling in the air around him. Whether it was his imagination playing tricks on him or an actual sensation he couldn't exactly tell. One thing that was pretty clear though, the local wildlife seemed to give the area a wide berth.

The clearing was relatively small and unassuming, so much so that it wouldn't have warranted a second glance during their planetary terrain survey. Measuring a scant hundred and fifty feet wide by seventy-five feet across, the only landmark was a large boulder sitting almost dead center of the clearing. The rock was nearly twelve feet tall and fairly wide, three sides were craggy and uneven with another nearly smooth and very flat.

He'd parked the ATV on the eastern boundary of the clearing and at first walked a wide perimeter around the area. The general consensus was that he was walking into a trap and he had been strongly discouraged from coming, particularly alone. His rebuttal was simple, based on all they knew about the Creators and their capabilities, if they wanted Finn or any of the rest of them dead or captured, there didn't seem to be much they could do to prevent it.

So he'd come, alone and armed only with a pistol. He'd even declined Jenna's idea to have a strike team on standby in case things went south. No, he knew deep in his bones that the Creator's hadn't set this up simply to ambush him.

Shadows were growing longer as day slowly gave way to dusk. Overhead, the sky was clear and crisp, the brilliant twinkle of stars along with the throbbing glow of the setting sun provided more than enough light that he could still see unaided for long distances.

He wasn't sure what to expect, a large, heavily armed welcoming committee, a handful of thralls or maybe even an appearance from the Creators themselves, but it was evident whatever was going to happen there seemed to be no urgent rush.

His back was to the rock when he sensed rather than observed a change in the atmosphere around him. Glancing over his shoulder, he saw the flat side of the rock starting to pulse with a gentle blue glow. Turning around and facing the spectacle, his hand drifted subconsciously to his side where it gripped the butt of his holstered pistol.

The glow gradually intensified until it formed a rectangular outline. As suddenly as it appeared, it was gone and, in its wake, a beckoning doorway leading to a stairwell that disappeared downward.

Finn approached cautiously, his pistol remained holstered but his senses were alert and taking in every detail of his surroundings. Stopping just short of the doorway he found himself staring down into a bland stairwell lit with a soft bluish glow. It was nearly identical in design to the stairwell they'd followed only a short time ago into the bowels of the Creators warehouse complex.

"Well, here we go." Finn said aloud as he crossed the threshold and began traipsing slowly down each flight of stairs.

Minutes seemed to pass and he continued descending. The only difference he noted between this stairwell and the one into the production facility was that there were no doorways on any of the landings he passed. The only option was up or down, he continued on.

Fifteen flights down and he paused for a minute to listen while he pressed his hand against the cold concrete of the wall feeling for any indications of mechanics or activity within the structure. It was deathly quiet, eerie in many ways, he could hear his heart beating inside his chest and the longer he stood there listening he could actually hear the sound of his blood passing rapidly through his arteries in response to his elevated pulse rate. The air pressure around him had remained the same along with a constant temperature, hinting at some level of environmental control but there were no indications of vents or even a sensation of flowing air, nothing but the walls, stairs and subtle blue lighting. He forced himself to continue moving.

Twenty floors down and the he stepped off the bottom stair onto a wide metal grate and a solid but completely blank wall, no doors, no windows, no controls, just nothing but a sudden end to an otherwise uneventful descent. His shoulders sagged and his breath came heavy, his leg muscles had started to burn as the initial indication of muscle fatigue swept over him.

"Son of a bitch." He exclaimed as he stepped forward and reached to slap his hand against the wall to his front.

There was a brilliant flash of blinding blue light and his hand fell through empty space where the wall should have been. He felt a momentary sensation of weightlessness and vertigo followed almost immediately by a sinking in the pit of his stomach and an urge to vomit.

Finn tried taking a step forward but his knees were weak and rubbery and as he stumbled and began to fall forward a pair of hands grasped his arms and a familiar voice cried out,

"Finn!! Oh my god!!"

Lauren helped ease him onto a small cot extending from a nearby wall. As his vision cleared his eyes darted around taking in his surroundings. He was in a room, four whitewashed walls, a floor and ceiling but otherwise stark, cold and mostly empty. The cot and a single toadstool desk situated a few feet to his left were the only embellishments in sight.

Lauren crouched on the floor alongside him, smiling from ear to ear, she appeared healthy, happy, unharmed and most of all, free of mechanical implants.

"Try and sit still for a minute." Her voice came to him jumbled and shaken inside his head, he felt as though he'd been drugged and was only now starting to regain consciousness.

"That transporting mechanism plays hell on our physiology. It will pass in a few moments."

"Lauren?" Finn slurred. "Are you...are you...ok?"

"Oh god yes!" Lauren exclaimed as she wrapped his arms around him and squeezed tight enough that he thought his ribs would surely crack.

"Sit still, let me get you a drink." She stood and walked to the toadstool table, waved her hand in the air above the surface and suddenly the space in front of her was filled with a transparent floating control panel. Lauren's fingers tapped at the controls and in a moment a panel on the wall beside him suddenly opened with an extended metal tray containing a ceramic mug full of ice water.

The water was cool and refreshing, he felt his senses returning.

"Where are we? What happened? What did they do to you?" He started all at once.

"Easy there soldier. Slow down, take it one step at a time." Lauren replied sitting down on the cot next to him.

"I'm not exactly sure where we are, but I suspect its deep inside the planet, like miles deep inside the planet. I don't even know how I really know that, I just do. Tell me something though, how long have I been gone? I have zero sense of time, there is simply no way to judge if it's been hours, days, weeks, it's very disorienting."

"Five days exactly." Finn replied before launching into a brief overview of the attack on the colony and the Revati compound. He explained how the thralls has made use of specialized material to cloak themselves from satellite surveillance as well as the gas attack against the cave complex, surprising everyone with non-lethal measures. He finished by explaining how Marcela and the other colonists once held by the Creators and now living amongst the Revati had actually been something akin to sleeper agents, their implants activated remotely giving the Creators complete access to everything they saw and did.

Lauren cut him off as she exclaimed, "Marcela and the others! Finn, it wasn't their fault. They had no idea they were being used like that. Please tell me you didn't take any action against them?"

"No, nothing serious. We figured it out a short time later. Well, Dutch got to the bottom of it actually. She was so distraught at thinking Marcela could have betrayed us. With Marcela's consent, she cobbled together a converter allowing a direct connection between the cybernetics fitted to her head and our computer systems. Once Dutch got into the root coding, she was able to see how the Creators could remotely access those devices, turning them on and off at will. The individuals not only had no knowledge of it, but they also lost all control of their own motor functions while it was happening. Now, we have confined all of them to quarters, under guard, at least until Dutch finds some way of permanently deactivating those remote systems. But Dutch was able to convince me that there was no ill intent on Marcela's part in this whole thing."

"Believe it or not, after all we've learned the last few days, Dr. Hughes will probably be the leading authority of how to work with that equipment." Lauren added.

"Dr. Hughes? Is he here too?"

"He is, just not right here." Lauren tried to explain. "I've seen him only briefly since we arrived, I think he is in a similar room across the hall, but I can't be certain. I don't think he's hurt though. They seem to want different information from both of us, medical knowledge from me and scientific and technological from him."

His senses now fully restored Finn took in what she was saying but instead of filling in the gaps, all it did was introduce a hundred more questions. He forced himself to relax somewhat, seeing that she was unharmed and that at least for the moment, neither of them appeared in imminent danger.

"Maybe you should back up and start from the top." Glancing around the empty room and noticing the lack of exits, windows or obvious ways out he added, "it looks like we're not going anywhere anytime soon, so take your time and try not to leave anything out."

"Actually, it might be easier if I show you something first." Lauren said, a mischievous smile suddenly crossing her lips.

She rose and returned to the toadstool table, the floating controls appeared once again and her fingers moved quickly as she entered commands. A section of wall at the far end of the room suddenly began glowing with the familiar blue light. The outline of a large square materialized in the center of the wall. A moment later, the light began to fade, in its place a window suddenly appeared. Instead of glass, a crackling energy field separated them from the view beyond.

Finn took two involuntary steps backwards and released a shocked gasp as his senses were suddenly overloaded with input. The window looked out over a vast cityscape stretching as far as he could see. Although recognizable as a city, not a single structure could be considered anything close to a familiar design. Towering to dizzying heights, the array of shapes was both disorienting and fascinating at the same time. Many of the buildings were cylindrical, wrapping around themselves repeatedly from the bottom until ending in pointed spires at the top. Others were fat and round like gigantic puffballs, their disk-shaped roofs festooned with antennas and decorative sculptures. Additional buildings were composed of four separate triangular structures joined at several levels with tubular abutments that he imagined served as passageways of some type. The entirety of the city bathed in a soft blue light originating above, below and all around every structure, presenting the entire picture in a mystical radiance that was simply breathtaking and awe inspiring at the same time.

The window gave them a sweeping overview of the magnificent city from an elevated location several hundred feet above even the tallest of the colossal structures. It was like looking down on a view of New York City from an aircraft soaring high overhead. Finn's head began to spin with a sudden bout of vertigo as his mind tried to process the unexplainable sights as it also recognized the dizzying height they were peering down from.

"Incredible, isn't it?" Lauren beamed as she gazed out over the majestic city below.

"What is this?" Finn breathed, his voice barely above a shocked whisper.

"Believe it or not, it's only one of a hundred similar cities scattered all around the world. These cities are actually ancient, somewhere in the neighborhood of tens of thousands of years." Lauren replied, "These are the homes of the Creators."

For several long moments they looked out over the city in silence, soaking in the panoramic view. Smaller details were now becoming evident as the initial shock wore off. Finn noted the buildings were all interconnected at intermittent levels with closed in walkways as well as wider arteries that could only be roads of some kind, although from their altitude it was impossible to tell if anything was moving along any given segment. It was a surprisingly elegant and efficient means of construction allowing for maximum use of every ounce of available real estate. Although it was impossible to discern the function of any individual structure, he could easily see a population of close to a million people living and working comfortably within the metropolis.

As he began regaining his senses questions filled his head faster than he could prioritize them, he decided to start off simple with, "What's with the blue lights?"

The answer came from behind them as Dr. Hughes replied, "the Creators cannot tolerate any form of UV emissions, the blue light is completely devoid of even miniscule radiation discharge."

They turned and found the Doctor standing several feet away towards the middle of the room. Finn's hand instinctively started reaching for his pistol as soon as he realized he wasn't alone.

There were eight figures standing several feet behind Dr. Hughes. They stood shoulder to shoulder, and for the second time in only a few minutes, Finn once again found himself in shock and at a loss for words. Discovering the Revati and cybernetically altered humans had been a jolt to his senses to be sure, but what stood before him now defied any rational explanation.

The figures were humanoid in shape, meaning they each had two arms and two legs extending at the correct locations from a central thorax and a round head mounted on top of squat little necks. From there the differences were nearly too numerous to count. First, their skin, if you could even call it that, was the same blue color as the lights inside and outside the city, but it was also nearly translucent in that you could actually see through their forms. Finn corrected himself, you could almost see through them, what he could see was inside them. Bone structure, organs, sinewy pathways that had to serve as their cardiovascular system were all clearly visible.

There was no mouth, no nose and no ears visible, although small nodules on the sides of their heads could have been ears, Finn had no idea. The entirety of the facial features were a pair of normal looking eyes, at least normal in size and distance from each other when compared to humans. Their rounded heads were hairless, in fact there was nothing anywhere on them that mimicked hair, fur or feathers of any kind, no eyebrows, no body coverings, nothing.

Next, Finn noted that there were no visible sexual organs nor navel cavity, simply nothing but blank slates. They were somewhat taller than average for a human male, each standing close to six foot five inches, almost like a miniature basketball team. They were slender, not exactly gaunt or emaciated, simply lacking any discernible muscle mass but despite that oddity they stood steadfast and stable.

Seeing Finn's hand drop to his pistol, Dr. Hughes held his own hands out in front of him and pleaded, "No, don't draw your weapon. They mean us no harm."

"NO HARM!" Finn exploded, "we're still digging graves and patching wounded! They enslaved tens of thousands of human beings and then murdered them simply to make a point! They kidnapped both of you for god only knows what purpose! Tell me again how they mean us no harm!"

"Greetings Captain Brian Finnegan of the armed forces of the United States of America." The voice boomed inside his head like a sonic blast dropping Finn to his knees as he squeezed both hands against the sides of his head in agony.

"Finn!" Lauren cried out as she dropped down and grasped his arm.
Glaring towards the spectral images she shouted, "Tone it down! You said you wouldn't hurt him."

A line of blood trickled from Finn's nose and he appeared ashen and weak as Lauren gently helped back to his feet and then guided him across the room onto the cot.

224

"What the hell was that!?" Finn cried out not realizing he was shouting near the top of his lungs.

"It's ok, give it a minute, it will pass." Lauren urged as she wrapped an arm protectively around his shoulder. "It's how they communicate with us. Some form of telepathy. It takes them a moment to regulate their volume to not cause us injury."

"Christ that hurt." Finn groaned. Turning to face the Creators he asked, "What is this? What do you want from us?"

The eight figures remained passive and still, staring at him with blank faces that gave away no subliminal clues to help decipher emotions or intentions.

"It's as I thought" Lauren replied, "They're species is dying. We were their last hope and they finally accept that there is nothing that can be done for them."

"What? I don't get it." Finn fumed, his rage starting to boil over, "What does all this mean? What does any of this have to do with us? Why bring us all this way simply to enslave and kill us?"

Dr. Hughes glanced over his shoulder and for several minutes nodded silently back and forth towards the Creators as they silently communicated. Finally, he turned back to face them and said, "they have asked me to help explain things in a way that will make sense to you."

When neither Finn nor Lauren offered any objections, Dr. Hughes continued, "While we have come to call them 'Creators', the name is actually somewhat misleading. They have no direct connection to this planet or our own. Centuries ago their own home world suffered a cataclysmic event, a solar eruption that exposed their people to heavy doses of radiation. They were eventually forced to flee their home and seek sanctuary here."

"Sounds familiar." Finn muttered suspiciously.

The Creators continued to stare silently back at him, Finn had the impression they were studying him in the same fashion they might have observed a lab rat.

"Yes, in a way." Dr. Hughes continued, his enthusiasm at imparting his new-found wisdom clearly overcoming any misgivings he held at being held captive the last several days. He was in his element and actually seemed to be enjoying himself.

Finn considered kicking him square in the balls for a moment but managed to let his disgust and anger pass while he sat quietly waiting for him to continue the lecture.

"A space fairing race, with highly advanced technology, they were already aware of this planets existence and its capability of supporting life. They arrived here with the hope of starting over, but by then the damage was already done. At that point, their species was actually very similar to our own. Within a few generations, mutations within their DNA began manifesting. Their lungs lost the capacity to process oxygen, preferring a carbon monoxide rich environment instead. Their bodies also lost all natural protections against UV radiation forcing them to seek refuge deep under the surface."

"While this is a wonderful history lesson Doctor, it doesn't explain what we are doing here and why they have been drawing humans here only to enslave and torture them." Finn interrupted.

"In a way it does." Lauren interjected, "As Dr. Hughes explained, they were once very similar in all respects to Earth born humans. The mutations in their DNA, passed on from generation to generation over centuries have basically transformed them into what they are now. However, the progressive nature of the mutations indicate that their race is headed towards total extinction. A sterility factor is rapidly gaining ground, and in another three or four generations, they anticipate losing the ability to reproduce. At that point they will simply cease to exist as a species."

"They had hoped that commonalities between our species would allow them to introduce genetic scripts that would ultimately be used to reverse or at least slow the process within their population." Dr. Hughes added.

"Had hoped?" Finn asked skeptically.

"Yes, that's kind of where Dr. Hughes and I come in." Lauren said, "when we introduced the code to create that liver for Tayte, they recognized the level of medical achievement within our people that they had long hoped would eventually occur. I am not exactly sure how they do it, but for the last several days, they have literally picked through our brains collecting every scrap of medical and scientific data available. We were able to help them reach the conclusion they had long suspected. The mutations in their genetic structure have gone too long for our species to be of any practical use in finding a solution."

"Well, that's both comforting and a bit insulting I guess." Finn replied.

"Knowing that humans would only be able to travel to his planet in small numbers and only after reaching a certain stage of development, they designed the temporal vortex. By making this planet available to humanity throughout a countless number of alternate universes, they have been drawing us here for over a thousand years now." Dr. Hughes said.

"So now what?" Finn asked, "Now that we are no more use to them, what happens now?"

"Nothing." Dr. Hughes replied bluntly, "they will allow us to leave here and from this point forward, our people will be free to live our lives on the planet's surface while they continue their own journey in their underground cities."

"Just that simple?"

"Yes." The unfamiliar voice rang out in his head once again, the volume was keyed much lower this time, the mental intrusion was unnerving but no longer painful.

Finn looked down the line of eight aliens, he could not distinguish one from another and there were no outwards signs to indicate which one was doing the talking. He now realized that like the energy field of the window, the figures were not physically in the room with them. What he was seeing was closer to a hologram or projection of some type, an extremely detailed and realistic projection.

"We leave the custody and care of this planet in your hands. Our technology will aid you in guiding your fellow humans here. We have watched and learned much from you Captain Brian Finnegan. You are a noble and honorable person. One day we may meet again, but for now we leave you with one parting thought. Learn from your mistakes as we have done, care for this world and build a society to serve as a beacon of hope for other lifeforms throughout the galaxy. Yours is a unique species, but far from the only forms of intelligence. This planet will draw others and it's now up to you how those encounters will unfold."

With that, the figures suddenly began fading into a dissipating mist.

"No! Wait!" Dr. Hughes cried out as he reached towards the dimming figures, "I have so many more questions…"

As the last embers of the images winked away, Finn felt a growing fog within his head. Looking at Lauren, he saw her reaching her hand towards her temple, her eyes squeezing shut as the same sensation began to overtake her. Dr. Hughes suddenly dropped to the floor; his eyes closed tight, his face contorted in pain. The fog gave way to darkness and a sensation of falling overcame him. His eyes closed as he allowed himself to sink deeper into the rushing gloom.

A cool breeze lapped softly at his cheek and he could feel a growing warmth across his body as sunlight beamed down over him.

Willing his eyes open, he blinked against the intensity of the sun's glare. He was flat on his back, soft tufts of grass and bare dirt underneath him. Sounds of insects and the rustle of leaves were accompanied by the refreshing scent of fresh air, pine and other pleasing woodland scents.

Opening his eyes, he stared up a crystal blue sky directly overhead, the sun was high on the horizon making it close to midday but he couldn't tell if it was simply the following day or even weeks later, his sense of time was skewed and out of sync.

Pulling himself up on his elbows, he took in his surroundings to find himself laying in the same small meadow where he had started his journey into the land of the Creators. Lauren and Dr. Hughes were both laying in the grass next to him slowly coming around.

"What happened?" Lauren asked as she stood on her wobbly and unsteady legs, "I feel like I just woke up with a hangover."

"Not sure." Finn replied as he walked around in slow, cautious circles while the dizziness sluggishly faded away. "We're back where I started last night."
Gesturing to the boulder he explained, "There's a stairwell behind the flat face of that rock."

Lauren studied the rock from all angles, her head finally clearing enough that her senses had returned nearly too normal. "Nothing here."

"It can wait." Finn added, "I suspect we will eventually learn how to open those doors."
Glancing towards the East he continued, "we've got a pretty long ways home, we should get started if we want to get back before dark."

Grasping his hand Lauren held it tight and looked up into his eyes with a renewed sense of determination and hope burning brightly across her face. "I think we're going to be ok. I think we're really going to make a new home here."

"As long as we don't repeat our own mistakes." Finn said as the words of the Creators echoed in his head, "I think they'll be watching us and I certainly don't think we've seen the last of the Creators."

Look for Part 2 of the series, coming May 2022

Enjoyed this book?

Please consider leaving a review on Amazon.com

Questions and comments are always welcome.
Contact the author at:
sganley@yahoo.com

Also available from Amazon:

Zombie Nation
The beginning

The Dead Don't Bleed Series
Part 1: The Outbreak
Part 2: The Aftermath

The Infected Series
Part 1: The Infected
Part 2: Gerald's War
Part 3: Rise of the Zombies

Scott Ganley
© 2021, S.Ganley
sganley@yahoo.com

Made in the USA
Coppell, TX
27 December 2021

70207936R00136